A FATEFUL PLATEFUL

A FATEFUL PLATEFUL

AUNTIE CLEM'S BAKERY #16

P.D. WORKMAN

 **PD WORKMAN**

ISBN: 9781774682173 (KDP Paperback)

ISBN: 9781774682210 (KDP Hardcover)

ISBN: 9781774682227 (KDP Large Print)

ISBN: 9781774682203 (Lulu Paperback)

ISBN: 9781774682180 (Kindle)

ISBN: 9781774682197 (ePub)

ALSO BY P.D. WORKMAN

Murder Meringue Pie

A Fowl Play on Christmas Day (Christmas crossover story)

Cinn-Full Secrets

Muffin to Lose

Custard Cream Conspiracy

Mock Apple Alibi (Coming Soon)

Chocolate Eclairvoyant (Coming Soon)

Quiche Me Goodbye (Coming Soon)

Recipes from Auntie Clem's Bakery

Parks Pat Mysteries

Police Procedural Set in Canada

Out with the Sunset

Long Climb to the Top

Dark Water Under the Bridge

Immersed in the View

Skimming Over the Lake

Hazard of the Hills

Knows the Hills

Spanning the Creek

Sanctuary in the Stream

Echoes of the Engine

Bench with a View

Beneath the Icy Depths

Grounded in the Wind (Coming Soon)

Reservoir of Secrets (Coming Soon)

Peril in the Blooms (Coming Soon)

AND MORE AT PDWORKMAN.COM

For those with a lot on their plate

CHAPTER 1

*E*rin brushed her forehead with the back of her wrist to wipe away a bead of sweat as she walked from the kitchen of Auntie Clem's Bakery to the front store space where her customers were gathering. She smiled in greeting.

"How are ya'll this morning?"

"You're sounding like a regular Tennessean," Mary Lou Cox observed, giving Erin a brief smile. She smoothed the fabric over the hips of her pantsuit.

"I've been giving her lessons," Vic offered cheekily. "Trying to train her on the proper grammar and etiquette that a business owner in Tennessee should know."

Mary Lou nodded and looked into the display case to see what the bakery had on offer that morning. "Hmm. Half a dozen of the cheesy rolls. Half a dozen brownies. Pizza shell… and a loaf of multigrain bread."

Erin started to pull the order together while Vic rang it up on the till. She knew that the multigrain bread was for Mary Lou. Everything else would probably be consumed by Joshua, her younger son. They were the only two left at home and Mary Lou watched her figure carefully, rarely allowing herself a baked treat. But Joshua was a

1

growing teen and was still getting back in shape after being kidnapped and starved.

"How is Joshua?"

Mary Lou rubbed the back of her neck, considering her answer. There were other people around, so her response would probably not be as open as it would be if she and Erin had been alone.

"Everyone says that kids are resilient and he will be back to his old self in no time." Her eyes were distant. "But it's been a long time since Joshua was 'his old self.' All of the trials that he and Campbell had to go through when Roger..." She trailed off, not putting it into words. They all knew how Roger had lost all of the family's money and had tried to commit suicide. And about the brain damage the attempt had left him with. The boys had been forced to grow up and become men way too quickly, and it had taken its toll on both of them.

Erin hadn't lived in Bald Eagle Falls then, so she had only known the boys after the spate of family disasters. She liked them both. They had been responsible and hardworking until, eventually, they just couldn't keep it up anymore. Cam was now in the city, living with friends in a lifestyle that Mary Lou definitely did not approve of. And since his kidnapping, Joshua had also dropped out of school and was having trouble getting over everything that had happened.

"What about counseling?" Erin suggested. "Is he seeing someone?"

"No. He won't have anyone in town knowing his personal thoughts and feelings and says that he doesn't want to go all the way into the city. It's too far. I told him I would take him, of course, that we would make it work, but... I know it's just an excuse. And at this age, I can't really force him. I can't exactly throw him over my shoulder and drag him off anymore."

Erin smiled at the image this brought to mind. Joshua was taller than Mary Lou, lanky and still regaining his weight, but certainly too big for Mary Lou to physically force into anything.

Though Erin had known families in the past who would have used other methods to force their will on a recalcitrant teen. Having grown up in the foster system, she had seen her share of domestic violence and other coercion.

"Well... tell him hello for me." Erin put a couple of extra brownies into the bag for him. Chocolate and carbs might not heal every ill, but they wouldn't do him any harm. "Tell him I'm thinking of him. And if he ever wants to talk..."

Mary Lou nodded once. But she probably wouldn't tell Joshua that part. She would prefer that Erin and Joshua did not get too close, convinced that Erin would do more sleuthing around Bald Eagle Falls and would drag Joshua into something he shouldn't be involved in. She would prefer that he would just work things through and go back to school in the fall.

Vic smiled warmly at Mary Lou and gave her the total. Mary Lou counted out her cash carefully and gave her exact change. Erin couldn't help but wonder how much Mary Lou struggled financially. Joshua's medical bills on top of the bankruptcy Roger had caused... Mary Lou worked at the General Store, which probably didn't bring in much money. She had only herself and Joshua to take care of, but even that must have been difficult.

"Y'all come back now," Erin told her, and winked at Vic.

Erin tucked a stray lock of dark hair back under the baker's hat, rolling her eyes at how her hair was always pulling out of whatever clips she tried to tame it with. On the other hand, Vic always looked sleek and professional, her fine blond hair done up in a bun or a French braid, makeup perfect, each line of her clothing lying just the right way. Erin always felt like an ugly duckling when compared to her transgender employee and best friend.

Vic gave her a smile of sympathy, and they turned their attention to the small mob of Fosters waiting to be served.

The Fosters were Erin's favorite customers, if she allowed herself to pick favorites, which she knew she shouldn't. But she couldn't help herself. Most of the reason was young Peter Foster, the oldest of the children, who had severe celiac disease. Erin opening up the gluten-free bakery in Bald Eagle Falls had changed his life for the better. He now had the choice of anything in the store, instead of being limited to the single brand of dry gluten-free bread that the grocery store carried and boxes of commercial gluten-free cookies, which only came in a couple of varieties.

He tried to herd his younger sisters and to direct them as to what they should do, helping Mrs. Foster out the best he could. Still, sometimes his attempts backfired and he ended up causing a fight with the girls instead of keeping them in line.

"Choc'late!" Traci insisted, getting her fingerprints all over the display case as she pointed insistently at the chocolate chunk cookies at her eye level. "Want choc'late. Choc'late!" Her voice rose insistently. The baby of the family until just recently, she was used to getting her way. It must be hard for her to understand why the new baby in Mrs. Foster's sling had changed everything so much for her. Somebody else was the center of attention now. Everyone fussed over him, and he stole Traci's mother's time from her.

"Okay!" Peter told her, trying to shush her. "I hear you, Traci. You want the chocolate cookie." He rolled his eyes dramatically at Erin. "Can Traci please have a chocolate chunk cookie for her kid's club cookie?" He looked down at Traci and tapped her on the top of the head. "Say 'please!'"

"Pwease?" Traci demanded, looking at Erin and jabbing her finger in the direction of the chocolate chunk cookies several more times for emphasis. "Pwease? Choc'late? Dat one?"

Erin followed Traci's pointing finger through the glass and touched one of the cookies with her gloved hand. "This one?"

"No! Dat one!"

Erin moved over one cookie. "This one?"

Traci nodded. Erin pulled it out and put it into a napkin for Traci. "Okay. And how about the rest of you cookie monsters?"

Karen and Jodi laughed at this, and each picked out which cookies they wanted, ignoring Peter's attempts to try to get samples of as many different kinds of cookies as he could. Not that he hadn't already tasted everything Erin had on offer. It was about time to mix things up and add a couple of new varieties of cookies to get people's attention. And some Easter cut-outs.

"How is everything?" Erin asked once the children were munching on their kid's club cookies more quietly. "You're getting back into the swing of things?"

"Trying to," Mrs. Foster agreed. "It seems a little bit harder this time. Maybe I'm getting too old to keep doing this. Maybe we should stop at five."

Erin shook her head. "You are amazing with them. I can't imagine being able to wrangle that many. Even just thinking about how I would fit one baby into my life... I don't think I could do it."

"It gets easier after the first two or three." Mrs. Foster jiggled and looked down at the baby cradled in the sling. "Until you end up with one with colic or who has a more... demanding personality. After Peter and the girls, I thought I had it all figured out. It was easy. But this one..." She bounced Allan up and down. "He has his own ideas of how things should be done. Like what time he eats and sleeps. I think he has allergies."

"Oh, no. What about celiac disease? You don't think he's celiac like Peter, do you?"

"We'll have to get him tested, I guess, once he starts eating solid foods. He shouldn't be getting gluten through my milk. But he definitely reacts negatively to some of the stuff I eat. Like peppers. This little man does not do well with peppers."

"Poor guy. Well, if you need anything special for your diet, you be sure to let me know. You don't need to worry about peppers in anything here but the pizza bread, but if you identify anything else... I'll make sure you still have other options."

Mrs. Foster smiled and nodded. "You are so accommodating to everyone. I have no idea how you do it. Everything tastes so good and has a good texture, even though it is gluten-free and sometimes vegan or something-else-free. You're a lifesaver."

Erin couldn't help beaming at that. That was precisely the reason that she had wanted to start the gluten-free bakery. So that people like Peter and Mrs. Foster had delicious choices and didn't have to feel left out. She wanted there to be something for everyone at Auntie Clem's Bakery.

Mrs. Foster placed her order, and Erin was busy for a few minutes getting everything packaged up.

"Mom? Blueberry bagels?" Peter pointed out. "Can we get some? Please? I'll eat them for breakfasts."

"I don't want you harassing me to buy out half the store," his mother warned.

"I won't. That's the only thing. I won't ask for anything else."

Of course, he knew everything else that his mother had already ordered. There was no need for him to beg for the regular bread, rolls, granola bars, or other things she had already ordered.

"Fine," Mrs. Foster conceded. Erin knew that she always left a little flexibility in her order, knowing she would need to deal with Peter's negotiations. "We'll take a bag of the blueberry bagels as well."

Erin added it to the order. After Vic rang up the order, she helped to pack everything into a box for Mrs. Foster. "Let me carry that out to the car for you. Then you don't need to juggle it and the baby at the same time."

Of course, she would have to once she got home, and Peter and the older girls would be at school so they couldn't help her. Mrs. Foster nodded. "Well, all right."

Peter led the family out of the bakery like so many little ducks walking in a line.

CHAPTER 2

*E*rin took advantage of a momentary lull in customers to go to the kitchen and get a couple more batters mixed up. It was always nice to have something fresh out of the oven at the end of the day when the after-school and before-dinner rush came around.

There was a knock on the back door. Erin checked through the peephole, then opened the door.

"Adele! Come in!"

The tall, dark-haired woman slipped into the kitchen. She glanced around briefly.

"I want to take advantage of your day-old bread program," Adele told Erin.

Erin raised her brows in surprise. In trying to help the rural homeless in and around Bald Eagle Falls, a community very difficult to identify or get close to, she had set up a program where anyone could ask for day-old baked goods, which Erin normally saved up to take into one of the homeless shelters in the city, and they would be provided free of charge.

A lot of the church women had rolled their eyes at this and insisted that there were no homeless in Bald Eagle Falls or the surrounding wilds and farmlands. And if there were, they were clearly homeless by choice and should get paying jobs to support their families and pay for their own food. But Erin had seen some of the home-less families with her own eyes. Women, often on their own, taking care of thin children with old eyes. Women who were doing the best they could to eke out a living in a society where even the most basic of homes or lands cost more than a person on minimum wage could afford. Especially if they weren't able to work two or three jobs because of childcare.

Adele had become acquainted with one of the families who had been camping out in Erin's woods, the treed lands behind Clemen-tine's house that she had inherited along with the house and the store-front for Clementine's old tea shop, the first iteration of Auntie Clem's Bakery. So Adele was not one of the parties who rolled her eyes and suggested that anyone willing to work should be able to earn a living wage.

Erin employed Adele as the groundskeeper for the woods, tasked with keeping away trespassers who might light fires, dump trash, or hold Erin liable for some ill that befell them while camping out or taking a hike through her property. In exchange for this service, Adele lived in the summer cottage rent-free and was able to spend her time wandering in the woods, picking herbs, and doing whatever it was that Wiccan women did at night under the full moon. Adele had already been run out of other towns in the Bible Belt when people had come to suspect or know that she was a witch.

"Are you... not making enough to survive on?" Erin asked guiltily. Adele sold herbs and handicrafts made from nature in the General Store and online. Erin didn't suppose that it made a lot of money but, since Adele didn't have to pay rent and harvested some of her own food, her living expenses were very low.

Adele gave her a reproving look. "I thought the policy was 'no questions asked,'" she pointed out.

"Oh. Well, yes, of course. Sorry. I was just surprised. I didn't mean to pry. What can I get for you? Bread, rolls, dessert?"

"I think... bread and maybe some muffins?"

"Absolutely." Erin went over to the chest freezer. "How much?"

If it were just for Adele, then all she would want was one loaf and a few muffins. But she ended up picking out three loaves of bread and a couple of bags of muffins. She was feeding someone other than herself.

That was exactly why Erin had started the program, so she wasn't going to do anything to sabotage it.

"Come back whenever you need more. I don't want anybody in Bald Eagle Falls going hungry. We should take care of our neighbors."

Adele nodded. "You are the only one I know of who puts your money where your mouth is. It's funny that all of these Christian women, who believe in a Jesus who said to feed the hungry, find so many excuses not to help."

Erin shrugged.

She didn't care what anyone's religious beliefs were. She was happy to let others believe what they wanted and hoped that they would let her live life the way she wanted to. But it seemed like the most vocally religious ones were the same ones who refused to take action when there was a clear need for it. They were good about collecting Christmas presents for needy children in December. Erin knew that they went as a group to serve at one of the big soup kitchens in the city at least twice a year. Still, those token efforts seemed to satisfy them that they were doing all they could and that no one closer to home needed their help.

"Thank you for helping out," she told Adele. "I'm glad that someone is taking me up on my offer."

Most of the families that Erin had reached out to had turned down her offer of "charity," saying that they didn't need anything from her and could provide for themselves.

Adele gave one brief nod and headed for the door. "Change happens slowly," she pronounced, "but it is possible over time."

～

Vic had taken out the Fosters' purchases and was back at the front counter when Erin finished with the batters she would want later in the day and returned to the storefront.

"There you are," Vic commented. "Wasn't sure what you were up to."

Erin glanced around. There were a couple of customers waiting, but no one who looked impatient or like they had been waiting for a long time. She hadn't really been in the back long enough for anyone to be upset about the wait. Small town life in Bald Eagle Falls was a slower pace.

"Just dealing with some day-old bread," Erin commented.

Vic frowned and looked at her. "I thought it was all in the freezer already."

"It was. But someone needed it."

"Who would—" Vic caught on suddenly. "Well, that's good. Glad someone is coming by to get what they need. We had enough?"

"Plenty and to spare."

"Good job."

Erin nodded. She was inordinately happy that *someone* was taking advantage of her offering. She turned her smile onto Betty, one of her older customers. She always took her time making choices and could drive Erin crazy with her endless questions. Still, she was a good, steady customer who always came back looking for something for dinner or for the next event she was planning. Bridge night with the girls or the grandkids coming over for Easter. There was always something going on.

"What can I get for you today, Betty?"

"Oh, I already told that nice young lady," Betty assured her.

Vic already had a bag started. She pointed to the seeded bread. "One of those, and then we're done."

Erin wrapped it up while Vic rang everything up on the register. Betty paid for her purchase, carefully putting coins down on the counter as she added everything up.

"Thank you. See you again soon."

"Goodbye, Betty. Have a good day."

The customer waiting patiently for Betty to finish was Beaver.

Rohilda Beaven was a federal agent, living part of the time with Vic's older brother, Jeremy, who had come to Bald Eagle Falls to get away from the family and their involvement with the Jackson clan, an organized crime syndicate operating in the Moose River area. Jeremy had been in and out of trouble, but that didn't seem to faze Beaver a bit. Maybe she liked flirting with the wrong side of the law. At any rate, she and Jeremy got along together like a house on fire, even though Beaver was a number of years older than Jeremy was.

"Hi, Beaver," Erin greeted. "What can I get for you today?"

"Actually…" Beaver chewed vigorously on her omnipresent wad of gum, her strong jaw working up and down. "I came to talk to Miss Victoria."

Erin raised her eyebrows and turned her head to look at Vic to see whether she had been expecting this. Vic looked just as surprised to hear that Beaver needed to talk to her as Erin was.

"You want to talk to me? What's up?" Vic's eyes went over Beaver's serious face. "Is something wrong? Did something happen to Jeremy?"

It wasn't that long since Jeremy had been shot on his job at Crosswood Farm, protecting a valuable ginseng crop. He had recovered quickly, and he hadn't quit his job there like Erin thought he would. Apparently, he liked it enough or made enough money at it that a little thing like a bullet was not going to deter him.

Beaver held up her hand. "It isn't Jeremy."

Vic swallowed and licked her lips. "Then who?"

"It's your father."

CHAPTER 3

"*M*y father?" Vic leaned on the counter. She shook her head. "What about my father?"

Beaver glanced over at Erin. Erin tried to read Beaver's expression but, as usual, found it difficult to tell exactly what she was thinking. She was good at what she did, which meant that she could mask her true feelings and give nothing away.

"Do you want me to leave?" Erin guessed. "Did you want to talk to Vic alone?"

Beaver shook her head. "Just the opposite. I want to make sure… she has someone here."

Erin put her arm around Vic's shoulders protectively. "Of course. I'm always here for her. What's going on?"

"Jeremiah Jackson is in the hospital," Beaver revealed, choosing her words carefully and speaking very slowly and distinctly so that there could be no misunderstanding. "He is in critical condition. They don't know whether he will make it through the night."

Vic just stood there staring at Beaver. Erin was silent, waiting for the information to sink in and for Vic to decide what she wanted to do about it. If anything. Vic was estranged from her parents, and her response to Beaver's news might very well be "good riddance" or whatever Tennessee slang was the equivalent.

Vic's fair skin turned even paler than usual. She was still holding on to the counter for support. Erin grabbed the stool nearby that she sat on when she was at the till for too long and her feet started to hurt. She slid it in behind Vic so that she could sit down rather than fainting.

"Are you okay, Vicky? Do you want me to get you a drink of cold water?"

Vic didn't even glance at Erin and didn't respond to the stool bumping the backs of her thighs. "No. Yes. I don't know."

Erin nodded. "I'll get you one. Just… you might want to sit down. I don't want you fainting on me."

"I'm not going to faint," Vic dismissed. But her knuckles turned white as she hung on to the counter.

"Come on," Erin urged, bumping the stool into the backs of Vic's legs again. This time Vic responded automatically, sitting down. "Good. Now just stay put while I get you a drink."

Erin moved as quickly as she could without risking bumping into something or smashing or spilling the glass. She was back at Vic's side again in seconds. Her own heart was thumping away at high speed.

She had only met Pa Jackson once, and that had been enough. She didn't like the man and had hoped never to see him again. He wasn't a nice or pleasant person and had treated Vic horribly. So her heart wasn't racing because she cared about whether the man lived or died, but simply because she had a hard time seeing her friend's shock over hearing about her father's condition. Was Vic sad? Upset? Angry? She might never see her father alive again. How did she feel about that? Maybe she was even relieved that the old man would be out of her life permanently.

Erin handed Vic the glass of water and rubbed her back gently. "Are you okay? What do you want to do?"

"He wouldn't come to see me if I was in the hospital."

Erin bit her lip. It wasn't exactly an answer. But Vic was working through it the best she could.

"Is he really that bad?" Vic asked Beaver.

Beaver chewed and nodded.

"This isn't just some kind of con? He really is… dying?"

"He may or may not," Beaver said carefully. "There is no guarantee that he will die. But things are not looking good, and it is quite possible that he will."

Vic just stared at empty space. Erin tried to put herself into Vic's place. She had been rejected by her family. She had run away or been kicked out at seventeen because they disapproved of her gender transition. They had refused to call her by her preferred name and had preached at her or hit her when she had gone back to them for answers in a case that Erin was working on, trying to clear her half-sister Charley's name of a murder charge.

Vic had been devastated when she had left there, as well as being in physical pain from her father hitting her with his cane. Erin didn't want Vic going back there. She didn't want Vic going anywhere near the guy. Vic was much better off without him.

"What happened?" Erin asked. "Was it a farm accident?" It seemed like she was always hearing about tractors rolling over people or other horrific accidents with combines or balers. A farm could be a dangerous place. Jeremiah Jackson wasn't exactly an old man, but he already had one disability, some kind of injury to his leg or foot that necessitated his using a cane to get around. Maybe he had moved too slowly to get out of the way of a piece of equipment, or maybe he had tried to pry something that was stuck with his cane, ending up with his arm being crushed.

Beaver shook her head. "They're not sure what it is at this point. At first, maybe the stomach flu. Some kind of gastritis. But it has been very severe and he is getting weak. He had a heart attack today. The doctors…" She shrugged dramatically, chewing on her gum. "They're at a loss. Maybe not even be able to diagnose him before he dies, at this rate."

"A stomach bug?"

"Worse than a stomach bug."

"I can't understand this," Vic said in a far-away voice. "I don't understand what's going on. How do you know about this, Beaver?"

Beaver didn't reveal her source. "I've told Jeremy. He's going to get a few things together and go say goodbye. Stay for a night or two until it's all over."

"Why would Jeremy go there?"

"It may be his only chance to say his piece. If there's anything you want to tell him... then you might want to go see him too. It may be the only chance you get."

"I don't want to talk to him. And he sure as heck doesn't want to talk to me."

"That's up to you. Jeremy said to not even bother telling you. But I thought... it was your right to know."

"How did you even find out about this?"

Beaver just chewed. She had a long nose and too-generous mouth. Not a beautiful woman by society's standards, but she had a certain attraction that was difficult to ignore. She was the kind of person who always did what she wanted to do, not caring about what other people thought about her or how society judged her. That boldness and unswerving loyalty to her own principles were so rare, it pulled people in.

"I think I have a right to know," Vic challenged.

Beaver cocked her head slightly, then shook it no. As a federal agent, she had plenty of sources of information, and it made sense that she wouldn't want to compromise them. Especially not for a little fish like Pa Jackson and his family. She had much bigger things to worry about.

Erin looked at Vic. "So... what do you want to do? Did you want to go see him?"

"No."

"Okay."

Vic looked at Erin, surprised. "What? No lecture on how this is my only chance, how I need to make my peace with him now before he passes? Reconcile with my family?"

"No."

Beaver shrugged. "Call Jeremy if you change your mind. He'll be going tonight. Has to arrange things with work first. If you want to go together..."

"I'm not going," Vic said stubbornly.

"Okay."

Nobody argued with her. This seemed to throw Vic off-balance more than anything else. She expected them to tell her what to do. Expected them to insist that family was more important than her personal feelings and that it was important for her to make up with her father before he passed over.

But Erin saw no reason why Vic should reconcile with a parent who had clearly been abusive. If Vic wanted to go, she should go. But if she didn't want to, Erin saw no reason why she should have to. She had a good life in Bald Eagle Falls, and her family and the extended Jackson clan would only cause her grief.

Maybe if Pa Jackson were gone, Vic's mother would be more accepting of her. Maybe she could have a relationship with one of her parents. But Erin wasn't betting on it. Vic's mother had seemed pretty hard-line on her own.

Beaver nodded a goodbye to Erin. "See you around."

"Do you want something?" Erin asked, looking at the baked goods in the display case. "A cookie or brownie? On the house?"

"I'm good," Beaver assured her. "Just wanted to talk to Miss Victoria and let her know what was going on."

CHAPTER 4

hings were awkward for the rest of the day at the bakery. Erin didn't bring up Vic's father to her, waiting to see if Vic wanted to talk about it herself. But Vic was obviously thinking about it, needing to be told orders twice, ringing items up wrong on the cash register, or banging into Erin walking through the doorway into the kitchen. Since the customers did not know what was going on with her, they showed irritation at her mistakes. Erin did her best to smooth things over and keep everyone happy.

Bella Proust came in during the afternoon for a shift to help with the after-school rush and preparations for the next day.

"Do you want to go home?" Erin asked Vic when they were all in the kitchen. "Bella and I can handle things."

Vic shook her head. "I don't want to have to think about anything. It's better if I can just keep working."

Erin shrugged and didn't push it or point out that Vic was going to have to think about it after work anyway. It wasn't a matter of whether she was going to think about it, only of when. But if Vic wanted to delay that moment as much as she could, Erin couldn't blame her for that. They would have to just keep tripping over each other until the end of the day.

Vic returned to the front of the store and Bella turned her gaze toward Erin. "What's going on?"

"She just got some news," Erin told her. "I don't think she wants to talk about it right now."

"Is everything okay?"

Erin shrugged. "No. But she'll be all right." She didn't want to give any details to anyone else. It was Vic's news to share or not share as she chose. Erin didn't want to invade her privacy. Many people in Bald Eagle Falls knew Vic's family, so word would probably spread sooner or later. But hopefully, people knew that Vic was estranged from her family and wouldn't bring it up with her.

Erin sighed, shaking her head to herself. She knew very well that the church ladies would be all over the news and wanting to talk to Vic about it. Of course they wouldn't just leave her alone. They would want to *help* her and hear all the details of Vic's dysfunctional family relationships.

Once home, Vic retreated to her loft over Erin's garage without much more than a wave. Hopefully, she would feel better after a bit of time to herself. Maybe after a good cry or screaming into a pillow. Erin paused to watch Vic go around the house to the backyard before opening the front door.

Terry was home, so she didn't need to disarm the burglar alarm. He was sitting in front of the TV with a large orange cat on his lap and didn't get up to greet her. Erin couldn't believe how big Orange Blossom had grown since she had discovered him as a tiny, scrawny kitten.

Orange Blossom yowled a greeting at Erin, but didn't get up either, too comfortable where he was.

"I've been taken hostage," Terry told Erin. "I can't get up. Do you want to give him a T-R-E-A-T?"

Erin stood with her hands on her hips, looking down at him. "Can't the big, brave policeman just push the itty bitty kitty off his lap by himself?"

A dimple appeared in Terry's handsome face as he smiled at her. "Well, I would, ma'am, but that would be rude."

Erin bent down to scratch Orange Blossom's ears and then leaned over Terry, supporting herself with a hand on the back of the couch to give him a kiss in greeting. "How has your day been?"

"All quiet. I did fix that window that you wanted me to. And ended up helping Willie with repairs on his truck." This, Erin thought, was offered because he didn't want her to think that he'd just been lazing around watching TV all day while she had been working hard. But he didn't need to justify himself.

"Thanks. Maybe now it won't rattle all night when the wind blows. You're on shift tonight?"

He nodded and looked at his watch to check the time. "I have a couple of hours still."

"Good." Erin pushed herself back up to standing. She saw K9's tail and back end protruding from where he was lying behind the couch. "What is K9 doing?"

Terry looked over in his direction. "I *think* he's trying to cuddle with Marshmallow."

Erin frowned, not sure whether to believe that. She reached down to pet K9. "What are you doing, boy? What's going on down here?" She immediately worried that K9 might be sick. Animals did that sometimes, crawling into corners or dark places when they were sick, separating themselves from the people they usually loved to be with. She remembered finding Orange Blossom crammed in behind the toilet when he had been ill. He had, luckily, recovered from being poisoned.

K9 crawled backward and poked his snout into Erin's hand for more love, alleviating her fears. She scratched his ears. "Were you just visiting with Marshmallow? Is that it?"

Marshmallow liked to sleep behind the couch and, when Erin peered down and around the furniture, she saw that was where the brown and white rabbit was. Sleeping right where K9's nose would have been. So maybe Terry was right about his just wanting to cuddle with Marshmallow.

"Well, I suppose he might as well cuddle with Marshmallow,

since I'm pretty sure he's not going to be cuddling with Blossom any time soon."

As if on cue, K9 poked his nose toward Orange Blossom and got a hiss and growl in response to his friendly overtures.

"Okay, let's get everyone a treat," Erin said in the higher tone she usually used to cue the animals that she was talking to them. Six ears pricked up and swiveled in her direction. By the time Erin reached the kitchen, an orange streak had overtaken her and K9 was right at her heel. Marshmallow followed more sedately.

"Ahhh." Terry stretched his arms and shoulders and put his feet down on the floor, moving from side to side to work the kinks out. "I've been in that same position for way too long."

Erin laughed. "Like I said, just push him off." She went to the pantry to get out a couple of Orange Blossom's treats, and sent them skimming across the floor for him to chase. K9 sat and waited politely while she got a gluten-free dog biscuit out of the cookie jar for him. Marshmallow sniffed around the base of the fridge, waiting for Erin to find him a juicy carrot.

"Did you hear anything about Vic's father?" Erin asked Terry over a dinner of soup from a can and rolls from the bakery.

"Vic's father. No. What about Vic's father?"

"Oh. Beaver knew, so I wondered if it was through law enforcement channels."

"She has different channels than I do. What happened? Is he in trouble?"

"Apparently in the hospital on his death bed."

"Oh, I'm sorry to hear that. Is Vic okay?"

"She's not going to go see him. I think she's upset, but she really isn't saying anything about it."

"Well, from what you and she have said, I'm guessing he wasn't that nice of a guy. Her feelings about him are probably mixed."

"Yeah. Dads like that are..." Erin shook her head, trying to find the words. "He was so mean when she went to see him. Trying to shame her, telling her how disgusted he was with her. Threatening Willie. And when he hit her…" Tears sprang to Erin's eyes. She had a hard time keeping her composure. "He hit her so hard with his cane, it hurt her for weeks. And if Willie hadn't been there to stop him, it would have been worse. What a horrible, nasty old man."

"Makes me grateful for my upbringing. My dad might have seemed strict, and I can remember being spanked as a child. But abuse like that… poor Vic."

"And the others, too. She's the youngest, and the baby of the family is usually spoiled. If he treated her that way, just imagine what the others had to go through."

Terry spread some jam on his roll. They were trying out some artisanal jams from a store in the city since they had run out of Jam Lady jams, and there were not likely to be any more produced in the foreseeable future.

"It's possible that he was fine with the others. It might just have been Vic's transition that triggered him. Some people are… very intolerant of that kind of thing."

Erin remembered the other boys telling Vic that her father's bark was worse than his bite. But Vic had also said that she had been whipped worse before as a child. She hadn't come out until just before leaving home at seventeen. Erin shook her head. "I don't know. I don't think it was just that."

Terry nodded. "Maybe not, then. She knows that you're here if she needs someone to talk to about it."

"I know. I just wish there was more I could do to help. If it was me, she would know just what to say. I always feel… awkward. I don't know what to say to make her feel better."

"She's your friend. It doesn't matter if you bumble your way through it."

Erin had a bite of her roll and blinked a couple of times to keep the threatening tears at bay. It wasn't that she was a powder-puff, just that she cared so much about Vic and she knew what it was like to deal with an abusive parent. Everyone would think that Vic should go see him and make up before he died, but if it were Erin… she didn't think she would.

Terry and K9 headed off to work, and Erin turned the TV on just because the house felt too quiet. She had no idea what was even on; she just wanted some background noise while she read through one of Clementine's old genealogy books. She had found some fascinating stories about her ancestors. Having grown up in foster care with no family stories except the few memories she had of when she was a little child, she was amazed to find how much history there was and how much she could learn about her grandparents and great-grandparents and so on back through time. She had a deep well of history she had never known about before.

And she was always surprised and enthralled when she found the names of other families in Bald Eagle Falls in her genealogy. Coxes and Prosts and many other familiar names. As Mary Lou had once told her, "If you're kin to Clementine, you're kin to half the mountain."

The back door opened.

"In here," Erin called before Vic could even *yoo-hoo.*

Vic walked through the kitchen into the living room, where Erin was sitting with the heavy volume.

"Hi." Vic looked at the TV. "You busy?"

"No. You can turn that off. It was just for company."

Vic pressed the power button on the TV, then sat down on the couch, lifting her feet up onto the cushion and wrapping her arms around her knees. A defensive position, shielding herself from the outside world.

"I think I have to go."

CHAPTER 5

$\mathcal{E}$rin wasn't surprised. As Terry had suggested, Vic was bound to have mixed feelings. She was attached to her parents, even if they had been abusive. Sometimes the cycle of abuse and one person's survival being dependent on the changeable moods and whims of another forged even stronger bonds than a normal, healthy parental relationship.

"When? Tonight?"

Vic rested her chin on top of her knees, studying Erin. "You're not even going to give me a lecture about how I said I wasn't going to go, and now I'm thinking about it?"

"People are allowed to change their minds. It's a big decision. It takes some time to think it through."

Vic grunted an acknowledgment. For a while, neither of them said anything. Erin figured Vic would talk sooner or later. She'd come over to say something, and Erin was sure there was more to it than just "I think I have to go."

"It's so hard," Vic sighed. "I want to just stay here in Bald Eagle Falls and not think about it. I don't want to see him. I don't care if he dies. Life would be a lot easier without him around."

"Yeah."

"But what about my mom? I don't want her to be all alone. The boys aren't going to ask her how she's feeling about it. They'll just… joke around and punch each other in the shoulder and act like it doesn't matter. But it will matter to her."

"You want to show her your support."

Vic nodded. "And… I know I said I would never go back there. And he said never to go back, or he would shoot me. But… all of that is in the past now. Everything has changed."

"If you want to go, you should go," Erin affirmed. Then she reworded it. "If you feel like you should go to help your mom, then go. It's up to you. It doesn't really matter what anyone else thinks."

"If I thought those buffoons who are my brothers would be of any help to her, I wouldn't worry about it. Maybe Jeremy might give her a hug and get her a cup of tea, but…"

Erin nodded. Jeremy tried, at least. He was the only one who had reached out to Vic since she had left home and who made an effort to call her by her chosen name. She didn't know the others, Joseph and Daniel, and had only seen them once. "You want to make sure that your mom is okay. There's nothing wrong with that."

Vic closed her eyes, thinking. "You think I'm being unforgiving about Pa," she said. "You think I should make up with him."

Erin was shocked. "I do not! Don't put words in my mouth."

Vic's eyes opened. She looked at Erin. "Really? That's what everyone is going to be thinking. That I should make up with my pa because he's dying. I hope he's already dead when I get there, so I don't have a chance to."

If she were expecting Erin to be horrified by this, she was wrong. It made perfect sense to Erin. "You don't *have* to do anything. What do you care what anyone else thinks about it? People already—" Erin cut herself off.

Vic cocked her head. "What were you going to say?" She paused, thinking it through. "People already think that I'm a bad person because I'm transgender?"

Erin's face burned. She tried to repair any damage that her thoughtless words might have caused. "No, they already know that you're strong-minded and don't care about any gossip. You're not concerned with what society says you *should* do."

"Like pretending that I'm something I'm not."

"You should be able to be your true self," Erin said firmly. "No matter what it's to do with. Your gender, your relationship with your father, whatever. You shouldn't have to pretend something that isn't true."

Vic stared off into space for a while, and Erin wasn't sure whether she had gotten through to Vic or not. She had never told Vic that she should do something or be something she wasn't comfortable with. She'd seen too many kids in foster care who were forced to follow the roles that their parents set out, and things rarely ended well.

"You're right. I really shouldn't care," Vic agreed eventually. "It's the same old biddies as already think that I'm going to the devil for being transgender. I don't care what they think about my gender, and I shouldn't care what they think of the relationship I have with my pa either."

"I really didn't mean to put it that way."

"No. It's freeing. These are people who will never approve of me, so why am I so worried about it? I can do what I want because they're never going to approve of me either way."

Erin shrugged hopelessly. "I just… hope that you don't think that I meant…"

"It's all right. People don't approve of me. They think I'm the worst kind of sinner. So what does it matter what else they think I have done or not done?"

Erin shrugged. "Don't Christians believe that everyone is a sinner? So *they* are too."

Vic chuckled. "You always pretend not to know anything about religion, but you know plenty. Yeah, everyone sins. But some sins are worse than others."

"And being transgender is a sin?" Erin rolled her eyes. "I still don't get that."

CHAPTER 6

There was a lot to be done. Erin pulled her new planner out of her purse and flipped over to a new page.

"We'll need to make sure that all of the shifts are covered at Auntie Clem's. Figure out what to pack and where we're going to stay. Terry can look after Orange Blossom and Marshmallow. Do you want him to take care of Nilla too?"

Vic's brows drew down. "What are you talking about?"

"Getting ready to go to Moose River. Do you think you will only be one day, or should we arrange for the whole week? If there is a funeral, you won't want to come back here and then go back out there again. You'll just want to stay there."

"I'm..." Vic sputtered for a moment. "You're coming?"

Erin stopped scribbling items on her list and looked at Vic, the blood rushing to her face again. "Well, I... yes... I thought we would go together."

"Erin... you don't need to come. This is my family. My deal."

"Well... if you don't want me to come, then okay... but I thought... it would be easier if you had someone there with you to support you. Is Willie going?"

"I was just going to go by myself. I didn't think... I didn't think anyone would come with me."

"I'd like to." Even though the thought of facing Pa Jackson again gave Erin a shudder, there was no way that she was going to let Vic face the challenge alone. Not unless she insisted. "Wouldn't it be better if you had someone with you? We can go to a hotel after seeing him or talking to your mom and watch a movie or something. Chill out away from everyone else."

Vic made a noise that seemed like half-laugh and half-sob. "You know what, that sounds like heaven. That would be so much better than having to stay at the farmhouse with everyone else."

"It's okay, then? I don't mean to push myself on you. I just assumed that we would go together. If you don't want me to..."

"I never thought you would come. It would mean a lot to me if you would."

"Really?"

Vic nodded. Erin leaned over and gave her a tentative hug around the shoulders. Vic hugged her tightly in return, so hard that it hurt and, after a few moments, Erin pushed gently back to make her loosen her grip. Vic had tears in her eyes. Erin rubbed her back.

"It's going to be okay, Vicky. Really. I don't know what's going to happen, but it will all work out. We'll make sure of it."

"Yeah. It will be good." Vic didn't sound sure at all, but at least she was saying the words. They had to start somewhere.

Erin sat back again and picked up her planner. "So... Nilla? Are we going to take him? Or do you want Terry to look after him?"

"I don't think we'd better leave him with Officer Piper. He doesn't really get along with men. He and Willie have a sort of an understanding, but I don't know if they'll ever really get along with each other. Maybe he was abused by a man in the past."

Erin nodded. "Okay. So we need to take Nilla and his things. We shouldn't be more than a few days, so one suitcase each?"

"I'm going to need more than one for my beauty routine," Vic countered.

"Well, okay, one suitcase and one smaller bag?"

"I suppose so. Why does it matter how many suitcases we have? We're not going on an airplane and there will be plenty of room in the hotel for whatever we need."

"I don't think there's enough room in the bug for much. If we have Nilla's kennel—"

"Wait!" Vic held up her hand. "We're taking the bug?"

"Well, we can't really take Terry's truck. Not for that long. And I'm sure Willie wouldn't want us taking his for that long either. And one of them driving us there and then coming back to Bald Eagle Falls wouldn't be very efficient."

Vic knew that Erin had been having some work done on Clementine's old Volkswagen Beetle to make sure that it was roadworthy after having been left to sit in the garage for several years. The mechanic had changed all of the fluids, replaced the battery and any other worn parts, and given it a tune-up. He claimed that it was in excellent condition and shouldn't cause her any trouble. Better than the clunker that Erin had come to Bald Eagle Falls in, which had been totaled at Christmas, several months previous.

Terry was happy that she would have her own vehicle again instead of coordinating with her to borrow his truck when she needed something. He wasn't so sure that the old bug was the best solution, but he'd tried not to complain too much about it.

"Wayne says it's all ready to go," Erin said with a shrug. "We might as well take it out on a road trip and find out."

"A road trip," Vic repeated, sounding pleased. "This is starting to sound more like a vacation. Two girls out on the road together, staying up late to watch stupid movies, sleeping in every day. You are going to sleep in, aren't you?" She fixed Erin with a serious look.

"I can't promise anything except that I'll try. But my body is used to getting up early and I can't say for sure that I'll be able to sleep in later than my usual time."

"If you stay up late, you have to sleep in."

"I'll try," Erin repeated.

"A road trip," Vic said again, grinning.

"Two girls and a *dog*," Erin reminded her.

~

Erin went to bed as usual, but her ideas and lists were buzzing around in her brain, making it very difficult to settle in and get to sleep. She eventually did drop off but, when Terry got home from his shift, she was immediately wide awake and sitting up with the lamp on when he came into the room.

"What are you doing up?" Terry asked, not used to this kind of reception. Normally, he was lucky to get more than a few grunts of greeting from Erin. And he did his best not to wake her so that she would still be able to get to Auntie Clem's in the morning and not be wrecked by a short night.

"I just wanted to talk."

"Hmm." Terry sat down on his side of the bed and began removing his duty belt and uniform. "That sounds like a dangerous thing."

"Dangerous? Why? I just want to talk."

"That's the way that it starts. Then the next thing you know, I'm out on my own and we're just *friends.*"

Erin gave his shoulder a playful shove. "I'm not breaking up with you!"

"Are you sure? Because that's what it sounds like. It always starts with a *talk.*"

"No. I promise. I just wanted to tell you that Vic changed her mind. She is going to Moose River to see her father before he dies. Or after, if he doesn't make it through the night."

"Okay."

"We'll be leaving in the morning. You'll be able to take care of the animals? We're going to take Nilla with us, so you don't need to worry about him."

"We? You kind of skipped over the part about why you're going along."

"For moral support. I don't want her to have to deal with those people on her own."

"Those people are her family."

"I know who they are. And I know what they're like. Or at least, what they were like when we were there last time. And I'm not leaving her at their mercy."

Terry smiled and resumed undressing. "You're always the one looking out for everyone, Erin."

She shrugged. "You don't mind, do you? It will only be a few days. Depending on when he dies and when the funeral is."

"She's going to stay for the funeral?"

"Yes." Erin shrugged with one shoulder. "At least, that's the plan right now. If she has to escape, we'll just split and come back home."

"How is she? She must not be too happy about going back."

"No. It was a hard decision because she doesn't want to see him and have people telling her that she has to forgive him and make up with him before he dies. But she wants to help her mom and be supportive of her. So in the end, she decided to go."

"With the help of her friend."

"I didn't tell her to go."

"No, I didn't mean that. I just meant that you're going along with her. To help her."

"Yeah."

"She's lucky to have such a good friend. Lucky that she chose your store to shelter in after leaving Moose River."

"Yeah." Erin smiled, remembering with fondness her discovery of the girl who had been hiding out in her store. Who would have guessed back then that they would end up being such fast friends? "Lucky for both of us."

"She's good for you too," Terry agreed. "You both lucked out."

"So you don't mind taking care of Blossom and Marshmallow for a few days?"

"As long as I don't have to take care of that terror. No problem."

"I hope they don't miss me too much. I don't think they will, with you still here. It isn't like they'll be in an empty house."

They had been gradually consolidating their belongings in Erin's house, intending to eventually sell Terry's place. He was barely there anymore, except to pick up the odd possession or take care of the house and yard. She was sure he would be happy with one less yard to mow.

"They'll miss you. But they'll be okay," he assured her.

"Yeah. Okay." Erin lay down like she was going to sleep. But her body was tense and her brain spinning with all of the plans and thoughts of what would happen over the next few days. What if Pa Jackson's death hit Vic harder than she expected? What if her family tried to talk her into going home? Or there was some kind of complicated inheritance that she had to take care of? More worrisome than that, what if Vic's family and extended family said things that hurt her? She knew that they would be cruel, whether intentionally or not, and she hated to think about how that would affect Vic.

She squirmed around, trying to find a comfortable position. Terry finished getting ready and leaned across her to turn off the lamp. Then he molded himself against her and held her close. Erin tried to relax and go back to sleep.

CHAPTER 7

*B*y the time Vic came by in the morning, Erin had all of her things packed and had been over the lists she had made to plan for their trip several times over.

"Charley will be in charge," she murmured, running through the arrangements, "and she and Bella can handle most of the shifts. They can call someone else in to cover the others. Am I crazy to leave Charley in charge?"

"Well..." Vic shrugged. "She is half-owner of the bakery, so I don't know how you could tell her that you were putting someone else in charge. But I understand why you're nervous about it."

Erin nodded. "She's really learned and grown a lot, but... I still worry about her. She's not responsible like you are. If she doesn't make it to her shift, then who is going to take over? She can't just do her own thing and expect everyone else to cover her."

"Did she say she would do it?"

Erin nodded.

"Then you have to let her try, right? Maybe being put in a responsible position, she'll step up to the plate and surprise you. Some people never really show their true colors until you trust them and let them run with the responsibility on their own."

"Yeah. Yeah, she'll do fine. And Bella is really good. She knows everyone's schedules, and she can call someone in if she needs to. And she's an excellent businesswoman. That's what she wants to go into. Running her own business."

"And if Charley doesn't show up, then she'll get a taste of what that is really like," Vic said with a smile.

"Uh-huh. Good educational experience for her. As long as she doesn't decide it's too much and run away."

"She's not going to do that. Not Bella."

Erin agreed. "I know. She wouldn't do that. She's very responsible. She'd at least call before she ran away."

Vic giggled. She looked at Erin's packed bags. "I just have a few more things to pack up, and then we can go."

"What about breakfast?"

"We're going to stop at the first fast-food restaurant we see and get their breakfast sandwich."

"Really?" Erin asked doubtfully.

"Are we going on an adventure or not?"

Erin took a deep breath and let it out slowly, like one of the breathing exercises in her tai chi practice. "Yes. We're going on an adventure."

CHAPTER 8

*I*t had been a while since Erin had been to Moose River. She hadn't had any reason to go there; the closest she had come was going to Crazy Theresa's house during the investigation of Bo Biggles's murder. That had been back in… October. It seemed like a long time ago, and it seemed like just yesterday. So much had happened since then, but Erin found herself flashing back to memories of finding Terry and Jack Ward injured, and all of the terror that had surrounded the experience. She gave a shudder but tried not to let Vic see how she was affected by it. Vic had been there too, and if she could be strong, then so could Erin. Although it hadn't been Vic's partner who had been lying there unconscious.

Before that, she had been to Moose River several times after finding out about the existence of her baby sister, Charley. Charley had come a long way since Erin had first found her and she had been a murder suspect. From working with a Tennessee crime family to helping to bankroll Auntie Clem's Bakery 2.0 and helping Erin with the running of the business. She was still tough, sassy, and not particularly ready to settle down to domesticity, but Erin had grown to like her. And even to entrust her with Auntie Clem's Bakery while she went along with Vic. At least Erin would only be a couple of hours away if there were an emergency. She could get back quickly. And she was only a text or phone call away if Charley had questions about how anything should be done.

Not that Charley took instructions well. She tended to rebel and want to find her own way to do things, even if it meant failing a few times before finally settling on what she thought worked best. It was frustrating, and Erin thought she understood a little bit what it would be like to be a parent, trying to provide direction and yet having to just step back and let her child make the mistakes she was going to make.

She was eight years older than Charley, but it felt like a lot more.

"What are you thinking about?" Vic asked.

"Me? Nothing. Just enjoying the scenery." Erin forced herself to look at the beautiful deep green trees that lined the highway. Tennessee was a beautiful place; she couldn't deny that. "I've never really lived out in the country. What was it like living on the farm?"

Vic gave her a sideways look. "About how you'd figure. Early chores. Helping to look after the animals and the garden and the crops. Learning how to fix things and shoot. Swimming at the watering hole."

"Did you have any pets?"

Vic ran her fingers through Nilla's fluffy white fur as the dog snoozed in her lap. "We had lots of animals growing up. Not inside, though. Dogs guard the place and chase off any wildlife that threatens the chickens. Cats keep down the mouse population in the barn. There were kittens in the hayloft or shed every year; that was always fun. I loved playing with or watching the kittens."

It was a very different childhood from Erin's. "That sounds nice."

"That part was. I can tell you, though, I didn't enjoy having to get up before the sun to get started on chores."

Vic liked to sleep in as late as she could. Even though they had to get up early for the bakery, Vic still timed it down to the last minute she could to get out of bed and be ready for her day. Erin preferred a less-hurried morning routine.

"And what about school? Was that in Moose River? Did you have to take the bus?"

"Yep. You better believe it. I was on the rusty yellow school bus every morning to ride to school."

"With your brothers."

Vic nodded. "All the Jackson boys," she agreed. "There's only one school in Moose River, so we all were on the bus together, even though they were older than me."

"And you were the baby. Did they tease you a lot?"

"Teased and tormented me something fierce. But if someone else tried to bully me... you know who was there to look after me. They wouldn't let anyone else bully the baby of the family. That was their job."

Erin smiled. She was glad that they had been close that way. She hoped that Vic would be able to get along with her older brothers after her father's death. She got along very well with Jeremy, who had been accepting of her gender transition and made an effort to always call her Vic and refer to her as his sister rather than his brother. Hopefully, once the other boys had been around Vic and Jeremy a bit, they would be able to do the same.

"So what *were* you really thinking about?" Vic asked.

"What do you mean?"

"I mean, you wouldn't be sighing like that if you were just admiring the scenery."

"Oh... nothing. Just remembering being here before."

Vic nodded. She didn't bring up the visit to Theresa's. Or to Vic's family farm before that.

"I'll have to give you the grand tour when we get there. Show you all the super-secret places I used to hang out."

"Super secret?"

"Well, maybe not so secret. Kids always think they invented sneaking out of class to smoke or pass around a bottle of whiskey stolen from somebody's pa's liquor cabinet. Never mind that their parents probably did exactly the same thing and had exactly the same hideouts."

"Small town life." Erin shook her head. Vic had grown up connected with her community and her history, walking the same paths as her parents and grandparents before her. It was hard to believe that people still lived like that. It made her think of the old-timey TV shows. *The Waltons* and *Little House on the Prairie.* "So different from the way I grew up. I lived with so many different families and went to so many different schools…"

"It must have been exciting, though," Vic suggested. "And being able to wipe the slate clean and start somewhere else without everyone having preconceived notions about you. New experiences, new friends…"

"No… it wasn't exciting. Sometimes it was a relief to get out of a family. But usually… it just made me anxious about what it would be like in another new family. Sometimes sad to have to leave if it was a family that I got along with. And as far as starting somewhere new with no preconceived notions…" Erin shook her head. "People knew that I was a foster kid the moment I arrived, so people had all kinds of ideas about where I had come from and what kind of person I was. People didn't really want to be friends with someone who might be emotionally disturbed or would just be leaving again at the end of the school year. And a lot of foster kids would steal or make things up… so that made people pretty leery about becoming friends. Why would you want to be friends with someone like that?"

"But you weren't like that. People must have figured it out sooner or later."

"There wasn't always a later. I might only be there for a few months or a year. And I wasn't an angel."

"You're a good person."

"I try to be. But… a lot of people influenced me in the wrong direction, especially if I really wanted to have a friend. I'd do pretty much anything to get along. And I wasn't exempt from the behaviors that other foster kids fell into. Hoarding, stealing, telling lies to try to impress the adults or get them off my back."

"You?" Vic's tone of disbelief made Erin laugh. "I can't believe that you would do any of those things."

"You think I was born perfect? How would you act if there were different rules everywhere you went, and you didn't have a permanent family or anyone to love you? I got in my share of trouble. I try to do the right thing, but I always had to look out for my own interests."

"And now you're just the opposite. Always looking after everyone else."

Erin frowned, thinking about that. She didn't see herself that way at all. She still saw herself as a selfish person, the girl who had to take what she wanted to survive and thrive. A couple of close brushes with the police had taught her the value of staying on the right side of the law, so she always did her best to be a law-abiding citizen. When Clementine had died and left her the store and the house, she had been eager to step up and take something for herself. And when Charley had offered to help her to rebuild Auntie Clem's Bakery after the fire, she had taken it, hadn't she? She hadn't stopped to consider that maybe she should go in another direction and let someone else more deserving go into business with Charley. She had hardly been able to tolerate Charley, but she'd been eager to take her money.

"You are," Vic insisted. "You started up Auntie Clem's because you wanted to be able to provide safe food for people with gluten intolerances or allergies, so they wouldn't have to get sick and die just to fit in or to be able to eat what they wanted to. You're always stepping up and helping when you think someone has been unjustly accused. Helping to find Joshua. Offering free food to the homeless."

"Well… that's all true," Erin admitted slowly. But those didn't feel like big things. They had been easy choices for her. Just part of the person she was. She had been hungry, been down on her luck and almost out on the street. She'd been unjustly accused more than once. And she couldn't bear to think of anyone else dying like her foster sister Carolyn had, because she didn't have adequate food choices and kept eating foods that damaged her body. "But… I always look after myself first."

"I don't know about that. You've put yourself in risky situations plenty of times."

Erin thought of that more as a failing than a positive character trait. Her foster parents and social workers had certainly never praised her for getting into the middle of trouble to help someone else.

They drove in silence for a while.

"I'm glad you're here with me, anyway," Vic said. "You're a real friend."

CHAPTER 9

*T*he hospital in Moose River was not a big concrete structure like Erin had been to in other cities over the years. It was more like the one that she had been to in Whitewater. A low, single-story brick structure like a retirement home. If Pa Jackson's condition was as bad as Beaver had suggested, Erin was surprised that they didn't have him in the nearest city hospital. But then, maybe his family hadn't wanted him to be so far away and had insisted. There was no reason a small rural hospital couldn't give end-of-life care. Keep him comfortable until he passed.

"Lordy, the memories here!" Vic said, still sitting in the car and looking at the building. "The number of times that I came here for a cast or stitches…!"

Erin looked at her. *And how many of those times had been because of something her father had done to her?*

"Farm kids," Vic said with a shrug. "Always falling off of something or getting snagged on barbed wire. And I had three brothers. You can bet that we weren't all quiet little bookworms."

From what Erin had seen, none of them had been quiet little bookworms. Vic seemed to have been the quietest of them, and she still had some hair-raising stories to tell.

Eventually, Vic opened her door. Erin followed her lead, and they entered the building. Erin was not at all sure the hospital staff would allow Vic to walk in with Nilla on leash, but they would deal with that if they were confronted.

The woman in hospital scrubs at the reception desk looked up at the swishing of the automatic doors. "How can I help you?" she asked pleasantly.

Vic grinned. "Mary Alice! As I live and breathe."

She looked at Vic in confusion. "I'm sorry... I can't place your face..."

"It's Vic—when you knew me, I was James Jackson."

Various emotions flashed across the nurse's face as she tried to make sense of this. Recognition, confusion, disapproval, joy at seeing Vic—they all warred together as she tried to sort out an appropriate response.

"As I live and breathe," she choked out finally, echoing Vic's words. She stood up and leaned over her desk to give Vic a brief hug around the shoulders. "I was sorry to hear about your father. That must have been quite a shock."

Vic stepped back slightly, giving herself a little more of a personal buffer. "Has he passed, then?"

"Oh, no. I'm sorry. I didn't mean to make you think that. He is still with us. Fighting the good fight."

Vic shook her head once. "That would be a first."

Mary Alice giggled. "Don't be naughty, Ja—er—Vic?"

"Vic. So is he making your lives miserable? Or is he unconscious?"

Erin suppressed a smile at the implication that if Pa Jackson was awake, he was making someone's life miserable.

"He's in and out. A little stronger today, I think, but he's still in a tenuous situation. I'm sorry to have to be the one to tell you."

"I didn't think he'd still be around today, the way Beaver was talking. I suppose the man is just too ornery to die when people think he should."

"You shouldn't talk about the man that way. He is your father!"

"Which way? I suppose I ought to go say hello to the old cuss, if he'll let me. I don't hear him yelling, so which way...?"

Mary Alice pointed to their right. "Just follow the blue line on the floor. He's in the cardiac unit. Someone will direct you once you get there."

Vic took a deep breath, and they followed the blue line on the floor, watching for the sign for the cardiac unit.

"Beaver said he'd had a heart attack, didn't she?" Vic said. "Everything is kind of jumbled. I remember she said he had the flu. How does that end up being a heart attack?"

Erin shook her head. "I'm not sure. I know that they say that sometimes a heart attack can feel like indigestion. Maybe he went in thinking that he had the flu and it turned out to be a heart attack?"

"Yeah, maybe."

They found the cardiac unit and another nurse smiled politely and pointed them in the direction of Vic's father's room.

Vic paused when they reached the door and looked back at Erin. Erin nodded encouragingly.

"It's okay. It will be okay."

Vic took a couple of steps into the room with Nilla, and Erin followed.

Pa Jackson lay in the bed closest to the door. It was quieter than a hospital room on TV, where there was always a heart monitor beeping away. He was hooked up to several tubes and an electronic monitor, but Erin wasn't sure what everything on the display meant. She supposed they were watching all of his vitals carefully so that they would know if he had another heart attack.

The woman sitting beside the bed turned her head, apparently having heard their approaching footsteps. She saw the dog, then looked at Vic for a moment with blank eyes. Then recognition entered her features. Her fingers tightened on the railing of the bed.

"James?" She asked tentatively, then grew more certain. "Oh, thank goodness you came. You don't know what good it will do your pa to see you again."

Vic cleared her throat uncomfortably. "Hi, Ma. It's Vic now."

"Victor. James Victor. I always did like that name."

"Just Vic."

Erin gritted her teeth over Ma Jackson calling Vic by her old name, her "dead name," but she kept quiet about it. She was there to support Vic but not to make a scene and fight her battles for her. Vic was there to support her mother.

Vic looked over at the form in the bed, her lips tight and face pale. "How are you?" she asked her mother.

"I'm hanging in there. The Lord giveth and the Lord taketh away, but I'm hoping that it's not Pa's time yet."

"I heard it was pretty bad."

"They told us to say goodbye last night, just in case... but he made it through the night, as you can see." Ma's voice raised hopefully. She reached over and patted Pa's arm. "He's a fighter, your pa."

"He always was," Vic agreed, mouth twisting into a wry smile that didn't reach her eyes.

"Come here and give your mother a hug. Let me take a look at you."

Vic obediently stepped closer and bent over to give her a hug. She was clearly uncomfortable under her mother's scrutiny, shifting and looking away from her. The last time, when they had gone back to the farm, Vic had done her best to look more like they would want her to, scrubbing off her makeup and wearing a shapeless hoodie that hid her figure. This time, she was there as herself, with no concessions to her family's sensibilities. Pretty, feminine Victoria Webster. Erin always felt like an ugly duckling beside her. Or a goose. She didn't have Vic's polish and presentation.

Ma shook her head slowly. "I don't understand it. I don't know where we went wrong with you. We raised you just like the other boys and none of them would ever have considered such foolishness. We spoiled you too much."

"Spoiled me?" Vic gave a short laugh. "You never spoiled me. I had chores and responsibilities from the time I could walk. Had to follow the house rules just like anyone else. You never gave me any special treatment because I was the baby of the family. Pa was always putting his hand in, trying to get me to toughen up."

"Then maybe it was that. Maybe if he hadn't been so hard on you, expected so much from you, you would have been happier. You wouldn't have felt the need to rebel like this. You always were a *sensitive* soul."

By the way she said it, Erin assumed that being a sensitive soul was right up there with being effeminate. Something that shouldn't be tolerated in her sons.

Vic looked over at Erin, rolling her eyes. "Mom, you remember my friend Erin Price?"

"Yes… you came with James the last time. It was nice of you to come with him again."

"Victoria," Erin corrected.

She didn't acknowledge the correction. "Now the two of you…" her finger flicked from one to the other and back again. "You aren't a couple…?"

"No, Ma," Vic said with frustration. "You know that I'm with Willie. William Andrews, you remember? Neither of you was very happy about it."

"That man." Ma Jackson shuddered. "I don't know how you can even touch him. He's so disgusting."

"He's not disgusting. His skin is stained from mining and processing minerals. From *hard work*, Ma. You should be proud that he's such a hard worker."

"I've heard he is lazy. Just a bum."

"That's not true! It isn't true at all. He has lots of different ventures. He's working all the time."

"A bum will always tell you he is working," Ma dismissed. "He's always got his fingers in a dozen different pies and tells you all of the wonderful things he is going to do in the world, but it doesn't go anywhere. You can't let yourself be deceived by him. He's just taking advantage of you."

"Taking advantage of me how?" Vic challenged. "You think he's living off of me?"

"How would I know if he was or wasn't? It isn't like you write to us and tell us what's going on. But I have eyes. I can see how he is leading on someone half his age! He's closer to your father's age than yours. A dirty old man who has told you things that aren't true and led you away from the Lord's straight path."

Vic shook her head in disbelief. "Nothing could be further from the truth! I love him. He's kind and unselfish and hard-working. He didn't pursue me or lead me into a life of sin. You know I left home before I ever met him."

"And if he hadn't led you away, you would have come back home," Ma said with certainty. She had clearly made up a story of her own to explain why Vic had never returned to the farm. It had to be Willie's influence, or Vic would have surely returned on her own after a few days or weeks.

Vic turned away from her mother and took a few steps in the opposite direction, looking frustrated and agitated. She closed her eyes, rubbed them with her palms, and let out a slow breath. She petted Nilla for a minute, then turned back to her mother to try again.

"I didn't come here to talk to you about my personal life. I wanted to make sure that you were doing okay. That you had the support that you need."

"To make sure that we were both okay," Ma amended. "Your pa is the one who is sick."

"And I didn't know if he'd even be alive when I got here. Where are the boys? Why are you here alone?"

"I sent them away. I don't need a room full of restless boys horsing around and making a lot of noise in here. There's a certain *decorum* that I would expect in a hospital room. Especially with..." she looked in the direction of her husband and trailed off.

Especially with someone who was dying, Erin guessed.

"Someone should be here with you. Or take over for you while you take a break. When was the last time you ate?"

"I don't know... I've been picking. Tea and snacks from the machines."

"You need to do better than that. There's a cafeteria, isn't there? I remember Barbara Jean's mother worked there when we were in school. They had good food."

"She still works there," Ma said with a smile and a nod. She looked over at her husband. "But I really can't leave him alone. If he wakes up and I am not at his side..."

"If he woke up and found out that you'd been sitting beside him wasting away, he'd tell you to go get something to eat, woman!"

Ma smiled more widely at that. "You're right about that," she admitted.

"Then go get something to eat. I'll sit here while you're gone. If he wakes up, I'll send you a text message and you can come right back."

"Are you sure?" Ma asked, fiddling with something in her purse. She appeared to be getting ready to go and just needed a little more reassurance that Vic would stay there and watch and that Ma couldn't be accused of having neglected her husband in his time of need.

"Yes. I promise. Give me your phone number and I'll text you if anything changes."

"Oh, I don't know…" Ma looked back at Pa Jackson as if seeking his reassurance.

"I promise," Vic repeated.

"It's just…"

"He'll be okay while you get something to eat."

"But he said not…"

Erin saw that she was touching her phone in her purse, trying to decide whether to take it out or not. A lot of older people weren't comfortable using cell phones. Maybe she was embarrassed not to know how to text.

Vic looked from her father to her mother, brows drawn down.

"He told you not to give me your cell number?"

CHAPTER 10

*E*rin couldn't believe it.

Ma Jackson dropped her eyes to her phone, nodding. A flush spread over her cheeks.

"He's afraid that I'm going to talk to you? Tell you my side of the story? What, *corrupt* you?"

"We both love you so much," Ma said apologetically. "But we can't let ourselves be swayed by that. What is right is right. And what is sinful… is sinful."

"So you can't talk to me because you love me too much to hear what I have to say."

"We're just trying to do what is right. You know we didn't raise you *that way*. We taught you to be a man. Like the other boys. Strong and faithful and willing to put in a hard day's work. It is my great shame that you… made this choice. My great shame."

"I didn't *make this choice*, Ma," Vic said, taking a step closer and addressing her in a controlled voice. "I can't help the way that I was born. I can't help the fact that I was born in a male shape. That's just the outside. I have always been female on the inside."

"No."

"Even when I was a little kid. I knew that I'd been born in the wrong body. I didn't understand it, but I knew it was wrong. I didn't choose to be transgender. The only choice I made was whether to tell anyone else and live my life honestly."

"You should never have done that. You should have stayed like you were, and found a nice girl to marry, and settled down and had children. That's the way it should be. That's the way that everyone else does it. But you had to do this instead." Ma shook her head. "If you stayed the way that you were, you would have been happy. That's how you find fulfillment. That's the way that it works."

"That would never have made me happy. I want to be myself, Ma. The person I really am. What would make me really happy is if you would accept that."

There was only silence in reply.

"If you don't want to give me your cell number, then don't," Vic said flatly. "Just go have your meal and come back here when you've had a rest and gotten something into your stomach."

"It isn't because I don't want to," Ma said, heaving herself to her feet and made her way ponderously toward the door. "It's just…"

"That you can't talk to me or you might start to see things my way."

Ma Jackson nodded and left the room.

Erin and Vic both waited a couple of minutes, until they were sure that she was out of hearing.

"Man, oh man, can you believe that?" Vic demanded, her eyes shining with angry tears. "I can't even have my own mother's phone number. I'm *that* bad."

"Well, bless her heart," Erin said in her best Tennessee twang.

Vic burst out laughing. "Oh, yes. You nailed it that time, Erin. Bless her heart. My mother, folks. She's one of a kind."

Vic turned to look at the chair that her mother had vacated. "I guess this is mine, since I promised. Do you want to grab a chair from the other side?" She stretched her neck to look around the curtain that divided one bed from the other. The second bed was occupied, but there was no one visiting the sleeping stranger.

Erin tiptoed over and grasped the tubular metal chair. She sneaked back to Vic's side with it and put it down close to Vic's. She looked closely at the man in the bed for the first time. To begin with, she had only seen the bed and the medical equipment and had not paid any attention to Pa Jackson himself. She had done some home care for the elderly and knew her way around a sickroom.

When she had last seen Jeremiah Jackson, he had been upright, hale and hearty other than his game leg. He used a cane, but he used it for more than standing and walking, wielding it as a weapon against Vic when she stood up to him. In the bed, with all of the tubes and equipment, he looked much smaller and more vulnerable. An oxygen tube fed into his nose. He had an IV in his arm and a sensor clipped onto his finger.

He was pale, his farmer's tan looking painted on. His face was much more deeply wrinkled than she remembered it.

"Does he look like he's dying?" Vic asked. "I've never sat next to someone who might die before. If he dies and I'm the only one here with him, the whole family is going to hate me."

"That's not going to happen," Erin assured her. Though, of course, there was no way to know when her father would choose to die. Often it was when someone was left alone for a few minutes. A bathroom or coffee break, and when their family member or caregiver returned, there was no more breath. No more anything. "He's still going to be alive when your mother gets back."

"He'd better be, or I'll kill him."

The joke fell flat. Vic rubbed her face. "I don't know what to think. I don't know what I was expecting. I guess... I wasn't expecting him to still be alive. I thought I'd just be here for planning the funeral."

"He could still pull through. Beaver said it wasn't a sure thing. We should talk to the doctor while we're here. Sometimes... things get mistranslated when they come through several people."

"Okay," Vic agreed, nodding. "I hope I didn't come here all for nothing. If all he's got is a sick stomach and everybody is just blowing it out of proportion..."

Erin shook her head, looking at Pa Jackson. "No, I don't think so. He looks like this was quite a bit more than just a sick stomach."

"Yeah." Vic leaned with her forearms on the rail of the bed and her head hanging down. "I'm as weak as a kitten. Isn't that stupid? Shaky and weak from talking to my own mom? How ridiculous."

Erin rubbed her back soothingly. "It's been very emotional. That takes a lot out of you. Be kind to yourself."

~

They didn't have much conversation, but mostly just sat there waiting for Vic's mother to return. She was taking longer than Erin would have expected. She thought that it would only be a few minutes while Ma went to the hospital cafeteria, grabbed a cold sandwich, and either wolfed it down there or returned to the room with it, not trusting Vic to be alone with Pa for that long. But time passed, and Erin realized that Ma must have decided to take Vic's advice and to rest and relax away from her husband. She had needed a break, even if she hadn't acted like she appreciated it.

"What are *you* doing here?"

Erin jumped. Vic, still leaning against the bed with her head down, raised her head slowly to look at her father, scowling at her from the hospital bed. She tried to arrange her face into a pleasant smile.

"Pa, how are you feeling?"

"Feeling mighty puny. I asked you a question."

"I heard that you were poorly. Thought I'd come to see if Ma needed anything."

Erin was inordinately pleased that Vic didn't say she had been worried about him or that she had come to see him. She hoped that Pa noticed that detail.

"I told you never to come back. Not unless you gave up this female nonsense." He continued to glower at her. "Which you clearly have not."

"I'm not at the farm. I'm at the hospital. And since they had the sense not to let you bring your shotgun with you, you can't run me off from here."

Pa's eyes flitted around the room as if hoping that his gun or his cane would materialize somewhere he could reach them. But he didn't move, not even turning his head.

"Where is your mother?"

"I sent her to the cafeteria to get something to eat. She's not going to keep body and soul together if she's just sitting by your bedside night and day."

Pa grunted. "Good. Can't stand having people hover over me."

"So, I hear you had a bit of a sick tummy."

Erin smothered a snort. She covered it up with a cough and turned away from Vic and her father.

"A sick tummy," Pa scoffed. "'bout puked my guts out. Sick as a dawg. Doctor said it was a good thing I got here when I did. But then..." He rubbed his chest, remembering. "I s'pose I had a heart attack."

"You suppose?" Vic repeated. "You don't know whether you did or not?"

He grunted. "I know I did."

"Do you remember it? Did it hurt?"

"Course it hurt. It was a heart attack."

"I've just heard that they don't always hurt. Sometimes people don't know when they've had a heart attack, or it's just pressure, or they think it is just indigestion. I just wondered... if it was really a heart attack. And how it felt."

"Felt like a durn elephant was sitting on my chest, crushing me. That's what it felt like."

Vic nodded. She didn't tell him that she was sorry for what he had suffered. She just continued to talk to him casually, as if this happened every day and was no big deal.

"And do they think that the stomach bug is related? Or are they two separate things? Were you sick because you were having heart problems? Or did being dehydrated cause the heart attack?"

"They don't know. Ignorant doctors in this Podunk hospital don't know anything. If they were any good, they'd be working at one of the big city hospitals. Not here."

"Do you want to be transferred to the city hospital?" Vic asked, raising one eyebrow as if she already knew the answer.

"No," Pa growled, sullen as a child. "That's where people go to die."

Vic smiled sweetly at him. "So you don't think the doctors here are any good, but it's the ones in the city who will kill you?"

"Don't be such a smart aleck."

"Maybe you just want to go home. Who needs all of these machines and medicines?"

"Would if I could."

"But you can't. Because the doctors here are keeping you alive."

He said nothing.

Footsteps progressed down the corridor outside, and then a young, shaggy-haired blond man stopped in the doorway and looked in. He blew out his breath in a whistle.

"Land sakes, he's awake. Morning, Vic, I didn't think you were coming."

"Jeremy!" Vic jumped to her feet, and they met in the middle of the room and embraced. "How are you?"

Nilla ran up to Jeremy excitedly and got some ear scratches from him.

"Fine as a summer day," Jeremy answered. "What about you? You and this old coot getting along?"

Vic looked over her shoulder at the hospital bed. "Well... there ain't been any bloodshed."

"Yet," Erin added in a murmur.

Jeremy looked at her and laughed. "And Erin is here to keep the peace. Or to defend you if there is bloodshed." He reached out a hand to shake, and Erin used it to pull herself up and give him a hug as well.

"How about you? How are you doing?"

He nodded. "Fine, fine. Where's Ma?"

"At the cafeteria getting something to eat."

"How did you convince her to do that? I did everything I could to get her to go earlier, and she outright refused."

"Just used my charms," Vic said with a smile. She motioned to the chair she had vacated. "You want to sit down?"

"Nah. Best to stay on my feet until I've woken up properly."
Jeremy yawned widely.

"Until you've woken up?" Vic repeated. "Did you just get out of
bed?"

Jeremy ran his fingers through his hair, swiping it back. "Well, I
didn't *just* get out of bed. But... yes."

"I didn't raise my boys to be lazy," Pa growled from the bed.
"Where are Joseph and Daniel? What's going on at the farm?"

"Nothing is going on at the farm," Jeremy said with a shrug. He
turned around to face his father. "I don't know where Joseph and
Daniel are. Maybe off with the clan."

CHAPTER 11

*T*here was silence for a few seconds as everyone looked at everyone else. Erin was the outsider and felt that she got the worst of the suspicious looks. She wondered if she should leave the room to give them some privacy to talk. Vic could apparently read this in Erin's eyes and made a small hand motion for her to stay where she was. She sat back down in the chair that she had previously occupied.

"None of my concern if they are off on clan business," she commented. "What's that got to do with me?"

"Is that what they told you?" Pa demanded of Jeremy. "Did someone talk to them?"

"How would I know? I'm not part of that world anymore. Don't want anything to do with it."

"The Jackson clan is the reason you had a roof over your head and food on the table," Pa growled. "If it weren't for them…"

"Then you would have actually had a producing farm," Jeremy finished. "Instead of pretending you were growing enough crops to support a family."

"Farming is a hard business. A few years of droughts, and where do you think the money comes from? The clan saved our bacon more than once."

"For a price."

Pa Jackson didn't appreciate this. "We would not have survived without the help of the clan."

"Then how do the rest of the farms survive? They're not all members of the Jackson or Dyson clans. Dysons hardly bother with farmers. The only reason the Jacksons do is because of family members like you who won't leave their farms. If they could get you into town, they would."

"What do you know? You don't know anything about how to run a farm or a business. You left. You decided you were too good for the clan and you ran away."

"I didn't want to end up in prison."

"Am I in prison? Are your brothers? The clan takes care of its own. We're not going to end up in prison."

"Because nobody in the clan does?" Jeremy challenged. It was clear from the rise in his voice that he knew better than that, and so did his father. Erin tried to imagine what it must have been like to live with an organized crime syndicate always in the background of their lives. Always there waiting to get them to do a job or take care of something. Knowing that the only thing that stood between them and losing the farm or ending up in prison was the clan. As long as they stayed in the good books of the men leading the clan. Growing up associating with criminals being treated as family. Or criminals who were family.

"You don't know what you're talking about," Pa repeated. His voice was getting weaker and his breathing more labored. Erin suspected he would fall asleep again within another minute or two. Talking was tiring him out.

Ma Jackson appeared in the doorway and looked in, past everyone else to her husband. "Is he awake? Pa? Pa, how are you feeling?" She moved past them, pushing herself in between Vic's chair and the bed.

"Tired, Mother. Need to close my eyes."

"Are you in any pain?" She leaned over him, shaking him. "Should I get the doctor?"

"No. Just let me rest."

He closed his eyes and drifted back off to sleep. Ma turned to Vic. "You said you would call me if he woke up! Why didn't you call me?"

Vic's jaw dropped. She looked at Erin in disbelief, then back at her mother again. "You wouldn't give me your number. How was I supposed to call you?"

"Well then… you should have come to get me. Or sent your friend to get me." Ma nodded in Erin's direction. "What is she here for? It isn't her family."

"Erin is here to support me. She's my friend. I could have sent her to go get you, but she doesn't know her way around here, and he was only awake for a minute. By the time she found you, he would have been asleep. You were already on your way back from the cafeteria anyway."

Ma Jackson shook her head, her mouth a straight, determined line. She had already decided that someone was to blame for her not being there when her husband woke up. She shot a look at Jeremy. He held his hands up defensively.

"I just got here. Just barely walked into the room."

Vic gave a dramatic shrug. "Whatever. I did what I could. I sat with him, so he wasn't alone when you were gone to eat. And you got to have a bit of a break. What else can I do for you? Do you need me to get you anything?"

Vic got up and gave her mother her chair back.

"Nothing is being done at the farm," Ma fussed. "No chores. No cooking. No shopping. Everything is just sitting there. I came to the hospital and I haven't gone home."

"What are those no-good brothers of mine doing? Don't they help out with anything?"

"With shopping and cooking? No! And chores are for kids; they don't think they have to do them anymore. They're out at all hours of the night or for days on end, and I can't rely on them to get anything done. They think the only ones they have to listen to are the Jackson clan. Ma and Pa don't count." Her voice broke slightly at the end of the tirade.

Vic nodded slowly. "Tell me what you need me to do. I'll go back to the farm and take care of things."

Erin unzipped her purse and pulled out her planner. She turned to a new page and held her pen over the page, ready to begin a list.

~

Half an hour later, Vic and Erin were climbing back into the bug. Vic patted her lap for Nilla to jump up.

"Well…" Vic drew the word out long. "What do you think of my dysfunctional family now?"

Erin put her purse in the back and settled into the driver's seat. "I've seen worse. They're stressed. People are more anxious and irritable when they're under stress."

Vic stretched her neck, turning her head back and forth. She rolled her shoulders. "Well, they're stressed, all right. Do you mind helping out with some chores?"

"Put me to work. That's what I'm here for. We should probably do the shopping first. Pick up what we need and take it out to the farm."

"Except I don't know what they already have. With Ma, something like 'the fridge is empty as Mother Hubbard's cupboard' might just mean that she's almost out of milk."

"There are four people living there, plus now you and Jeremy are going to be there at least part of the time for a few days, and there will probably be neighbors dropping by to express their condolences or ask how he's doing. So we should at least get the basics of what they will need for the next few days, and then we can look at the supplies when we get out there and make a list of what else needs to be purchased. You can visit the hospital again after we're done with the work. Get a good night's sleep at the hotel. Tomorrow we can do another supply run before we go back out to the farm."

Vic nodded. "Yeah. that all makes sense." She smiled. "You sound like you come from a big family. I'd never guess that you grew up without any family."

"I come from a lot of different families. Some of them big and some of them small," Erin pointed out. "I do have experience *with* families. I've just never had any of my own."

"I never thought of it that way." Vic pulled her door shut, buckled her seatbelt, and got Nilla settled. "You need me to direct you to the grocery store?"

"I think I remember where it is." Moose River was bigger than Bald Eagle Falls. Still, Erin had learned the basics of its layout on her previous visits there while trying to help Charley and taking care of her pet.

Just thinking about the gecko, with its sticky tongue, eyes that could roll two different directions, and the scampery little crickets he ate made Erin shudder.

She was *so* not a lizard person.

She put the car into drive and set out to find the grocery store.

CHAPTER 12

There were a lot of chores to be done at the farm, but not as much as Ma had made out needed to be done. She kept the place spic and span, so a couple of days away from home hadn't exactly resulted in the house turning into a disaster area. There were dirty dishes in the kitchen, mostly confined to the sink, and Erin didn't see much else that was out of place. They dutifully vacuumed the rugs, washed the dishes, and wiped down the counters, but there was no need for much more. Vic went out to the barn to take care of the animals. She shook her head at Erin's offer of help.

"No, I know how to take care of things and I don't need some city girl slowing me down," she drawled with a smile to let Erin know that she was not actually being disparaging. "You can just put your feet up here for a bit and relax."

Nilla pattered across the floor toward the door with Vic, his claws clicking on the floor.

"Oh, no you don't," Vic told him, pushing him back when he reached the door. "You stay inside with Erin. I don't need you getting kicked by a goat or eaten by a cat."

Erin laughed.

"You've probably never seen a farm cat," Vic said, "or you

wouldn't think that was quite so funny. They can be mean. Keep him inside with you; I don't want anything happening to him."

"All right," Erin agreed. "We'll keep each other company."

She walked over to Nilla and held on to his collar while Vic exited the kitchen. She let Nilla go, and he stood on his hind legs at the screen door, watching Vic go. He whined and looked back at Erin.

"She'll be back," Erin assured him. "Just put your paws up and relax."

Nilla didn't. He kept whining for a while, yapped to call Vic back, and whined some more at Erin to let him outside. She ignored him and, eventually, he curled up on the mat inside the door and waited.

Erin went to work baking. That was how she handled stress. She always felt better if she were mixing together a savory or sweet dough, breathing in the smell of the spices, the room heating with the warmth of the preheated oven. That was her heaven.

Though the Tennessee heat wasn't heavenly. It reminded Erin more of the depictions of that *other place*, which she didn't believe in any more than she believed in heaven. The devil would have been very comfortable sitting beside the oven as she put cookies in to bake. She had to keep sponging her forehead off with a clean cloth. She missed her air conditioner and fans at Auntie Clem's Bakery. Why wouldn't a farm in Tennessee have the convenience of central air conditioning?

When Vic returned to the farmhouse, Erin was putting in the last sheet of cookies. Vic sniffed at the air.

"Something smells good!"

Nilla barked and danced around her legs, earning a few pets and ear scratches.

"I thought I would make your dad some cookies," Erin explained.

"He could use some sweetening up, all right."

Erin laughed. "No, I just thought that with a sick stomach, he probably doesn't feel like much. Ginger helps to settle down nausea and it will probably help him to have something in his stomach, even if it's only a few bites."

Vic gave Erin a quick hug. "What did I say? You're always thinking of others."

"Actually, I just needed an excuse to bake."

Vic laughed. She went over to the cookies that were already on cooling racks and helped herself to a couple.

"Are you all done with your chores?" Erin asked. "Chickens didn't die with your mom being away for a day?"

"Unfortunately, no."

"Don't you like chickens? Your mom would have a fit if they died while she was gone."

"Maybe that's why I don't like them." Vic took a bite of one of the soft ginger cookies and gave a moan of appreciation. "Actually, I don't like the chickens because they're stupid and mean. They peck me, peck each other, and anyone else who gets close enough. Orneriest critters around."

"I thought chickens were smart. I've heard of people who have them as pets, train them like dogs, let them sleep in the house."

"Even my mother wouldn't let chickens sleep in the house. They're her critters and she's the only one that they like. Anyone else, they'd just as soon peck out your eyes. Or whatever other body part they could reach."

"Even your dad?"

"Especially Pa. You think he's nice to them? If he'd had his heart attack in the chicken pen, they would have pecked his bones clean. Chickens aren't quite as good as pigs at getting rid of a body, but give them a chance…"

Erin wrinkled her nose. "How did we get onto this topic? That's nasty. So, you fed and watered the chickens and all of the other animals?"

Vic nodded. "Yes, ma'am."

"And collected the eggs." Erin nodded to the pail in Vic's hand. "Where do those go? In the fridge?"

"There's room, so they may as well go in there until we're ready to do something with them."

"Do you sell them or just eat them yourselves?"

"Too many laying hens to just be eating the eggs themselves," Vic said slowly. "They must be selling at least some of them."

Vic found some egg cartons to put the eggs into and stacked them in the fridge. "Ma said that the boys didn't do anything, but someone at least milked the cows this morning. Not that there are very many to milk anymore."

"You did a lot."

"I'm not sitting on a stool milking by hand. Only takes a minute to get the machine hooked up. And most of the animals have auto-feeders; I just needed to make sure that everything was topped off." Vic sat down to eat the rest of her cookies. She stared out one of the kitchen windows. "Pa used a couple of the fields to start an orchard a few years ago, and he's still planting new trees. Not sure what he's growing out there or why he'd be changing the farm over to a new crop this late in the game." She shook her head.

"Maybe trees are more drought-resistant?" Erin suggested.

"Yeah, you're probably right about that. The trees themselves look okay, but the grass looks poor. Like there's something making them sick. It would be too bad if Pa plants something new, and then they all come down with the plague."

"The plague?"

"Whatever plague trees can get."

CHAPTER 13

*E*rin took one final walk around the house to make sure that everything looked acceptably clean and tidy. She knew that Ma Jackson probably had far more exacting standards than she did. Still, they couldn't be expected to do everything up to her expectations and to also do the farm chores that were normally Pa's purview.

As they headed through the kitchen to go back to the car, they were assaulted with the sound of a large engine as an ailing pick-up truck pulled up onto the gravel pad outside the door. Vic glanced out the window.

"Oh, boy. Well, more family time. Brace yourself."

They stepped out the door in time to hear one of the men getting out of the truck asking who they knew that drove a yellow Beetle.

"That would be Erin's," Vic informed them, head up and voice confident and clear. She had Nilla in her arms to ensure he didn't run out to meet the farm animals or the men. Nilla didn't like men very much.

"Well, well, well," one of them said, looking Vic up and down. It was disconcerting how much he looked like Jeremy. But he didn't have Jeremy's smile. His face was much harder and set into deep lines around the mouth and eyes. Lines that did not go up. "The prodigal son returns, eh? And did Pa kill the fatted calf for you?" He guffawed. A harsh, bullying sound.

Vic ignored the comment. "We did some cleaning up for Ma, and I took care of the animals. Fed and milked, eggs collected. Thanks for doing the milking this morning."

"We didn't do it," the second man said. He was, Erin thought, the oldest one. Joseph? She was pretty sure that the oldest was Joseph. "Neighbor must have come over and done it. Parker, maybe. Ma looked after their animals when Missus Parker was poorly."

Vic's mouth tightened. So they hadn't even had the decency to milk the cows when they knew very well that it would need to be done.

Both of the boys were staring at Vic. It was understandable, Erin thought. They weren't used to seeing her as a woman. It was probably hard to reconcile the James they had known growing up with the Victoria she was now. Her face and body so different from what they had been.

"There are cookies," Erin offered. The way to a man's heart was through his stomach, wasn't it? She was sure that they wouldn't turn down freshly baked cookies. "I'm taking a few to your Pa, but there are plenty left here. Help yourselves."

"Cookies. Well, that's awful nice of you. Nice James found someone so domestic. Are you one of *those* too?"

Vic's face flushed red. She might have been prepared to face some rude or teasing comments from her older brothers, but not for Erin to have to face them too. She opened her mouth to blast them.

"No, I'm not transgender," Erin told Joseph calmly. "How about you?"

Joseph sputtered and Daniel nearly busted a gut laughing. Vic closed her mouth and grinned at Erin.

"I'm still just as God made me," Joseph eventually managed, his voice both angry and embarrassed at the same time. "I'd be happy to show you any time you please."

"Don't be disgusting," Vic snapped at him.

"Mebbe a little fatter than God made you," Daniel suggested.

Joseph shot his brother an angry look. "You wanna say that again?"

"No." Daniel headed for the door. "I'm fixing to get some cookies. Can't let you get a weight advantage over me."

Joseph strode toward the door in an attempt to beat Daniel there. They wrestled on the concrete step outside the door, each trying to push the other out of the way to get in the door first.

Vic rolled her eyes at Erin and motioned toward the bug. Best to get going while the brothers were still occupied with each other.

"And those are my other two darling brothers."

When they got to Pa Jackson's hospital room, they found him awake, the head of the bed raised so that he could see around the room. He scowled when he saw Vic and Erin.

"Didn't I tell you to go home?" he asked. "You're not welcome around here as long as you're dressing up as a girl. Look at you. You're disgusting."

It hurt Erin just to hear him talk to Vic that way. She couldn't imagine how much it must hurt Vic to hear someone she had been taught to love and respect talking to her like that. Her face was pale as she looked back at him and didn't address the attack.

"Now Pa, you stop that," Ma corrected, shaking her head. "James and his friend came to help, and they've been doing chores up at the house for me. Unlike those other two good-for-nothings who can't be expected to lend a hand doing anything anymore."

"They have *important* things to do. They don't have the time to do your work too."

"I can't do all of the cooking and cleaning and be here with you," Ma pointed out, her brows drawing together in a scowl.

"What cooking? All you've been making lately are those gosh-awful salads. I told you they would be the death of me! A man needs meat and potatoes. And biscuits. And gravy. I can't subsist on rabbit food."

While Pa looked frailer than he had when Erin had seen him the last time they had visited the farmhouse, he did not look like he was wasting away to nothing. If Ma was insisting that he eat healthier, more power to her. She had obviously been correct about the state of his arteries.

"I brought you some cookies," Erin said tentatively, holding up the plastic container she had borrowed from Ma's kitchen.

"Cookies?" His eyes went to the container, then his frown deepened. "No. Thank you, but I don't need those."

"I didn't know whether you would be up to eating yet or not. They're ginger cookies, so they might help with the nausea."

"Who told you I was nauseated?"

Erin fumbled for words. "I thought... I was told that this all started with a stomach bug. You were throwing up. I just thought... I've always found ginger to be a good remedy to settle my stomach."

"Don't bring me any food. I don't want any of your food."

"Umm..." Erin looked at Vic, helpless. "Okay."

"You don't need to be so rude, Pa," Ma remonstrated. "She went to all that work just to bring you something nice. I'll have one of the cookies, Miss..."

"Erin Price. Just Erin." Erin popped the lid on the plastic container and offered them to Ma.

She took one out and nibbled at it. "They are still warm from the oven. How lovely. They're very good."

Pa watched her eat it, his eyes narrow and angry. His hand went to his chest and he breathed hard, expelling an *ugh* sound as though he had been kicked.

"Pa?" Ma leaned closer to him. "Are you okay? Are you in pain?"

He nodded, eyes watery. Ma hit the call button beside the bed.

"Come quick!" she shouted toward the door. "Somebody needs to come here! Help!"

It was only a few seconds before a nurse looked in the door. A quick response time. She looked at Pa and moved into the room.

"I need everyone out, please," she ordered. "Right now."

She lowered the head of Pa's bed and checked the vital statistics on the monitor. "Mr. Jackson, you're having a mild cardiac event," she told him in a loud voice. "I'm going to give you something to make you more comfortable and page a doctor. I need you to try to stay relaxed, do you understand?"

Vic and Erin both moved out of the room, Nilla's tags jingling quietly. Ma was another minute behind them, wanting to stay with her husband, but finally leaving at the nurse's insistence.

Another nurse on the unit motioned down the hall. "There is a visitor room down there where you can sit down," she said. She shook her head. "Cardiac patients are limited to *one visitor* at a time, and we ask that you not do anything to get them excited or upset them." Her eyes fell on Nilla but, surprisingly, she made no comment about pets not being allowed. "Please follow the rules. We have them for a reason."

"I don't think—" Vic started to protest.

"Go down there. I don't have the time to argue. We need to see to the patient."

They obeyed, walking down the hall to find the visitor room. They each sank into one of the upholstered chairs in a small grouping, anxious about Pa and irritated by the nurse's words.

"We weren't doing anything to upset him," Vic said, burying her face in her hands, elbows resting on her knees. "Offering the man a cookie is something upsetting? No one said we couldn't be in there."

Nilla stood on his hind legs, front paws on Vic's knees, in order to be able to reach her face, nudging and licking her anxiously.

"They said earlier that only one person was allowed in there at a time," Ma confessed. "I didn't think it would matter."

"Well, that's not what made him take a turn," Vic insisted. "Erin and I just barely got there, and we didn't do anything to upset him. It's not our fault."

"Of course not," Ma agreed. "He does tend to get riled up about your..." Ma made a helpless gesture toward Vic. "You dressing like that. And if he told you not to come back, then maybe you shouldn't have. I know you just want to make sure everything is okay, but..."

"He didn't tell me not to come back." Vic shook her head, face still in her hands. She swore under her breath.

"Maybe if you got rid of these things. Started behaving like a boy again. Then he'd be happy."

"I can't do this." Vic stood up and headed for the door. Erin scrambled after her.

Ma didn't make any attempt to call them back. They walked back down the hall the way they had come, past Pa's hospital room, where several medical professionals were working over him, relaying information back and forth to each other in what almost seemed like a choreographed dance.

CHAPTER 14

*E*rin followed Vic out to the hospital's main reception area at a brisk pace, Nilla scampering to keep up. Mary Alice was sitting at the reception desk again and smiled in Vic's direction, but she didn't notice. There were a few people sitting around, maybe waiting for doctors or waiting to be escorted to see loved ones. Vic stopped abruptly and whirled around to face Erin.

"We shouldn't have come. I should have gone with my first instinct and just stayed away. Let the ornery old coot die in peace without having to see how his precious *son* had turned out."

Erin didn't try to argue with her. She hadn't tried to convince Vic to come to see her father, and she wasn't going to force her to stay. If she wanted to go back to Bald Eagle Falls and Auntie Clem's Bakery, then that's what they would do.

"I'm sorry for the way they've been treating you. It's inexcusable."

"That's my family. That's my loving, crappy family. They're not going to change. What made me think that they would ever bother to grow and learn anything about being transgender? That they could give up their stupid beliefs and prejudices and consider that they might actually be wrong about something? It's never going to happen. They've got their neighbors and church friends all telling them that they are right and that if

68

they'll stay firm and tell me what I'm doing wrong that I'll see the light and mend my ways. Then everybody will be happy, right?"

Erin blinked at her. "*You* wouldn't be."

"What does it matter how Vic feels? Vic's feelings don't matter about anything. A person is whatever his parents say he is. They are always right. Anything else is just a *sin* and I sure as shootin' better repent and go crawling back, begging their forgiveness."

Erin was aware that everyone in the waiting area was watching them, listening in on the tirade, even if they were looking in the other direction or pretending to use their phones. Every ear was pricked to hear what Vic had to say next. Then they would go home and tell their families about all of the crazy stuff that happened while they were at the hospital.

A dark-clothed figure moved toward them. Erin startled, jerking her head around to look at him, her jumpy brain telling her that they were about to be attacked. But it was a security guard. A man in his sixties, neatly dressed in a black uniform, weaponry on his duty belt that he probably had never had the opportunity to use.

Vic followed Erin's gaze and saw the guard approaching them. She swore and shook her head as he got within speaking range. "I'm not going to cause any trouble. I'm just upset. My pa is in there dying and, according to the nurse, it's all my fault."

"It's okay," the guard said, his voice a soft bass, "but people can overhear you. There are more private areas—"

"We're not staying. We'll go outside. No point in disturbing anyone else with my troubles."

"I'm not saying that." The guard put a hand on Vic's arm, but he wasn't grabbing her to put her under arrest or hustle her out. It was a calming gesture. "Listen. *I* overheard what you were saying, and…" he hesitated, "I understand."

Vic rolled her eyes. "Thanks, but I don't think you could."

"When I came out, my family was the same way."

"You can't—" Vic started to argue before processing what he had said, then stopped. "When you came out?" she repeated. Her eyes went over the man, searching for the truth. "As… gay?"

"As a transgender man." His voice was hushed so as not to carry to the rest of the people in the reception area.

He and Vic looked at each other in silence for a few moments.

"There are more private places to talk," the guard repeated.

Vic nodded.

He removed his hand from her arm and motioned to a hall behind the reception desk. "This way." He stepped ahead of them and led them past Mary Alice—who was now looking at Vic with an uncertain expression—to a small meeting room that Erin supposed was used for consults or meeting with family members. They didn't sit down or close the door. Erin leaned against the back of one of the chairs and looked at Vic and the guard, trying to be invisible.

"You're trans?" Vic asked, not quite believing it.

"Derek Marshall," he introduced himself. "Formerly... Delphinium."

Vic grimaced. "That's horrible!"

Derek laughed. "I always thought so. Though Delf isn't too bad, at least it is more masculine."

"I'm Victoria Webster. Vic."

"Formerly Victor?"

"James Victor Jackson. Changed my last name too."

"Victoria is pretty." Derek hesitated. "Are you one of *those* Jacksons?"

Vic sighed. "I was. Yes. But I left the family and the clan." She looked down at herself. "You can see why."

"There are women who take an active part in the clan."

Erin remembered Crazy Theresa and shuddered.

"Not me," Vic asserted. "I didn't want to live that kind of life."

"Your dad is here now?"

Vic nodded. "Heart attack, I guess."

"It's not your fault."

"According to the nurse and my mother, it is. If I didn't want to give him another heart attack, I shouldn't go in the room dressed like this." She motioned to herself. "I should give it all up and go back to looking like I used to." Her nostrils flared. "I am *never* doing that."

"Some people aren't strong enough. They cave under all of the pressure and go back. I've seen it happen. Their families and old friends won't accept their transition, and they can't get over that abandonment. It's hard in the South, here in the Bible Belt. There's just so much hate and intolerance."

"And they're all so proud of themselves for being good Christians."

Derek nodded. "I think… the churches will have a lot to answer for, in the end."

"So what did you do? How did you manage it?" Vic asked curiously. "Things must have been a lot worse when you were young. At least there's a strong LGBT community, now."

"It's actually not that long since I transitioned." Derek touched his hair, short and speckled with gray. "I know I might not be typical, but as transitioning becomes talked about more openly, some of us who have been in hiding for a long time are finding the courage to come out. To be able to live our lives in a way that we never would have thought possible."

Vic let out a whistle. "It must have been a relief, after so long. Was it?"

"Yes… and no… also terrifying, heartbreaking… a huge loss as well as a huge gain." He blinked, his eyes shiny.

"You said that your family reacted the same way as mine. That must have been hard."

"I had always tried to have a good relationship with them. Not to disappoint them. Maybe overcompensating for the way I felt because I knew it would be repugnant to them if they ever found out. I lived my life for them for fifty years, being the perfect daughter. Trying to live up to all of their ideals in every way. I got married to someone I didn't love for all the wrong reasons. Dutifully got pregnant and had three lovely children." He stopped, scratching the back of his head and looking down at the floor. "I love my children, but getting pregnant was one of the most painful experiences of my life. The worst ever betrayal by my own body."

Vic wiped a tear from the corner of her eye, nodding.

"Up three cup sizes, pregnant belly, having to spend time in ultra-feminine clinics and obstetricians' offices. I tried to hide from my husband how depressed and suicidal I was. I never knew if I would be able to hold on and survive each pregnancy. My husband didn't know anything about dysphoria or what was going on; he thought I was just emotional from the hormones. Like all women."

"Are they still… in your life?"

Derek shook his head. "No. They all broke ties. My husband was the first to go, tired of a marriage that was a lie. He wasn't getting anything out of it. I wasn't getting anything out of it. The only reason we stayed together for as long as we did was to raise the children. When they were out on their own, he told me he wanted a divorce, and I didn't argue. Thank heavens he did. I don't know how I would have come to terms with my gender otherwise."

"And even your kids?"

"I thought that they would be confused, maybe angry, but that we were close enough that we could still be a family. But they couldn't accept it. A lot of that is the way we raised them. Church going. We'd always taught them that being gay was a sin. We really didn't have any concept of transgender back then. Any divergent 'sex' stuff was all just wrapped up in being gay. Women were expected to look like women, act like women, marry a man, and have children. Any deviation from that was a sin. So my kids took that to heart. One of them still contacts me every now and then. An email or a quick call. It's a secret. I'm not allowed to tell anyone. Maybe someday she'll come to accept me as I am. But probably not as long as she lives in the South. Not unless things really change."

"That must be so hard," Vic empathized. "It's been tough with my parents and brothers, but I can only imagine what it is like to lose your children too."

"I'm rebuilding a different kind of life. I've had to sever all ties with that old life. Maybe someday one of them will build a bridge back, but for now… that's another life. That's my past. And I have to live in the present, without a family but also without the pain of dysphoria. New friends, new experiences and opportunities. I lived for my family for fifty years and now it's time to live for myself."

"And your parents?"

"Father's gone. Mother's got dementia. She has no idea who I am, female or male. Those first few years after transitioning were so hard. I had been so close to them on the outside, but they had never known the real me. Who I was on the inside. I wanted them to know and love that person. But they didn't. They thought at first that I was crazy, told the police I was a danger to myself and tried to Title 33 me. They figured the doctors would give me a pill, and I'd be better, be my old self again. That didn't work, so they tried to have the pastor counsel me. Explain to me how I was going straight to hell if I didn't straighten out. A whiff of fire and brimstone, and I would give up my sinful ways."

"But you didn't," Vic said simply.

"But I didn't. Bless their hearts, they thought they could *convert* me into identifying as female. They had my best interests at heart. I had to cut them off. I couldn't let them control my life, to keep disrupting my chance at happiness."

"You think that's what I should do?" Vic used a tissue to dab at her eyes and then her nose, sniffling.

"I don't know what you should do. You're the one who has to make that decision. Everyone is different."

Vic gulped and nodded. "Okay. Yeah."

CHAPTER 15

*V*ic wiped her nose again and reached for her purse. She stopped with her hand out, looking for it. She looked at Erin.

"Where's my purse? Where did I leave it?"

Erin thought back. Had Vic had it when she left her father's hospital room? She was pretty sure that Vic hadn't put anything down in the reception area, so it had to be either in the hospital room or in the waiting room with Vic's mother.

"I think… probably in the hospital room."

Vic swore. "I don't want to go back there. Not now. I have to think about this. I need time."

"You can wait here or at the front. I'll go back and find it."

"I can't make you do that," Vic protested. But her distress was clear. She could not go back to that hospital room. Not before she'd had a chance to settle down and make a decision about her next action. There was no way she was going back in there to see her mother or father and have to deal with her father's condition, whatever it was.

"It's not a problem," Erin assured her. She didn't care what Ma and Pa Jackson thought about her. They'd already made it pretty clear that they would not approve of anyone who was friends with Vic and supported her in her transition. "It doesn't bother me at all. I'll go back and find it."

Vic nodded. "Okay. If you're sure."

"Just relax here… or back in the reception area. And I'll be right back."

Erin looked at Derek. He nodded. "I'll look after her. Go ahead."

She didn't know whether that meant he would keep her in the small meeting room or that he would escort her back to the main reception area once she was calmed down enough. But it wouldn't be hard to find them either way.

She walked back down the halls to find the cardiac unit and Pa Jackson's hospital room.

A tired-looking doctor and a couple of nurses, or maybe a nurse and an intern, were huddled together outside of Pa's room, looking at a clipboard the doctor held.

"I'd really like to know what is causing these episodes," the doctor commented. "For a man of his age and who has lived the lifestyle that he probably has, he is in remarkably good shape. His arteries are not occluded. So why is he having these cardiac episodes? What is causing them?"

"Maybe something genetic," one of the others suggested. "Maybe something that he's always had, but it's just being triggered now by age or stress."

"The wife says that his diet has changed recently," the nurse put in. "Maybe that has triggered them somehow? An allergy or intolerance?"

"Kounis Syndrome?" the doctor questioned. "A possibility. But he hasn't taken anything by mouth since he got here, has he?"

"No," the nurse agreed, frowning. "We've been trying to get him to eat, but he says he can't. He's still nauseated."

"Could a viral or bacterial infection have caused it?" the intern asked. "Both the stomach symptoms and the cardiac symptoms?"

"Both are possibilities. Bloods suggest liver and kidney damage, but from what? By all accounts, he hasn't taken any new medication. The changes in diet have been to a healthier, more plant-rich diet. Not something that should cause any damage."

"Do you want to transfer him to the city or get a consult? Maybe they would be able to suggest some lab tests that would point us in the right direction."

The doctor shook his head. "He's better off staying in one place. He's stable here. Moving him could make things worse. They're just going to do the same things as we're already doing anyway. Monitor his progress. Watch for triggers. Consult the literature to see what else we might be missing."

They each nodded. Erin saw the nurse look up in her direction and realize that she had overheard part of the conversation.

"Can I help you, miss?"

"Sorry. I just needed to see if my friend left her purse in the room."

They watched her as she walked by them to go into the room. Erin looked to where Vic had been standing and saw that she had, in fact, put down her purse on a chair and left it there when they were kicked out of the room. Erin looked anxiously at Pa Jackson. He was not watching her with an eagle eye, but was unconscious. The stats on the electronic monitor looked good as far as Erin could tell. The heart monitor was not making any alarming noises. He was resting quietly.

Erin picked up Vic's purse. It was lighter than hers, which she carried her new planner in. The planner helped organize her life much better than the scraps of paper that she had relied on until then. But it did make her purse significantly heavier. Vic said that she should use apps on her phone, which would not increase the amount she had to carry, but Erin wasn't ready to give up paper. It had worked for her, and she always felt calmer when she was writing down a list or a plan. Why change something that was working for her?

She walked out of the hospital room. The doctor and the others were still watching her. Erin raised Vic's purse slightly. "Got it."

They nodded and watched her walk away again. Erin kept her eyes pointing forward and didn't look back to see how long they watched her, and if they had their heads together talking about her before going to see Ma Jackson and give her an update on her husband.

~

"How are you doing now?" Erin asked as they got into the bug.

Vic held Nilla up to her face and pressed her mouth into the top of his head.

"You want comfort food?" Erin suggested.

"Oooh, I could go for some comfort food," Vic agreed. "What should we have?"

"You know the restaurants around here better than I do. Anywhere that you used to love to go to? Fast food or sit down, whatever you feel like. We can take something back to the hotel if you don't want to be around people."

Vic thought about it. "There's this soda shop we used to go to in high school. Burgers and milkshakes. They were so good. Probably a thousand calories each, but we lived on them when we were in school."

"Let's go for it," Erin agreed. "What's it going to hurt for one meal? Tomorrow we'll have lots of vegetables."

"It's only once," Vic echoed. "Why not? We're allowed to pamper ourselves every now and then. What's the point in going back to your hometown if you can't indulge in a little nostalgia?"

Erin nodded. Vic kissed the top of Nilla's head and scratched his ears.

"He's been so good on this trip. I was nervous about taking him to the hospital. Worried that he would be barking and growling at people."

"He's settled down a lot in the time that you've had him."

"He has. You're a good boy, aren't you, Nilla? You're much happier and calmer now."

He nuzzled her face, his tail wagging back and forth so fast it looked like he was going to take off.

CHAPTER 16

They were both feeling overstuffed and a little bit queasy by the time they got back to the hotel room. Vic held her hand over her stomach and groaned.

"I guess I can't eat like a teenager anymore. I can't believe that I ate like that practically every day through high school. That was my go-to lunch for years."

Erin shook her head. "Maybe we should have split a meal between us. Neither of us is used to eating like that. My body is rebelling!"

"No kidding. I could never understand why my mom made such a big deal of how much I ate back then. All of the boys ate a ton. We worked hard at chores every day and I had a teenage metabolism. I just thought it was normal to eat that much."

"Things change!"

"Ugh. Yeah." Vic looked down at the hotel beds and the one chair by the writing desk. "I can't sit down here. And if I lie down, I'm going to throw up. I guess I'll take Nilla for a walk. Maybe if I walk around a while, it will settle."

"Okay." Erin collapsed onto one of the beds. Unlike Vic, she felt like all she could do was curl up and go to sleep. "Do you want company on your walk?"

Vic surveyed Erin, hands on hips. "Yeah, you look like you're up for a walk."

"I can walk if you want me to come along."

"No. I've already got company." Vic gestured to Nilla. "And it would do me good to have some time by myself to think about things. Walking helps to get the brain unstuck."

Erin couldn't help but feel a little relieved that Vic didn't need her to go along. "Okay. If you're sure."

"Yeah, I'm sure. You go ahead and have a nap or watch TV. I'll be a while."

Vic called to Nilla and took him back outside. Erin curled up on the bed and closed her eyes. She wasn't going to go to sleep. Just to rest and give her body a chance to digest the enormous, fat-laden supper.

She awoke some time later, disoriented about how much time had passed. She felt a little better, but Vic wasn't back, and that worried her. She picked up her phone and looked at the time. She wasn't sure exactly when they had gotten back to the hotel, but she thought that Vic had only been gone for half an hour or so. She had a lot to think about and might easily walk for an hour or more.

Erin propped herself up with a couple of pillows and tapped on Terry's number in her favorites. He answered within a couple of rings.

"Erin. How are you?"

"I'm good. Except that my stomach hurts."

"Are you sick?" he sounded concerned. "Vic's dad didn't have anything contagious, did he?"

"I ate too much."

"Oh." Terry chuckled. "Then I guess you deserve what you get."

"You're supposed to be a little more sympathetic than that."

"Sorry. A little bit difficult to feel bad for you for overeating."

"Vic took me to her childhood burger joint." Erin burped, tasting the burger again. "They must have increased the serving sizes since she used to eat there."

"Maybe. Or maybe your stomach isn't used to eating like a teenager."

"That's what I told her."

"Then you don't need me to tell you."

"Well, maybe I do. How about you? Did you get something good to eat tonight? Don't tell me that you just had a sandwich."

"We had pizza at the police department. It was Melissa's birthday."

"Oh, well, that was nice. I'll have to tell her happy birthday." Erin could send her a text or an email later.

"Are you alone?"

"Yes. Why?"

"I just didn't hear anything in the background."

"Vic took Nilla out for a walk and to try to walk off her meal. I had a nap."

"And are you feeling better?"

"A little. Not so tired, anyway. It was a long day today."

"How is Vic's dad. Is he still…?"

"Still in the land of the living. At least he was when we left the hospital today. He had another heart attack. The doctors don't know why."

"They don't know why?" Terry repeated. "I assume because of his age and his diet."

"No, the doctor said that his arteries weren't blocked. He is having heart attacks for another reason."

"Oh. Maybe something inherited?"

"They said it could be. I guess they're going to run more tests. Look into it."

"How was he when you saw him? Was he awake?"

"A couple of times. Not for very long at a time. But awake enough to know who we were and to carry on a conversation. A short one."

"How was he with Vic? Was he glad that she had made it there?"

"Umm… no. He was pretty nasty, actually. Telling her how disgusting she looked and that she shouldn't be trans. You know. The usual."

Terry sighed. "I'm sorry she has to deal with that. I hoped that with his close encounter with death, he would just be happy to see her. Have his family gathered around him."

"They don't seem like they're a very tight-knit group. I mean... Ma and Pa seem close, but... not in a good way, if that makes sense?"

"What do you mean?"

"Like... she has to be at his side, but when she is, all they do is argue and snipe at each other. He says she's trying to kill him; she gets after him for how he talks. They're not really nice to each other."

"Like an old married couple."

"Well, they are... but I think that if that's the way you are toward each other when you've been married for thirty years or whatever... maybe it's not working. I mean, shouldn't they know each other better? Have worked out all of those arguments?"

"From what I've seen as a law enforcement officer... no, it's pretty common to just keep arguing and grousing at each other for decades. It gets to be a familiar, comfortable pattern. You try getting in between the two of them, criticizing one of them in front of the other, and then you'll see some fireworks. Then suddenly, the other person can do no wrong."

"So they love each other; they just don't like each other very much?"

"I'd say it's more a case of being afraid of what would happen if they broke up. They know what to expect from each other. They are each other's safety net. They're terrified of what would happen if something came between them. I prefer the ones that just argue and complain. The ones who try to break up and end up in a physical altercation are much more dangerous. The ones who keep breaking up and getting back together again, those are the ones who end up shooting each other. Or some innocent bystander."

"Are there people like that in Bald Eagle Falls? Really?"

"There are people like that everywhere. Bald Eagle Falls is not exempt from domestic disputes."

"Everyone seems so normal and... boring when they come to the bakery."

Terry laughed. "I don't imagine too many couples go to the

bakery and come to blows over what kind of cookies to buy. You can never be sure what goes on behind closed doors. People keep that part of their lives private. Other than, you know, when their fighting gets so loud that the neighbors call in a disturbance, or their fight spills out into the street. But not everyone is like that."

"I know. Sometimes no one would have any idea what was going on." Erin said it softly, not really wanting to acknowledge that part of her past.

There was silence from Terry as he considered that. "I suppose you probably have more experience in that area than you let on."

Erin didn't know what to say to that. She didn't really want to talk about it. There was a reason that she didn't talk much about her past.

"I am here if you want to talk about it," Terry offered.

It was easier when they talked over the phone, when she didn't have to look him in the eye and he couldn't see her face. And Vic wasn't there to overhear the conversation. She had privacy for a few minutes.

"I don't really. I don't even like to think about it."

"You were with several different families," Terry suggested, "so you have had a variety of experiences with the ways that couples or parents deal with their relationship or with their kids. I know a lot of stuff goes on in foster care that shouldn't. Things that no one outside of the home knows about, or they wouldn't be able to continue to be foster parents."

"Yeah."

Though Erin wondered, sometimes, how much the social workers had guessed. Some of the abuse was invisible. But sometimes, she thought that the social workers looked the other way because they didn't have anywhere else to place kids. There were only so many homes available, and admitting that they knew what was going on would mean fewer places for kids to go.

"Was there a lot of abuse? Was it common or the exception?" Terry prodded.

"I don't know. There are different kinds of abuse. Stuff that no one cares about or is built into the system. It's not just physical abuse, but... control. Raising kids is about control. About adults telling kids what to do and making them do it. Some people do that by physical force and some people do it other ways."

"I think there's more to parenting than that. A good parent knows that their child needs to grow to be an individual. To separate and develop independence."

"Maybe in a normal family. But in foster care, it's about making them behave the way the government and social workers say they should. Kids can't just decide to do what they want. The only way to do that is to run away. And stay away. Not get caught."

Terry considered that. He didn't argue, which was good. Erin knew what she was talking about. He'd asked her opinion.

A lot of people would have argued.

That was one of the reasons Erin wasn't keen to have kids of her own. That and the impact it would have on her business. She didn't want to be the adult on the other end. In charge of not only seeing to the care and feeding of a child, but also with making them comply with society's expectations. There were parents who didn't try to control their children, but that created a whole other set of problems. Erin wasn't sure she would be able to find the happy medium. If there even was one.

"So..." She sighed, returning to the conversation they'd been having before it went off track. "That's Vic's parents. I suppose they're happy together. They seemed comfortable with the kind of relation-ship they have, anyway."

"Does Vic want to stay there? Or has she had enough?"

"I don't know. See what she says when she comes back from her walk. We're here for the night, anyway. I don't think either one of us wants to drive back tonight. We'll sleep off our burgers and come back in the morning if she decides she wants to go home."

"Okay. Whatever is best for her. I miss you, but you're where you should be. Vic needs someone on her side."

"Yeah. I wouldn't want her to be here by herself. I mean, Jeremy's around, but he's kind of funny with them. He's not an outcast like Vic, but he did leave the family business, so he's still kind of an outsider."

"Maybe."

Erin frowned into the phone. "Maybe what?"

"*Maybe* he left the family business. We don't really know that for sure. He could still be operating covertly. It isn't as easy to get out of the family business as you might think. It isn't a matter of just walking away. A lot of people who try to leave... end up being recruited back, even if they do get away initially."

"Why would Jeremy ever go back? He didn't want to be involved."

"Life is easier when you are being taken care of. Their physical needs, at least, are met. They don't have to worry about living out on the street. They get the money they need to live well. That counts for a lot. Someone who has grown up living that lifestyle and suddenly finds themselves on the skids... it's much easier to just go back."

CHAPTER 17

*E*rin cleared her throat. She shook her head emphatically, even though Terry couldn't see it.

"Jeremy hasn't gone back. I'm sure of that."

"He might never have truly left. You know that there was still some question of just how much he was involved in what went on before we found out about The Bake Shoppe being used as a way station."

"He wasn't involved in that, and he isn't involved with anyone else in the clan now. He's just here to see their pa."

"Okay."

Erin could read his tone, though, and "okay" didn't mean that he was convinced she was right. Just acknowledging that she thought she knew what she was talking about and he didn't think it worth arguing about. Placating her.

She hated to be *handled.*

One day she was going to throttle him when he did that. But it obviously wouldn't be this time, since he was a two-hour drive away.

"Hopefully, the doctors will be able to figure out what's wrong with Vic's father," Terry said in his wrapping-it-up voice. "Get him on whatever medication he needs to be on or put in a pacemaker."

"Yeah. As dysfunctional as the family is, I don't think they really want him to die right now. He's not that old. Just... fifties or sixties. If they can figure out what's making him sick, maybe they can fix it. And he can go back to the farm and do whatever... plant more trees."

"Is it a tree farm? I assumed it would be soybeans or cotton. Maybe corn."

"He's been planting trees lately. Maybe the soybeans didn't weather the droughts very well. Trees are hardier than annual crops, right? And you don't have to replant them every year. I don't think the farm has been doing very well."

"I imagine that's stressful. Maybe this was all just caused by stress."

"Maybe," Erin agreed, thinking about it. That hadn't seemed to satisfy the doctor, and wouldn't he be the one who would know whether a sudden illness like Pa Jackson's could be caused just by stress? She knew that stress could cause heart problems, but throwing up like he had been? That didn't sound like stress. "I don't know. Maybe it was just a virus."

The doctor had said that it might be viral.

Something that Pa had said came into Erin's mind. He hadn't tried to pass off his illness as just a stomach bug. But he had complained about the change in his diet, about his wife making him eat salads rather than the meat and potatoes he was accustomed to.

"Do you think that a change in his diet could have made him sick?"

"I've heard that eating a really fatty meal can precipitate a heart attack. It actually makes your blood thicker."

Erin tried not to think of the meal that she'd just eaten and how slowly her blood was probably squeezing through her blood vessels now. No wonder she felt so sluggish.

"Actually, he was complaining that his wife was making him eat healthier stuff. Salads and vegetables."

"Oh... well, you do hear about people getting salmonella poisoning from salads sometimes. Because of the conditions that they are grown and harvested in."

"Wouldn't the doctor know that? Wouldn't they recognize food poisoning? I know it can make you throw up a lot. But can it give you a heart attack?"

"No idea. I would assume they would recognize food poisoning. It's pretty common."

"Yeah," Erin agreed. She smiled. "Maybe Ma is trying to poison him. That's what he said. That her salads would be the death of him."

Terry chuckled. "I think we can rule out Ma Jackson. She's put up with him this long; she's not likely to suddenly start poisoning his salads now."

Erin recalled how Pa had looked at her when she had brought him the cookies. As if she were offering him a snake. Why would he refuse to eat cookies? She could understand it if he had said that he was too nauseated to eat anything. But he had just told her that she shouldn't bring him anything to eat, he wouldn't eat it. Ma had been perfectly happy with the cookies, so it didn't seem like it was a territorial thing.

"What if someone *did* poison him? What would it look like?"

"There are a lot of different poisons. Vomiting is a pretty common symptom. But it is a common symptom of a lot of things. I wouldn't jump straight to that conclusion."

"But the doctors have checked for all of the usual stuff. Could it be poisoning?"

"Yes…" Terry drew the word out. "A lot of poisonings are never discovered until it is too late. And many poisons wouldn't show up in a run-of-the-mill autopsy. Doctors have to be looking for a particular toxin in order to find it. It isn't like on TV, where you just put a sample into the machine and it spits out a chart and tells you what it is, as well as the manufacturer's name and lot number."

Erin grinned. TV did make the process look pretty simple.

"But you don't think it really is poisoning, do you?" Terry asked.

"No, I guess not…" But why not? He had been throwing up, then had a heart attack? That sounded like poison to her. "But if he worked for the Jackson clan… then I guess he had enemies. People who might not want him around."

"He would have said something to someone if he suspected poisoning."

"To who? The police? He wouldn't want to involve them if it was something to do with the clan."

"To the doctor. If you thought you'd been given poison, wouldn't you want the doctors to know about it so they could treat you?"

As someone who had previously been poisoned, Erin had to admit that yes, she had wanted to help her doctor figure out what the poison was so that she could get the proper treatment and feel better and get out of the hospital. "Yeah. But if it was just a suspicion, and the doctors said they thought it was a virus... if I was a member of a criminal organization, I probably wouldn't want to bring it up. Just to be careful of what else I put in my mouth."

Like Pa had been, refusing to take her ginger cookies.

But he hadn't stopped Ma from eating one, so he obviously hadn't thought that Erin was trying to poison him. If he did, it was pretty cold-blooded to watch his wife eat a possibly poisoned cookie in order for him to determine whether it was safe or not.

"Erin?"

"Yeah."

"What are you thinking?"

"I think that he might suspect it." Erin told him about the cookies and Pa's odd behavior in refusing to have any.

"He might just have been feeling too ill."

"I know. That's probably all it was."

"If you really think that it might be poisoning, then you should talk to someone. More than one someone, actually, because you should talk to the hospital so they can test and treat him and talk to the police to put them onto the case."

"I should probably stay out of it. It's not really anything to do with me."

"Is this the Erin that I know and love? You're going to stay out of it?"

"Well... it's Vic's family, and I don't want to do anything that is going to make things worse for her."

"Uh-huh."

"I don't really have any reason to be suspicious of anything. Just because he didn't want my cookies? Not everyone likes cookies. And some people really hate ginger. It's a strong taste. Peter Foster doesn't like ginger."

"I'm not going to argue that you should be investigating a crime. I think it's a good idea for you to just stay out of it and let things take their natural course."

"If it was poisoning, then the doctor will figure that out on his own, right?"

"I'm sure he will."

But Terry had already said that poisonings were often missed by doctors until it was too late. That they could be very hard to detect. What if the doctor didn't figure out what was wrong with Pa Jackson, and the next heart attack killed him? Erin felt guilty without even having done anything. What if she said nothing and Vic's father died because of it?

She sighed.

"You know Jack Ward," Terry reminded her. "Drop in on him for a visit tomorrow. You don't have to tell him anything; just see how you feel about it. He'll be happy to see you."

"He might not be so happy if I tell him that I think someone is trying to kill Jeremiah Jackson."

"Do you think he would be happier if you thought someone was and didn't tell him about it?"

"You always tell me to stay out of investigations. Let the police deal with them."

"Yes. And that's the same thing as I'm telling you now. If you think there is a crime being committed, then tell the police and let them take care of it. You don't need to investigate on your own. No asking questions. No speculating. No looking into things. Just leave it alone and let Jack Ward and his men deal with it."

"I'll sleep on it. There's probably nothing there. I'm just imagining it."

"See how you feel in the morning," Terry agreed. "That's the best."

"And you won't ever mention this to Vic, right? If I decide there's nothing to it and I'm just being dramatic, you won't tell her that once I thought someone was trying to poison her father?"

"I won't tell her."

"Promise?"

"I don't need to promise. If I say I won't tell her, I won't tell her."

"Promise," Erin repeated firmly. She knew that what Terry said was true. He wasn't going to tell her that he would keep her secret and then go and blab it to Vic. She didn't need some kind of signed contract from him.

But she was anxious about it and wanted to make sure that he understood how serious she was.

"Fine," Terry said. "I promise not to tell Vic."

CHAPTER 18

*E*rin heard a jangling in the hall. It sounded like Nilla's dog tags. "I think they're coming back now. I'll let you go."

"Call me tomorrow and let me know how things are going."

"Sure. Talk to you tomorrow."

The jangling stopped at the door. Erin got up to unlock the door for Vic but, by the time she did, Vic had already swiped her key card and opened the door.

"Hey. How are you doing?" Erin asked.

Vic looked around. "I thought I heard you talking to someone?"

"Just on the phone with Terry."

"Oh." Vic looked at the phone in her hand. "Hi, Officer Piper!"

"I already hung up."

"Well, don't I look stupid talking to your phone for no reason." Vic shut the door and let Nilla off the leash. The little dog ran around the room a couple of times, as if he hadn't just spent the last hour walking. Vic sat down on the bed, then stretched out. "I am beat. I'm tired of walking and tired of talking."

"Were you talking to Willie on your phone?"

"No. Just been talking to Nilla. He's a pretty good listener, you know."

Erin laughed. "Probably better than most people." She sat back down on the bed and stretched out like Vic, snuggling into the warm spot she had previously occupied.

"Yup. Never judges me or makes fun of me for saying something silly. Lets me go on for as long as I like. Doesn't care if I cry. I don't know what I need a man for with him around."

"So, did he give you any advice? Did you come to any conclusions?"

"No. Just that I need to get a good sleep tonight. Then maybe in the morning, I'll be able to decide."

Erin chuckled, amused that it was the same conclusion she had come to. Vic tilted her head, looking questioning. "Nothing. Just that I decided the same. Have to make sure I get a good night's sleep. It's been a long day."

"Has it ever." Vic yawned. "You want to put something on the tube? Or just lie here?"

"I'm good with just lying here," Erin said, closing her eyes and relaxing.

~

Erin must have fallen asleep. She hadn't even brushed her teeth or changed, but she was so mentally exhausted that even just lying there making the occasional remark to Vic as things came into her mind, she had drifted off. By how long it was taking Vic to wake up and realize that her phone was ringing, she had also fallen asleep.

"Vic. Vicky. Hey. Your phone is buzzing."

"What?" Vic yawned, still not focused on the fact that someone was trying to reach her.

"Your phone is ringing."

"Oh. Thanks."

Vic fumbled for her phone, then finally found it in her pocket and lifted it to her face. "Unknown caller," she grunted, and moved like she was going to put it away again.

"It could be the hospital," Erin pointed out.

Vic swore. "You're right. But why would they be calling me?" She swiped the call and hit the speaker button, whether to ensure that Erin could hear the caller too or whether by mistake, she wasn't sure.

"Hello?"

"Victoria." The voice on the other end was female. Teasing. An accent identical to Vic's. Maybe Mary Alice, the receptionist at the hospital. "Victoria Webster. I hear your pa has been feeling poorly."

Vic's eyes suddenly went to Erin. Erin covered her mouth to hide her expression. She knew that voice too.

Theresa.

Crazy Theresa Franklin.

Crazy, murdering, on-the-run Theresa.

"Is this…" Vic gulped. "Tess?"

"Of course it is. Who else would be calling to express their condolences?"

Vic placed the phone on the bed and rubbed her eyes. "Condolences…? He hasn't passed."

"Just my condolences for him being sick," Theresa said, still a mocking, teasing note in her voice. "I know what it's like to have a sick parent."

"Oh? What happened with your parents?" Vic asked, keeping her voice upbeat.

They already knew Jack Ward's theory that Theresa had killed both of her parents and had buried them somewhere on the property.

"It was a short illness. Kind of like your pa's."

"And what happened? Did they get better?"

"Do you think they got better?" Theresa laughed. But she didn't fill in the details, telling her that they were dead or that they were off on a cruise somewhere, the story she'd been telling around town.

"Well, it was nice of you to call," Vic said. "I actually was sleeping, though, so…"

"I couldn't know what you were doing. Not unless I was there. Watching you."

Erin looked around the room, spooked. She got up and went to the window, parting the curtain just a crack to peer out and see if she could see a shadowy figure standing out on the sidewalk, watching them. Theresa might not actually be able to see into the room but, if she had been watching the room, she could know that the TV was not on and that their shadows had not crossed in front of the curtains for an hour or two. Easy enough to figure out that meant they were asleep.

Erin couldn't see anyone outside.

Maybe it was just a guess based on the fact that it was late and they'd had an exhausting day. Visiting people at the hospital made for an emotional day. Stressful emotions made people tired. Not exactly rocket science.

Erin shook her head at Vic to indicate she didn't see anyone. Vic nodded back.

"Are you back in town?" Vic asked. "I didn't know that. I figured… you'd stay away."

"I'm just like you. I couldn't stay away."

"I'm not here to stay. Just here to make sure that my mom is okay."

"Your mom?" Theresa sounded confused by this. "But it's your dad who's sick."

"I know. And he doesn't want anything to do with me. But I figure my mom will have a lot to do and need some support if he passes."

"*When* he passes," Theresa corrected. There was a smile in her voice as she continued. "You know that he's going to die sooner or later."

"Well… everyone dies sooner or later."

"Exactly."

Vic rolled her eyes at Erin and shook her head. That look that said, "Crazy Theresa." Erin had to agree. She gave a nod. Then she went to the hotel room door and folded over the lock to keep the door secure. She knew they could be foiled by an experienced burglar, but it was the best she could do for the moment.

"When I was told that he was sick, I thought he was going to die right away. But now I don't know. He's rallying. Maybe he won't die this time. Maybe he's got another twenty or thirty years in him, especially if eats more healthy, like Ma is trying to get him to."

"Healthy eating won't help him if it's his time to die."

"Well... we pray that it isn't."

"You ever get the feeling that God isn't actually in charge of these things?" Theresa asked, laughing.

"I know that Jack Ward survived. If God wasn't in that..."

Jack Ward had survived being stabbed in the back multiple times by Theresa with a hunting knife. Erin had to admit that it was miraculous. If she believed in an all-powerful being, she would undoubtedly have attributed Jack Ward's survival to him. Or her. But she didn't.

Theresa snorted. "God had nothing to do with that. Jack Ward was just too ornery to die. He had the devil on his side."

"Have you met my dad? If anyone can be called an ornery old cuss, it's him."

Theresa laughed, apparently liking this. "He is, at that," she agreed. "But I don't know if he'll be able to stand up against fate for much longer. Sometimes, the universe demands satisfaction."

Her voice was flinty. Judge, jury, and... executioner? Could Theresa have had anything to do with Pa Jackson's illness? Erin pushed the idea away from her. Pa and Theresa were both part of the Jackson clan, and the clan would not tolerate any infighting. It was one thing for Theresa to settle fights within her own family with violence, but Pa was older than she was and highly respected in the organization. Erin didn't know how high he sat in the hierarchy, but she knew he wasn't a foot soldier. Higher than a twenty-year-old could rank, even if she had been taking orders for a couple of years. Pa had decades on Theresa.

"You wouldn't do anything to hurt my dad, would you?" Vic asked, softening her voice as if she was having an intimate conversation with Theresa. As if they were both in the same room and Vic still had romantic feelings toward her. "We may not get along, but he's still my kin. My blood."

"You're better off breaking those ties. They're just going to hold you back. You don't owe him anything, the way he's treated you. I remember how tough he was when we were little kids. And I know how he acted when you came out. You don't owe that old coot anything."

"My mom—"

"Your ma is better off without him too."

"She'd lose the farm. She wouldn't be able to manage things without him."

"The clan would look after her. You wouldn't have to worry about that. They look after their own. Including widows and children."

"Just… stay away from him, okay, Tess? Really. I don't need you to do anything. You should stay away from all of us and just disappear. If the cops heard that you were back in town…"

"Those bozos couldn't find their—"

"Theresa. Please. Stay away from my pa and stay away from me. I don't need any help."

Theresa coughed and spoke in a grating tone. "Yeah, you don't need any help; you already got all of the help that you need from that Erin Price, right? She gives you everything you could want? That's how I hear it, anyway."

"Erin is my boss. She could never replace a friend like you." Vic rolled her eyes and shrugged at Erin apologetically.

"Why would your boss come with you to Moose River? I know you two are more than that. I see the way you look at each other."

"Tess, I have no romantic feelings for Erin. I promise you that. And she's just in town to look at some real estate. The bakery in Bald Eagle Falls is going really well, and she's looking at starting up one in Moose River, too. There are a lot of people here who need gluten-free, and they've got to drive into the city or all the way over to Auntie Clem's Bakery to get anything decent. You know what that stuff at the grocery store is like? It's like eating cardboard. There's a real killing to be made in this market."

A killing. Erin winced at Vic's choice of words.

"If she opened a store here, would you come home? Back to Moose River? You wouldn't have to live on the farm with your folks."

"Yeah, maybe I would. That would be kind of cool," Vic said.

"Running my own store in my hometown? Then people wouldn't look down on me anymore."

"People are always going to look down on you, babe. Doesn't matter what you do. Everybody is always gonna say that you got all the breaks, that someone helped you. That you were just lucky, instead of having smarts and skills. That's just the way the world is."

CHAPTER 19

*V*ic eventually begged off the phone call, telling Theresa that her battery was getting too low, and she had forgotten her charger in the car. When she disconnected the call—and double-checked her phone to make sure that it had really disconnected—she gave a long whistle and shook her head at Erin.

"Oh my. She's here in town."

"It sounded like it."

"She's here in town. And she'd better stay away from my family. What am I going to do?"

"Well, we're not going head-to-head with her, that's for sure. Call the police, tell them she's in town. They can get out there and look for her. She'd probably go right back to her house, wouldn't she? Maybe they can find her there. Take her in on the outstanding warrants for her assaults on Terry and Jack Ward."

Vic was hesitant to get the police involved, but she had to know, like Erin, that it was the only way to go. They couldn't keep it quiet. They couldn't try to catch Theresa or flush her out themselves. She was way too dangerous for anything smaller than an army to capture.

"They don't have 9-1-1 service, do they?" Vic asked, remembering the night they'd had to call the police out to Theresa's place. "Do you still have their phone number?"

"I have Jack's. It went to the dispatcher after hours last time." Erin pulled out her phone. She took a couple of deep breaths, focusing on breathing in and out like she did during her tai chi practice. Taking life-giving oxygen to every cell of her body and clearing out the carbon dioxide. In and out. She tapped the lowest number on Jack Ward's contact list. It was answered quickly.

"Moose River dispatcher."

"Is this Geraldine? I don't know if you would remember me, but last time I was here was the night that Jack Ward was stabbed, and I called for help. Erin Price."

"Well, shore, I remember you," Geraldine drawled. "How are you, honey?"

"Well… we just had a call from Theresa Franklin. And we think she's here, in Moose River."

"In Moose River? She wouldn't dare!" Geraldine muttered a couple of choice words, and Erin could hear rapid-fire computer keys typing in the background. "I'm going to get a unit over to you, and you can tell the officers what you know. Where y'all at?"

"At the hotel. Room 290."

"I'll have someone there in two shakes. If I's you, I wouldn't open the door to anyone without checking who it is first."

"Good thinking. We won't." The last thing Erin wanted to do was to open the door to Theresa and have her bust into their hotel room. The police wouldn't be able to get there fast enough to stop her from killing both of them. And Erin had no doubt that even with Vic's concealed weapon, Theresa would easily best both of them.

"Good. Y'all take care. Nice talking to you again!"

"Thanks, you too." Though Erin hoped that it was the last call she would need to make to Geraldine.

Erin hung up. She and Vic met each other's eyes. Despite how late it was, Erin was no longer tired. She might not sleep for another forty-eight hours, with how wound-up she felt.

"Do you have your gun handy?"

Vic's eyebrows went up. She knew how much Erin hated the weapon and the fact that Vic felt the necessity of carrying it. She slipped her hand into the bra holster and pulled the small gun out.

The last time they had faced Theresa, it had been down the sights of a huge automatic assault weapon. But Erin assumed she wouldn't carry something like that around town with her or walk into the hotel with it. This time, they weren't going to let Theresa Franklin get the drop on them.

They waited in silence, listening for the sound of an approaching siren.

The siren never came. Apparently, the police decided not to advertise to the whole town that they had been called to the hotel. Which, upon consideration, Erin decided was probably wise. They wouldn't want Theresa to know that they had called the police as soon as they hung up the phone from talking to her. If she wasn't watching the hotel, there was no need to advertise the arrival of the police.

Geraldine had apparently also called Jack Ward to tell him of Erin's call. He showed up not long after the officers and made Vic and Erin tell the story again from the beginning.

"Do you think that she could have anything to do with my Pa being sick?" Vic asked him, "Or was she just shining me on, acting like she was responsible for him having a virus or whatever has made him sick?"

"We'll have to look into it," Jack said with a shrug. "No way to tell without checking. I can't imagine what reason Crazy Theresa would have for killing your father, but... she's not called Crazy Theresa for nothing!"

"But probably not," Vic said.

"Probably not. Probably just taking advantage of the situation. Finding a way to get close to you, get under your skin. As you say— just shining you on."

"But she's probably in town or somewhere close," Erin put in, "or she wouldn't have heard about Mr. Jackson being in the hospital, right? She must be pretty closely connected to the grapevine."

Jack nodded. "We'll surveil her property from a distance, see if we can spot any sign of her being there. And listen for any gossip about her being back. I can't imagine why she would want to come back to somewhere it was known that she has warrants out. Moose River isn't that big a place. People she knows will see her."

"I hope she's not here. I don't like having to worry about her being around while we're going to the hospital or the farm." Erin gave a shudder. "I don't like to be looking over my shoulder all the time."

"There's probably no point in looking over your shoulder. She's not going to let you see her," Jack advised, with a roguish smile. "You might as well just carry on as if Miss Victoria hadn't heard from her."

Erin rolled her eyes. "Thanks, that makes me feel a lot better."

"I'm armed," Vic pointed out. "If she shows up, I'm not going to hesitate to protect myself."

But Erin couldn't imagine her shooting at her old friend in cold blood. It would take a lot of provocation before Vic was willing to take that action.

Vic was watching her face. "I won't hesitate," she repeated. "I've seen what she can do. I saw the knife she left in Jack's back and the bruises after she tried to choke you out. She's not going to get the chance to do that again. She's dangerous. If I see her, I'm shooting."

"Take care what you say in front of law enforcement," Jack warned, nodding to the officers who were there to take Vic's statement. He might agree with Vic's plan, but they did have witnesses who might not have the same perspective.

"I'll defend myself and the people I love," Vic said. "I'm allowed to defend myself."

Jack nodded. "Well, I think I've got all of the information we need. Will the two of you consider going back home? Is there really much that you can do here? Your mom will look after your pa. And they've got other hands to help on the farm. You'd be safer in Bald Eagle Falls."

"Maybe, maybe not. It's not that far away. If Theresa decided to follow us back, it wouldn't be hard. She already knows where we work. And everyone in town knows where we live if she was to ask. Or she could just follow us home."

"We have burglar alarms," Erin pointed out. "And a cop. And the dogs. It's safer than a hotel room."

"Do you want to go back?"

Erin looked down at her hands, thinking about it. She didn't want to take Vic away from her family. Or to leave her there on her own. "No."

"Are you sure? You don't have to stay here."

Erin shook her head. "No. We'll stay. See what's going to happen with your dad. You'll want to be here in case... anything happens."

"You've seen how he treats me. He's not going to care if I go home. Ma neither. And the boys don't want me around. So, if you want to go back to Bald Eagle Falls, we can. They won't care."

But Erin knew that Vic cared, even if her family didn't return her feelings for them.

"No. You're right. If Theresa wants to do anything, she would just follow us home. It doesn't make any difference to her whether we are here or there. She's gone to Bald Eagle Falls to kill before."

"Yeah. I guess she has."

CHAPTER 20

*T*here was no more sleep to be had. Even though they had each only managed to get in a few hours, neither Erin nor Vic could get back to sleep again. The disruption by Theresa and then talking to the police had been too much. Trying to go back to bed would just result in frustration.

So, they visited and watched some bad TV. Once it was their normal early wake-up time, they headed over to the nearest all-night coffee shop and ordered a couple of mugs of piping hot coffee. They sat in the nearly empty shop, watching the sky start to grow lighter. Nilla snoozed at Vic's feet.

"Funny how we're up before dawn every day, but never really watch the sunrise," Vic commented.

Erin nodded. Sometimes she noticed the pink streaks across the clouds outside, but usually, she was in the kitchen baking the day's goods or was too distracted by customers and ringing up sales to notice much of what was going on outside. "We should probably spend more time outside, watching nature, taking time to appreciate the sunrise. They say it makes you healthier."

"Nothing that says we can't take a ten-minute break to have a cup of coffee and watch the sun come up."

"Yeah. You're right. We'd probably be less stressed, not be so tired at the end of the day."

But Erin doubted that anything would change at Auntie Clem's Bakery. They would both get caught up in the work of the day and not take the time to appreciate the sunrise.

Vic sipped her coffee. "I thought I'd be really tired, but this is nice. I know I should be worrying about Theresa and whether she is out there right now watching us. But I just feel... alert. And glad to be alive." She looked down at her mug. "Wonder what they're putting in this coffee. Maybe we should get their recipe."

Erin laughed. She looked at the orange highlights across the sky, then searched the street for anyone out there watching them, biding her time and gathering information.

Erin and Vic looked in on Pa Jackson, but found him asleep and Ma out cold in the chair beside him. Best to let them get whatever rest they could. They backed out of the room and paced up and down the hall a couple of times, talking about the day ahead and waiting for the doctor to show up to do his rounds.

Eventually, Erin saw the same doctor that she had seen in the evening when Pa had had his second heart attack. He was at the nursing station, talking with the nurses and looking through charts while he asked them questions and got up to speed. He turned his head when he saw Vic and Erin. He studied them for a moment, then smiled and nodded in the direction of Pa's room.

"Found your purse? Did you ladies have a good night?"

Erin looked at Vic to see how she wanted to handle that one.

"Ain't no rest for the wicked!" Vic declared.

The doctor laughed. He looked through the charts and pulled one out. They were close enough that Erin could read the name on his ID card. Theodore Cousins. He reached down to give Nilla a pet. "I had a call from the police early this morning. Apparently, someone is wondering whether your father might have accidentally been poisoned."

Accidentally. Jack Ward had been discreet in his inquiries.

"Poisoned?" Vic repeated. "Do you think so?"

"I told him that a toxin wasn't out of the question," Dr. Cousins said slowly. "It is something that we're looking into. Sometimes people aren't aware of the toxins in their environment that could harm them. Or people practicing folk medicine don't realize the harm they could do." He raised his brows at Vic. "Does your mother practice herb lore?"

Vic pursed her lips. "Well… maybe a few old home remedies," she admitted. "Mustard plasters and poultices. Castor oil. Probably a few others that I'm not thinking of at the moment. She's not big on herbs, but…"

He nodded. "Does she make her own castor oil?"

"No. Always just bought it at the store. Do people around here make their own?"

"Not usually. But who knows; people get funny ideas sometimes. Castor beans also contain ricin, which is very toxic. Commercial castor oil doesn't have any active ricin in it. But if someone decided to press their own… that could be dangerous."

"I don't think so." Vic shook her head. "You can ask her."

"What about gardening and harvesting wild plants? Does she know enough to recognize all of the vegetables and herbs that she prepares? Or could she get a weed or look-alike plant mixed in with greens, root vegetables, mushrooms…?"

"I think she knows most of the poisonous plants around here. We're an old Tennessee family; the stories and warnings get passed down through the generations. Parents point them out to little kids. 'Don't ever eat that plant,' or 'Don't even touch the leaves of that one.' I guess people can make mistakes, but she's pretty sharp."

Cousins nodded. "Good to hear. I'll talk to her about it. If he has been poisoned and we can figure out what it is, we have a much better chance of treating him successfully. He's lasted this long, which is a good sign. He may do just fine if it wasn't a high enough concentration of the toxin and it works its way out of his system. But if it does more damage to his kidneys or liver, or he has another heart attack…"

Vic nodded soberly. "Can't you just do a tox screen? Wouldn't that tell you what he's been given?"

He shook his head. "A tox screen checks for common drugs and toxins. Not for everything under the sun. You have to know what you're looking for in order to get lab tests for specific substances. I'm thinking that with the heart issues he has been having, it could be something from the digitalis family."

Erin looked at Vic. Their eyes met, and Erin couldn't pull her gaze away.

Cousins tilted his head slightly. "That means something to you?"

"We just… we know someone in Bald Eagle Falls who was poisoned with foxglove. It was in a poultice that was supposed to be comfrey."

He nodded slowly. "Tragic. I'm sorry to hear that. But it does happen. As you have seen with your father, it can be difficult to identify what is making someone sick."

Erin didn't tell him that in that case, it had been intentional. Vic didn't seem to see the need to tell him about that part either. It was probably best that he continued to think that their former friend and Vic's father had both been poisoned accidentally. Tragic accidents. People made mistakes, misidentified one plant for another, and things like that could happen.

Cousins was silent as he continued to go through the clipboards. He handed them back to the nurse with a couple of cryptic comments, then gestured to Pa Jackson's hospital room.

"Let's see if we can find anything out."

CHAPTER 21

*E*rin and Vic exchanged glances, then followed him into the hospital room. Erin couldn't help feeling out of place there. It wasn't her family. And the way that they had been rushed out the day before and lambasted for having had more than one person in the room and triggering Pa's heart attack by getting him upset, she didn't feel like she should be there. But the doctor didn't seem to share the nurse's opinion.

He walked briskly to Pa's bedside and shook his arm. "Mr. Jackson? Mr. Jackson, I need you to wake up and talk to me."

Pa groaned and didn't open his eyes.

"Come on, sir. Wake up. I need to ask you some questions."

Ma straightened up and rubbed her eyes. She looked around blearily. "Oh. It's the doctor." She blinked and tried to focus on him. "Papa, the doctor wants to talk to you. Pa." She reached across and also shook Pa vigorously. "Wake up!"

"Unhand me, woman!" Pa growled, pushing her away and opening his eyes. "What's going on? What's the problem?" He looked at the doctor. "Well, I'm not dead yet, am I?"

"No, not yet," Cousins replied cheerfully. "And I'd like to keep you on this side of the sod, if you don't mind."

"You're the doctor."

"And I need you to answer some questions for me. Can you sit up a bit?" The doctor pressed one of the buttons on the bed rail, raising the head of the bed. "There, that's better, isn't it?"

Pa didn't look particularly pleased by this development. Erin watched the electronic monitor, where his heart rate was picking up speed.

"What are you doing, going around waking people up in the middle of the night? Don't you know that if we're going to get better, that we need to get a good sleep?"

"It's not the middle of the night, sir. It's actually getting on in the morning. If you were looking to get the worm, you're too late. Early bird has already been and gone."

"What is it, then?" Pa demanded, wiping his mouth and chin, which were slightly damp with drool. "What is so gosh-durn important that you have to wake me up the minute I fall asleep?"

"I want to ask you about what you ate before you came here. To the hospital. What did you eat the day before?"

Pa scowled. "Nothing but rabbit food. That diet Mother's got me on is about as appetizing as a bowl of weeds." He looked balefully in Ma's direction.

Ma, on the other hand, beamed as if he had given her a compliment. "If you want to live to a ripe old age, then you need to take care of your body."

"Don't want to live to a ripe old age if it means eating like that. Eating is one of my few pleasures."

Ma looked at Cousins, still smiling. "Don't let him fool you. I've been real proud of the way he's taken to this diet. I'll bet that he wouldn't have survived his heart attack if I hadn't been making him eat good, healthy food."

"So, what have you got him on?" Cousins asked, deciding that she was the more cooperative of the two.

"In the morning, toast and jam. If he's really complaining about how hungry he is or he has a lot of physical work to do in the morning, then a couple of eggs."

"Mmm-hmm. Your own eggs?"

"Of course! We don't have any need for store-bought."

"Coffee?"

"Tea. I've weaned him off of that nasty stuff. And he's been feeling a lot better for it. Gets a lot better sleep at night now that he isn't chugging that sludge all day."

"What kind of tea?"

She shrugged. "Whatever he wants. There are lots of choices."

"Do you make your own tea? Or from a package?"

"From a package. I remember my ma making herbal teas. She was very proud of her herbal teas, my ma. But I never really took to them. Don't like that stuff. Good for medicine, but give me some English Breakfast or Orange Pekoe..."

"Sure, sure. Have you given him any medicinal teas lately?"

"Oh, no. He's been feeling real hearty. Lots of energy since we started this."

"What else does he eat in a day? Particularly the day before he got sick?"

Ma frowned and considered the question. "Well, now. Lunch is salad. We've been eating lots of them mixed greens, along with berries and seeds. Some of that fancy dressing from the store. Not your ranch, but good, healthy sauces."

"And is that all store-bought? Or from your own garden?"

"Some from my garden. And I have a window box for the sprouts. You grow little bitty greens from seeds. Microgreens, they're called."

"So, just lettuce and vegetables that you have grown yourself?"

"Yes."

"Nothing that you've gathered somewhere else or that someone gave to you?"

"No. I have plenty in the garden."

"Do you think that any other kind of leaf might have gotten mixed in with the greens? From a weed or a flowering plant?"

"No. I'm careful. I pick and wash it all myself." Ma scowled at the doctor, then looked at Pa, who was watching and listening intently, as if he might catch her in a lie. "What is all this? You think that he got sick because of something he ate? He never ate anything bad. I prepared it all. Just like I'm telling you. Vegetables. Salad. Nothing bad."

"Do you know what foxglove looks like?"

"Of course I do."

"Do you have any in your garden?"

"You think I would feed him foxglove?" Ma's voice went from calm and measured to the shriek of a siren. "That is poisonous! I never gave him anything but vegetable greens. I told you, he was well and strong. I don't know what made him sick, but it wasn't anything I gave him!"

"I'm not accusing you of anything, Mrs. Jackson. It happens all the time. Something gets mixed in with your garden vegetables without you realizing it…"

"Not *me*!" Ma asserted. "I know what I'm doing. I've given him nothing but healthy foods."

"Ma, it's okay. He just has to check," Vic inserted.

Ma turned to look at Vic and Erin, who she hadn't seemed to notice before. "I'm not going to calm down when this doctor, who can't have been practicing for more than two shakes of a lamb's tail, starts throwing around accusations!"

"He didn't say that you poisoned Pa. He's just trying to figure out if anything Pa ate might have made him sick. You never know. He could have developed an allergy. You wouldn't even know what was going on. You'd have no idea that something he's been eating his whole life could suddenly make him sick like that."

"You can tell him to march right back out of here. I'm not going to abide this kind of treatment. I'll call old Doc Foley. He would straighten you out soon enough!"

"I'm sorry to have upset you, ma'am. That was not my intention. Maybe, Mr. Jackson, you ate something else. Something that your wife did not prepare. Maybe you were hungry because the salads didn't fill you up?"

Pa looked at his wife and shook his head. "No, of course not. I don't eat anywhere else." His eyes went over to Vic and Erin, narrowing. "I suppose you are the ones who suggested this. You don't know what you're talking about. I'd remind you to mind your own dang business."

"Don't you want to get better, Pa?" Vic asked. "If he can't find out what's made you sick, he can't fix it."

"Nothin' made me sick. It's just the flu."

"Did the doctor say you had the flu?" Vic demanded. She turned her head to look at Cousins.

"No, we know it's not the flu," Cousins said. "It could be another virus or bacterial infection. Or some weakness that was there before that has been triggered by stress or the dietary changes. Genetic, allergenic, we really can't tell. We haven't finished ruling everything out. But if the police say to check for poison, I check for poison."

Ma gasped.

Pa shook his head slowly. "You got the police involved in this." He stared at Vic. "Who do you think you are? What do you think you're doing?"

"I…" Vic scrambled for a satisfactory answer.

Cousins was turning red, realizing that he had unintentionally made things worse. "Mr. Jackson, I need you to stay calm. Your heart—"

"I can't believe you would go to the cops," Pa hissed at Vic. "I told you to stay away, to go home. I told you that you weren't welcome here. And instead of doing what you're told and going home, you get the cops involved! No child of mine would ever do something like that."

Vic swallowed. Erin wanted to pat her on the back or find some other way to comfort her. Pa Jackson had pushed her away before, and Erin knew how much it hurt Vic, even though she said very little about it. Disowning her completely was a step further than he had taken before.

Vic was struggling to keep her face impassive, to look at him as though he hadn't said anything that bothered her.

"You git out of here," Pa hissed at her. "And don't show your face here again. I don't care what you're dressed like or if you come back begging on your knees, you are not part of this family anymore."

"Pa," Vic's voice wavered, though she stood tall and put her shoulders back, trying to show him confidence and strength instead of what she saw as weakness. "Pa, I'm trying to help you. I came here because you were dying. And if the doctor doesn't find out what's going on, you still might die. I... I'm just doing everything I can to help. I'm there for Ma. Whatever she needs. And if someone did this to you..." She shrugged helplessly. "Don't you want to find out just as much as I do?"

"You have no idea about how I feel. You were raised right. You were raised to know how to behave, how things were run in the Family. It doesn't matter what happens to individuals. What happens to me or your brothers. What matters is the structure, the organization. The survival of the Family. *I* don't matter. *You* don't matter. Your Ma doesn't matter. You don't go back on all of your training and call the cops."

Vic shook her head. She didn't know what to say, and Erin didn't know how to help her or support her. She had nothing to say to Pa Jackson. It was clear that he didn't care anything about his daughter or himself, only about the Jackson clan.

CHAPTER 22

*V*ic took a deep breath in and then let it out. She turned slightly, nodding toward the door to Erin. They walked out together. Vic was shaking her head, eyes glistening with tears. Nilla looked up at her, whining.

"Wait. Wait!"

Erin put her hand on Vic's arm to stop her and turned to face Ma, who had followed them out of the room.

"James. James Victor, you wait."

Vic steeled herself and turned again. She looked down at her mother, waiting for her to say her piece. Erin didn't know whether she was there to second her husband's statement or to refute it.

"James!"

"It's Vic, Ma. Victoria."

"Please. He's not in his right mind. You know how it is when someone is sick. They get irritable. They say things that they wouldn't have said if they had been well. He's still in a lot of pain and he doesn't know whether he is going to get better or not. That's hard on a man."

"Yeah. I imagine it is. And I'm here. Where are the others? Have Daniel or Joseph even come to the hospital? How can either of you think that I don't care about the family? *Our* family, not the clan. If

113

something is going on, if someone did this to Pa, then I want to know who it was. I want them to be stopped. Rotting in prison."

"But you talked to the police. You had to know how your father would feel about that. You lived with us for eighteen years. You know how the clan works. You know that we would never involve the police on any family matter."

"What would you have done? What would you have done if someone called and threatened you and said that they had poisoned Pa? You wouldn't have called the police?"

Ma looked at Vic expressionlessly. "No."

Vic took a quick breath in and just looked at her mother.

What would Mrs. Jackson have done? Told her husband? Told someone else in the organization and asked them to take care of it? There were probably protocols for getting them to look into a matter and make sure that things were… sanitized.

"I would never call the police," Ma said evenly. "And you shouldn't have either."

Vic said nothing.

"If you think there is something going on, then you come to me. Or one of the boys. You don't call the police about anything."

Erin was still trying to wrap her mind around that. They would never call the police. Not for a burglary or a poisoning. No matter what crime was committed against them, they would go to the clan rather than the police. And the clan would take care of it. Just like on a mafia movie on TV.

Erin had never really believed in organized crime. She knew there were crime organizations. But she didn't believe in them as they were portrayed in fiction. She had seen unorganized crime on the streets. People acting for themselves, taking what they wanted, trying to find ways to keep body and soul together even if it were at someone else's expense. She had seen street gangs and all of the internal conflict that went on, people informing on each other, all of the distrust and one-upmanship that went on. And she thought that was how all organizations were. Not a regular, cohesive structure, but little bands of criminals bound together by a common cause. Because there was strength in numbers.

Maybe she had been wrong. Maybe strictly regulated crime organizations did exist. She had seen only glimpses of the workings of the Jackson and Dyson clans before. People struggling to gain more power and work their way up the ladder. Ma's and Pa's inflexibility was different. A lifelong dedication to following the organization's rules and an absolute refusal to break those rules, even if their lives depended on it.

"Ma... do you know anything? Do you know if he was poisoned?"

Ma shook her head, her mouth a firm, straight line. Erin wasn't sure whether it was an "I don't know" or "I'll never tell." Neither, apparently, did Vic.

"Ma, if you know, you would do something, wouldn't you? You wouldn't just let him die and pretend not to know what was going on."

No agreement or disagreement from Ma Jackson. Whatever she knew or didn't know, she wasn't telling.

"Well... you go back in with him, I guess. I can't be here."

Ma touched Vic's arm, and Erin hoped that she would say, "You'll always be my child, no matter what," or, "Don't worry, we'll figure this out."

But she didn't.

"Thank you," she said softly. "For the cookies."

Erin and Vic walked out of the hospital, Nilla pattering quietly at Vic's side. He didn't bark or strain on the leash to go in another direction to investigate something that had caught his eye. Or his nose. Maybe he sensed Vic's mood and knew that she needed him to be there for her, quietly supportive, not running around doing doggie daredevil stuff.

"You want to go back to the hotel?" Erin asked when they reached the car.

"I suppose. I need to think."

Erin hoped that meant they would be going home soon. There

was obviously little that they could do in Moose River. They might as well be back in Bald Eagle Falls, keeping themselves busy with baking and looking after the shop.

Erin's phone vibrated, and she pulled it out of her pocket to look at it before putting the car in gear.

It was a text from Bella. *Have you talked to Charley?*

Erin groaned. "You've got to be kidding me."

Vic raised her brows questioningly.

"Charley!"

"Oh." Vic gave a little shrug. "What happened? She sleep in or forget where she was supposed to be?"

"I don't know. I'd better find out what's going on." Erin hit the button to call Bella back, put the phone on speaker mode, and set it onto the dash mount.

It rang a couple of times and then Bella picked up.

"Hi, Erin. Have you heard anything?"

"No, I haven't talked to her. What's going on? Are you alone at the store?"

"No, it's okay. We've got enough hands here to run the store. Don't worry about that. I have the list of people to call in if we run into trouble. It's just that... she said she would come in, and hasn't. I tried calling to see if she was running late or had forgotten, and there's no answer. Her phone just keeps going to voicemail."

"Maybe she slept in," Erin said. She looked at the time on the phone screen. It was still only mid-morning. Charley had been known to sleep away the entire morning. She had promised that she would be responsible while Erin was away and had pointed out how much better she was at getting up in the morning. "Yeah, if she stayed up late, that's probably what happened. I wouldn't be too worried about it yet."

"She was just so excited to show you how well she was going to take care of everything while you were gone."

"She has good intentions," Erin agreed. "But her follow-through sucks."

Bella giggled. "Yeah. Okay. I won't worry about it then."

"Let me know if you run into any real problems. Remember that I'm only a couple of hours away. If I need to get back there, I will."

"I know. Everything is fine. You can stay there. How's Vic?"

"I'm here," Vic said. "You're on speaker."

"Well, thanks for telling me, Erin," Bella teased. "I might have really put my foot in my mouth."

"Yes, all of those terrible things you say when Vic is out of the room."

"How are you, Vicky?" Bella asked. "Is it really horrible?"

"Yeah," Vic agreed, nodding her head. "It really, really is."

"I'm sorry. We're praying things get better soon."

"Thanks, Bella. Hopefully, I'll be back soon."

But would it be because her father was dead or because there was no longer any point in staying in Moose River?

CHAPTER 23

*V*ic pressed her face down into the silky fur on the top of Nilla's head for a few moments.

"You know what? I don't want to go back to the hotel right now. All we're going to do there is sit around and stew over things. Can we go back to the farm? I should check on whether the boys are actually doing anything, and it's easier to think when my hands are busy."

"Sure." Erin nodded, understanding. She was the same way. She much preferred making a plan or diving into a new project or chore to sitting around thinking with nothing to do. She could do a little light cleaning in the farmhouse while Vic tended to the animals and outdoor chores.

When she pulled up to the farmhouse, there were no vehicles on the gravel pad, so Erin assumed none of the brothers were home. Had Jeremy stuck around town after seeing Pa Jackson, or had he gone back to Bald Eagle Falls and his place with Beaver?

Vic looked around. "I'll bet they haven't done a thing," she grumbled. "Why is it that Ma and Pa are always telling me how perfect Daniel and Joe are when they don't do a thing around here?"

"Do they live here? Or do they have their own places?"

"Live here, as far as I know. I could understand it if they had their own houses or families. Then they've got other responsibilities to take care of. But they don't. They could lend a hand. Especially while Pa is sick. I seriously think they would just let the animals die in the fields."

They got out of the car. Several dogs rushed them, barking warnings.

"Shaddup, git down!" Vic shouted at them, and they quieted at her authoritative commands, falling back and watching the two intruders warily.

Nilla jumped out of Vic's arms and, before she could do anything, he was rushing at the bigger farm dogs, growling and yapping. Erin wondered whether he thought his little voice was as deep and loud as the bigger dogs'. He certainly didn't seem to have any concept of the fact that he was so much smaller than they were. He ran around their legs and nipped at them.

"Nilla! Nilla, cut it out. Come back here!" Vic took a couple of steps toward the dogs, but didn't immediately rush in and grab Nilla. Erin supposed that would probably be a good way to get bitten. "Nilla, no! Bad dog! Stop!"

Nilla wasn't to be so easily deterred. He continued to growl and bark at the other dogs. Vic got in close to them and tried to separate Nilla out with her foot, pushing him away from the others. Once he was a couple of feet away, she bent down and attached the leash to his collar.

"I should have put that on you before getting out of the car." She shook her head and looked at Erin. "He just jumped out of my arms and went after them! Stupid dog."

"At least he didn't get hurt."

"Yeah. Come on, Nilla. If you want an adventure, you can come with me and see the livestock." She tugged at the leash. It still took a little more persuasion but, eventually, Nilla heeled, and Vic headed toward the barn. "I'll take him with me this time. You okay in the house?"

"It doesn't look like anyone else is here, so I think I'm fine. I'll do some dusting."

"If you want, you can just sit down with your planner or something. You don't have to do any work."

"I'd rather be working," Erin said with a smile.

Vic nodded her agreement and continued on her way down to the barn. Erin let herself into the farmhouse. People didn't lock their doors in Moose River. At least, Vic's family didn't. There was a slight odor of cigarette smoke inside. It was probably faint enough that others would not detect it, but Erin's nose wrinkled as she encountered the stale smell. She opened a window in the kitchen to help to air it out. The boys should know better than to smoke in the house. She was sure from her previous visits that Ma would not have allowed that if she had been home. There had been not a whiff of smoke the other times she had been there. Even if they smoked with the window open, it would still have clung to the soft furnishings of the room.

She walked around the house to take stock of what needed to be done. It was still neat and tidy. The others had apparently not spent much time in the common areas, sticking to their own rooms. Erin opened each bedroom door to see which was which. It was obvious which was the master bedroom Ma and Pa shared and which two were the boys'. From the looks of them, Erin suspected that Ma dusted and tidied those rooms as well, but she would not. She didn't want them to think that she was snooping or interfering. She shut their doors and left them as they were.

She found a duster and worked her way through the living room and other common areas, then around to the master bedroom. She wondered if Ma would want them to bring her a kit with some toiletries and a change of clothing. As far as Erin knew, she hadn't been back to the farm since Pa had been admitted. She would probably really appreciate a few things.

If they went back there. It would be pretty hard after the way that Pa had treated Vic. But maybe Ma could meet them in the parking lot, away from him. Vic clearly wasn't going to just abandon her family because of what her father had said. Maybe it wasn't the first time that he'd said something like that to her.

She lost herself in the rhythm of cleaning. She tried not to snoop, but couldn't help taking note of various things about the family as she dusted and tidied. She had been in a lot of different homes, both as a child and as a care worker, and she was good at reading things about people from their possessions and the way they lived.

Where had Vic's room been when she had been a child? There were only two children's rooms, and Erin hadn't noticed a basement or attic access. Probably the two oldest boys had roomed together and the two youngest, Jeremy and Vic, together. When Vic and Jeremy had left home, cutting their ties with the Jackson clan, one of the boys had switched rooms to take advantage of the available space.

But it meant that there was no trace of Vic in the house, which made Erin a little sad. There were a few family photos where she could see Vic's familiar face hidden by the boyish exterior, but nothing Erin could see that Vic had owned or left her mark on. Every other trace had been wiped clean.

Ma Jackson had a couple of the big, two-hole genealogy binders like Clementine had kept with her research in them. Jacksons and Websters and other names, many familiar to Erin now, stretched back over the generations. It was at least half a dozen generations before Erin started to see a few birthplaces outside of Tennessee. They had been there for a long time. Erin closed the book and continued to dust. There was no one around to see her, but she still didn't want to be accused of snooping.

After the dusting, she ran the vacuum through the rooms that she had cleaned. Once she had it put away, she took a peek at the bathroom and decided she'd better give it a quick wipe down. The boys were obviously not always careful and were used to having someone there to clean up after them. Erin probably shouldn't perpetuate the idea that messes were just magically cleaned up by fairies late at night, but she couldn't bear to leave it like that for when Ma returned.

CHAPTER 24

*W*ith all of the vital cleaning tasks done, Erin retired to the kitchen, always her favorite room of the house. There were dirty dishes to be cleaned, and she wiped down the surfaces covered with crumbs and coffee mug rings.

As she put the dish soap back into the cupboard under the sink, Erin had a sudden thought about poisons. What were the poisons most likely to be found in a kitchen? Not plants gathered in the wild, but cleaning solutions and pesticides. She opened the cupboard wide and checked to see what other cleaners Ma had on hand.

Even while she was checking the labels of the various bottles, Erin was challenging her own thought. Why would she be checking for poisons in the kitchen? Had she come to the conclusion that Pa had been poisoned in the kitchen? And if he had, then by whom?

She heard someone crunching through the gravel outside the kitchen door and quickly shut the cupboards and straightened up. Vic was approaching, Nilla still walking on the leash at her heel.

He was getting a lot better at heeling. For the first little while that Vic had had him, he seemed to have no idea how to behave on a leash, trying to run all over the place, sometimes running ahead and sometimes veering off to investigate something to the side or behind him. He was always pulling on the leash, winding it around Vic's or

Erin's legs or tripping over his body when he darted from one place to another.

"Good boy," Vic told him as she walked him into the kitchen. She bent down to unclip the leash. "Now, you can be free for a few minutes." She looked at Erin. "Unless you wanted to get out of here right away?"

"No. I'm okay, thanks. I think I'll look through the fridge next, make sure there isn't anything that should be thrown out. I suspect that your brothers are probably not great at making sure that leftovers get eaten and the milk hasn't gone sour."

"You would be right," Vic agreed with a chuckle. "That's women's work. Men put beer in the fridge and take it out to drink it. That's the extent of their relationship with the appliance."

Erin laughed. She opened the fridge door, and the first thing she saw was a six-pack of beer. That made her laugh harder. She went to work opening plastic containers to check the contents and checking each drawer to make sure that nothing was moldering.

"Finding anything that looks like poison in there?" Vic teased.

Erin had put up a couple of plastic containers of food that had started to turn. She pursed her lips, looking back at Vic, who had settled in a chair at the table. "Do you think he might have gotten food poisoning? From salmonella, I mean, or E. coli?"

"No... I think the doctor probably would have brought it up if the symptoms matched. He was talking about other stuff. Herbs. Foxglove. You don't see any foxglove in with the lettuce, do you?"

Erin removed a tub of greens turning to slime. "No." She kept it as far from her face as possible, trying not to breathe in the smell.

"I didn't think you would. Just thought I'd check."

"I was thinking..."

"Not too hard, I hope," Vic intoned, supplying the line that would normally have been given by Terry.

Erin didn't continue. Vic nodded at her. "Yes, you were thinking...?"

"Just... about what your pa said. And about Theresa and Jack Ward."

"Yeah?"

"If your pa was poisoned by something like foxglove, then who did it?"

Vic opened her mouth, then closed it again. She looked at Erin. "Huh."

Erin nodded and went back to her fridge review. She would wipe down the shelves and find out where to dispose of the rotting food-stuff, and then she would be done.

"You mean that Ma would be the first suspect," Vic said.

"I guess. The doctor was already asking her if she might have done it accidentally. If she didn't just happen to get foxglove in with her greens, then...?"

"Could she have done it on purpose?" Vic shook her head slowly from side to side, but Erin could tell from her expression that it was more a gesture of amazement than a negative answer. "I don't know. I know that must surprise you," Vic looked at Erin, her eyes round. "You thought I would say 'no way.'"

"Well... I kind of expected it," Erin admitted.

"She's not the kind of person I would think was a poisoner," Vic said slowly. "But is there really a 'type'? You hear stories about sweet old ladies being serial poisoners. Not that my mom is a sweet old lady." She wiped her forehead with the back of her arm. "She's... had to put up with a lot of stuff, raising a family. I think it would be bad enough with Pa and raising four sons. But then you add the clan stuff on top of that..."

"Did that have much of an effect? On your family life, I mean?"

"Yeah. It did," Vic admitted. "The clan was always there. Men coming to the door at all hours to see Pa, asking questions, telling him he was needed, taking him away on jobs. I never knew what he was doing. Probably don't want to know. But she would have. And raising us... always talking about how to behave with the clan, respecting our elders, knowing who was the boss and the boss's boss. And that whole thing about not calling the police. I guess in school now, they tell kids right from the time they're tiny about how to dial 9-1-1 and get the police if something is going on. For us, it was the opposite. You never call the police, no matter what anyone says. You call the clan, and they'll take care of it. Cops will just put everyone in jail. Right down to a two-year-old. I was convinced that it didn't matter how old you were, the cops would put you in jail for your involvement in… whatever."

"So if you thought there was a burglar…?"

"Yeah. You wouldn't call the police. You would call the clan."

"Wow."

"Yeah. It's hard for me to reconcile that with the way the rest of the world works. Or the rest of the country, anyway. You even have gangs calling the police to inform on each other. But not the clans. Not the Jacksons or the Dysons."

"That's really something. I had no idea it was such a big thing."

"So my mom had to deal with a lot. She might not have been in on exactly what Pa was doing with the clan or what other things were going on. But it still affected her. The violence that went on. The fear of the law. Pa's drinking and… behavior. He's a tough guy."

"I've noticed," Erin agreed.

"She'd stand up to him. Or get her own back in one way or another."

Erin gave a little chuckle.

"What?" Vic asked.

"Oh… just remembering a foster family that I was with. What was the name…? Goodale. Husband was a drunk. Would come home in the middle of the night, completely sloshed. I mean totally wrecked, And not a fun drunk, either. Mean. Bloody-minded and ready to take it out on anybody."

Vic nodded encouragingly. Nilla finished his explorations of the room and settled at Vic's feet.

"One night, he came home swinging. Shouting, slamming doors, knocking things over. Just spoiling for a fight. I could hear him and Mrs. Goodale up, and I peeked in. Wanted to know what was going on in case I had to run. Mrs. Goodale goes to the back door where all of the kids' gear is and picks up a baseball bat. Then she starts swinging for him."

"No way," Vic's eyes were wide.

Erin nodded. "Yes." Her heart was beating rapidly just repeating the story to Vic. She could remember how terrified she had been at the time, the mister and missus screaming at each other, threatening, swinging for each other. "With the baseball bat, she had the longer reach, and she got him good. Hit him in the head and shoulders a few times. She pushed him down the stairs to the basement, where he was unconscious, either knocked out or dead drunk. I thought she had killed him. I was sure that he was beaten to death at the bottom of those stairs."

"But he wasn't?"

"He woke up there in the morning. She told him he must have fallen down the stairs and hit his head. And he had no idea that she'd used his head for baseball practice."

Vic shook her head in wonder. "Unbelievable. The poor guy!"

Erin shrugged. "Don't feel bad for him. He was mean. Certainly gave her more than one black eye or broken bone. She just kind of… snapped. Wasn't taking it anymore."

"Well, I hate to say it, and I know I shouldn't when she's my own mother, but I could see Ma doing that. Or putting something in his food to make him sick. I don't know that she meant to kill him, but I could see her wanting to take the fight out of him."

Erin thought about this as she took the plastic bowls over to the sink and scraped the rotting leftovers into the compost bin. "So, you think it could have been her."

"I don't want to say that. But… maybe. I'm just saying it's not impossible. I could see it if she'd been pushed far enough. Without me and Jeremy here to help keep the peace, it's just Pa and Daniel and Joe against Ma. She could have been pushed too far."

"Would she use something like foxglove? I was looking around to see what else was on hand." Erin opened the bottom cupboard briefly to display the various cleaning solutions and pesticides. "There are a lot of noxious substances close at hand."

"I imagine there's even more in the medicine cabinet in the bathroom, or under the sink in there," Vic offered. "We've always had lots of chemicals around for cleaning or pests. Stuff to get rid of ants or moths or mice. Things are always getting in through the cracks or when someone leaves a door or window open to get some air. It gets hot in here."

Erin nodded and started to rinse the containers and fill the sink one more time. "If they're readily available, then it could be someone other than your ma who put something in his food, too."

"There's always been plenty of folks coming and going around the farm. Friends, business associates, neighbors, the clan. But usually, meals are just family. I don't think anyone else would have had the opportunity to put anything in his food. Ma would have been in the kitchen the whole time."

Erin didn't offer anything, continuing the clean the dishes. She squeezed out the dishcloth and took it to the fridge to wipe down the shelves, shifting the remaining dishes around to get under them.

"Are you talking about Joe and Daniel?" Vic said suddenly. "One of them could have poisoned him?" Her voice rose. "Why would they do something like that? What reason would they have?"

"I don't know," Erin said calmly. "I don't live here. I have no idea what kind of resentments there might be."

"Well, there isn't anything. Joe and Daniel may be loud and obnoxious sometimes, but they don't have anything against Pa. Not like that."

"Not like what?"

"Not like they would sneak around about. If they've got a problem with something, they just say so straight out. If they had a problem with something Pa was doing, they'd just confront him about it."

"He wasn't the enforcer? Didn't he rule the family?"

"Well... he was the patriarch, yeah. And he wasn't ever shy about laying the strap on someone. But the boys are too big for that now."

"Doesn't stop him from using his fists. Or his cane."

Vic winced at the reminder of how he had hit her the last time they had come to see her parents at the farm. He'd hit her so hard. Erin was sure if he had hit Vic anywhere else on her body, he would have broken a bone. Vic had been bruised and moved tenderly for weeks.

"Okay. So he rules with an iron fist," Vic admitted. She considered her own words. "And maybe the boys would resent that. I can see them taking him down a peg. Challenging him physically. He might be the patriarch, but they're bigger and stronger than him now. I don't see them using poison."

Erin accepted this. "Then I guess... we'd better hope that there could be someone else or that it can be explained away as accidental."

Otherwise, Ma could very well end up going to prison.

CHAPTER 25

There was the sound of a truck coming down the access road and stopping on the gravel pad outside the house. Erin took a deep breath and hoped that it would be Jeremy or a neighbor. But she heard the truck doors opening and then the voices of Vic's older brothers as they made comments to each other. They knew who the yellow bug belonged to now, so there was no speculation on who might be at the farmhouse.

The screen door banged open and the two of them walked in. They made no attempt to stamp the dust and dirt out of their shoes on the mat and just walked into the kitchen.

"What are you doing here?" Joseph asked Vic. "I thought you were going home."

"I didn't say that."

"Why would you stick around here?"

"Why do you?" Vic snapped back, "Seems to me that you're old enough to leave the nest."

Daniel guffawed at this, as if the shot didn't apply to him just as much as it did to Joseph. "*Burned*, Joe!"

"Shut up. I'm still here because somebody needs to take care of Ma and Pa," Joseph told Vic acidly. As if they were eighty or ninety and were too frail to look after themselves anymore. Until Pa was poisoned, they had appeared to have been doing just fine looking after themselves.

"You don't seem to be doing a very good job of it," Vic offered. "Pa's in hospital and you haven't been taking care of the animals or looking after things around here."

"Everything is fine."

"Not when you aren't feeding or milking the animals. And Erin's been doing all of the cleaning in here. Cleaning up after you slobs. Throwing out the moldy food. Ma's taught you how to look after yourselves, so why do you leave all of the work for her?"

"We're busy," Daniel told her. "We have important jobs. Things to do."

"That's news to me. Just what are these *important jobs?*"

Joseph and Daniel looked at each other. Measuring, warning looks. Each keeping the other in check.

"We have jobs," Daniel asserted. "What they are is none of your business. You don't live here. You're not part of this family anymore."

"Jobs with the clan or an actual outside job?"

"Jobs with the clan are real jobs. The clan pays the bills around here."

"The clan's never paid the bills. The farm pays its own bills."

Daniel shook his head. "No, it doesn't. Not for a long while now. You haven't been paying much attention if you think that."

"Why wouldn't the farm be paying for itself? Because of the drought? That's just temporary. They'll get back on their feet again."

"No. They won't. There's no way they're getting out from under. Not when they keep scaling down the farm operation. It hasn't been anything more than a front for years."

Vic had made comments before on how things had been scaled back. Not as many animals. Trees replacing the crops in the field. A much smaller operation than it had been when she had been younger.

"They're just being careful." Vic hesitated. "You really think it's that bad? That they'll never be able to support themselves through the farm?"

"Family farms are disappearing. There are too many big commercial operations. Family farms can't compete unless they get into some niche. Llama wool or gluten-free wheat or medicinal plants."

Erin opened her mouth to point out the impossibility of gluten-free wheat, then shut it again. Of course he already knew that. He was just exaggerating about how rare a product they would have to offer to survive against the big commercial operations.

"How much is Pa working for the clan, then?"

"Same as he has the last few years," Joseph said flatly. He looked at Erin and raised an eyebrow, plainly indicating that he would not be giving out any information about the family or clan business around an outsider.

It hadn't been that long since Vic had been living at home with them. But apparently, she had been too young or wrapped up in her own troubles to realize how much—or how little—of the family's income came from the farm and how much came from jobs done for the clan. Erin hated to think of what Pa might have been doing for the clan. What would be important enough for them to pay to support him and his family? He wasn't just offering them storage space in a barn.

"Did you know that they're talking about whether Pa was poisoned?" Vic asked, changing the subject abruptly.

Erin watched the two brothers for their reactions. They didn't seem surprised by this information. How had they already heard it? Had Ma called them as soon as Vic and Erin left? Erin wouldn't have been surprised. She needed someone to talk to about everything that was going on. Maybe she was closer to the boys than Erin had imagined.

"That's ridiculous," Daniel said. "Who would poison Pa? Why would anyone want to?"

"I don't know. That's what I'm trying to figure out. The doctor thinks it was poisoning."

"It's those dang salads," Joseph offered. "Healthy eating will kill you every time. Why is it whenever you hear in the news about someone turning one hundred, they've always been smoking and drinking since they were teenagers? All of the emphasis on healthy eating and exercise is what's killing people."

Vic rolled her eyes and shook her head. "You'd like that, wouldn't you? That's not the way it looks. Those are the cases that make it to the media because they're unusual. People who live to an old age usually do it *because* of healthy living."

"Not the stories I've heard."

"No one has any reason to poison Pa," Daniel repeated.

"No one?" Vic pressed. She didn't say that she thought it might be their mother. Didn't mention that they were the only other ones who had access to Pa's food. She just waited to see what they would come up with.

"No one," Daniel insisted. "He's just an old man. No one would kill him."

Vic nodded. She sighed and got to her feet. Nilla immediately jumped to his feet and shook, making his collar tags jangle.

"What's that?" Joseph asked, drawing back like he thought Nilla might be dangerous. "A rat?"

"You better be careful, or I'll sic him on you. He doesn't like men."

Joseph chuckled.

"Hey, wait," Daniel put his hand out. "Before you go…"

Erin and Vic looked at him expectantly. Maybe he had something to say about the possible poisoning after all.

"Are there any more cookies?"

CHAPTER 26

*V*ic giggled as she got back into the car with Erin. Erin looked at her to find out what was so funny. Maybe it was just a pressure release valve.

"Doesn't matter how old they are on the outside, they're still little boys on the inside. Can you believe that they ate all those cookies in a day?"

Erin smiled. "Well... I can, actually. I've seen kids go through cookies like locusts. Big men with appetites... no surprise to me at all." Erin started the engine, glad to be getting out of there.

"Why Erin, I think you just used Tennessee slang. And a Biblical reference, at that."

"Biblical?"

"A plague of locusts."

"I didn't mean it that way."

"Oh, you can't fool me. You're reverting to your roots. Way down deep there, you've got all kinds of homilies just bustin' to come out."

"No, I don't think I do." Erin hit the gas to back the car up, skidding in the gravel to start with. Then the tires got traction and jerked them back suddenly.

"You do," Vic assured her.

They bumped through the ruts in the gravel, and it was a relief when they reached the highway and smooth driving. Erin's phone rang, and she tapped the answer button before taking the turn onto the highway.

"Hello?"

It was Terry. "Hi, Erin. Listen… we have a little situation here."

Erin looked at Vic worriedly. *What else could happen?*

"You're on speaker," she warned, "Vic is here too."

"Morning, Miss Victoria," Terry greeted formally.

"Good morning, Officer Piper."

"It's about your sister," Terry told Erin, reverting to the situation in Bald Eagle Falls.

"Is everything okay? Bella called to say that she hadn't shown up at Auntie Clem's and she couldn't reach her."

"Charley is fine."

"But…?"

"She was picked up for public intoxication."

"What?"

Terry chuckled. "She's been… a little wild. This is the second day in a row that she's spent an overnight here. We prefer to transfer any detainees to the city; you know that we're not really equipped to handle overnight guests. But Charley is family, so I tried to give her a break. But giving her preferred treatment is obviously not the way to deter this behavior, so…"

"So…?" Erin was not sure where he was going.

"I wondered if it would help if you had a chat with her. Remind her that if she's trying to be a respected business owner in Bald Eagle Falls, she needs to cut out this juvenile behavior."

"Yes," Erin agreed, giving a nod. "I can give her a call. I don't know if she'll answer, though."

"She doesn't have her phone right now. I was kind of hoping you would talk to her face to face. A voicemail isn't going to change anything."

"Oh, well…" Erin looked at Vic. She was committed to being there for whatever Vic needed her to do.

Vic shrugged. "We don't have anything planned for the rest of the day. We might as well go see Charley."

"We?"

"If you don't want me along…"

"No, I do, but your family is here; I didn't think you would want to go back to Bald Eagle Falls."

"I could use a break for a day. I've already seen the boys, and you saw how welcoming Ma and Pa were today. We could probably use a break from each other. Who knows where Jeremy is? If he has any sense, he's probably already back in Bald Eagle Falls too."

"You're sure?" Erin checked. "You're not just doing that to make me feel better?"

"Can't I do things for you? If you can come to Moose River just to give me moral support, what's wrong with me going back to Bald Eagle Falls for a while when you need to take care of *your* family situation?"

"Well… okay." Erin raised her voice slightly to make sure that Terry could hear her. "I guess we're on our way back. I'll see you in a couple hours."

"Thanks, Erin. I appreciate it."

Erin said her goodbyes and tapped the phone screen to end the call. "Do you need anything from the hotel? Should we cancel our reservation for tonight?"

"Let's just go. I have everything I need at home. I don't feel like packing everything up just to spend one night back in Bald Eagle Falls. Unless you really want to. You don't need to stay with me in Moose River, you know. I don't know how long it's going to be or what the point is in staying. *They* don't want me there, so I don't know why I'm bothering."

"I think it's like raising teenagers," Erin said. "You have to be there for them even when they're acting out and say they hate you."

Vic laughed. "Yeah. Just like that. I'm okay with just going back to Bald Eagle Falls, then, and we'll come back tomorrow and see if anything has changed."

~

There wasn't much conversation on the way back to Bald Eagle Falls. Vic turned on the radio and closed her eyes and, in a few minutes, was fast asleep. Erin was amazed at how quickly she was out. They were both short on sleep, but it would have taken Erin a lot longer to fall asleep in the car, even in her condition.

Which was probably a good thing, since she was driving.

A couple of minutes after passing the "Welcome to Bald Eagle Falls" sign, she was cruising down Main Street toward the Town Hall where the Police Department had their offices. As Terry had said, they didn't really have a jail. A few interview rooms where a cot could be set up and the door locked if they had someone they needed to hold overnight, if transport to the city was no longer an option. Erin found a parking space outside of the brick building and she and Vic headed inside.

Clara at the front desk frowned at Nilla as they walked in, but she didn't say they weren't allowed to have a dog in there and just called Terry on the interoffice phone to let them know they were there.

Terry came out of the office he shared with Stayner, with K9 alertly at heel, as he always was when they were on duty. Nilla yapped excitedly, probably happy to see an old friend after his encounter with the farm dogs. He ran forward to sniff noses with K9, who deigned to lower his head to greet the smaller dog even though he was on duty.

"Thanks for coming," Terry said, giving Erin a smile that made his dimple appear and made Erin glad that she would be at home with him for the night. "I know this is a big pain in the neck."

"It's fine," Erin said, shrugging. "We were ready for a break from Moose River."

"From the Jacksons, you mean," Vic inserted. "I'm 'bout fed up with my family."

"That bad?" Terry sympathized.

"Take how bad you think it could be and double it."

Terry smiled again and nodded. He led them to one of the interview rooms and opened the door.

CHAPTER 27

"How long are you going to hold me here?" Charley demanded. "I have rights, you know, you can't just keep me here without a hearing—"

"Visitors for you, Miss Campbell."

"You can lose the 'Miss Campbell,'" Charley griped. She looked past Terry to Erin and Vic as they walked into the room, Nilla at Vic's side. "Oh, shoot! What are you doing here?" She looked around as if hoping for some avenue of escape, or at least a way to explain why she was there.

"We heard that you'd been detained," Erin said in a light tone.

"You're supposed to be in Moose River! What are you doing back in Bald Eagle Falls?"

"We heard that you'd been having some trouble."

"You shouldn't have come back here for me." Charley's cheeks were getting red. She and Erin were similar in looks. Both dark haired with similar facial features. Charley was taller and wiry, in better physical shape than Erin was. She'd been a member of the Dyson clan and had, Erin assumed, needed to be in good shape for her assignments with them. Or maybe she just liked working out.

But she had bags under her eyes that gave her a slightly haunted look. Probably hungover after a couple of days of drinking.

"I was worried. You're supposed to be taking care of Auntie Clem's while I'm in Moose River. Bella said that she couldn't get ahold of you. Then Terry said that you were here for two nights in a row. What's going on?"

"Nothing is going on." Charley looked at Terry. "Do you have to be in here, Officer Piper? Or can we have some privacy?"

Terry considered for a minute, then nodded. "Five minutes." He and K9 withdrew.

Erin knew that he'd give her however long she needed. Especially if it meant that Charley wouldn't be back again the next night.

"Now then, what's going on?" Erin asked. "Did something happen? Is something wrong? You said you would look after things while I was gone."

"I know I did. And everything has been fine. Bella and the others are on top of it. They haven't had any reason to complain about my management. Just… that I haven't exactly been there. But I've made sure that all of the shifts are covered each day, and they have all of the supplies they need. Everything has been running smoothly."

"You've returned Bella's calls?"

"When she leaves a message. Usually, she doesn't, and if she doesn't leave a message, I figure she's got things under control and we can just connect up when it's convenient." Charley pushed her hair back and rubbed her eyes. "I could really use a drink."

"What's up with the drinking?" Charley had had a few episodes since moving to Bald Eagle Falls after her boyfriend's murder. There had been a few binges and depressive episodes, but they had been short and seemed to just be Charley's way of working everything through. It was perfectly normal for someone who was grieving to have a few emotional outbursts. "You've been pretty good lately."

"Yeah, I have," Charley agreed. "So you don't need to worry about one or two drinks."

"One or two nights of drinking," Erin corrected. "I don't care if you have a drink with supper or before bed. But when you're drunk in public and get pulled in by the cops two nights in a row… that concerns me. First, because you're my sister and I'm worried about what's going on with you. But also because you're my business partner, and it doesn't reflect well on Auntie Clem's if you're making a fool of yourself in public."

Charley looked down at her hands. "I didn't mean to do anything that would make you or Auntie Clem's look bad."

"Well, you're a business owner. You need to think about that. This is a small town. People notice if you have a beer with your lunch. Carousing isn't exactly something people will overlook."

"Yeah, you're right. But I wanted to help you."

Erin frowned. "You wanted to help me." She wasn't sure she understood how this was a comment on or excuse for Charley's behavior.

"You." Charley was looking at Vic.

"Me?" Vic's brows came down. "Help me with what?"

"I'm not with the Dysons anymore, but I still have some contacts with them," Charley said. Her voice was low and she gave a little jerk with her head, indicating that they should come closer.

Vic exchanged glances with Erin, then went over and sat down on the cot next to Charley. Erin stepped closer so that they were all together in a more intimate grouping.

"What are you talking about?" Erin asked. "What do the Dysons have to do with anything?"

"Because they hear things. They pay attention to what's going on in the Jackson clan. You always have to know what your opponent is doing. Internal politics and operations inside the other clan are really important. How do you know what they are doing or what they are going to do unless you have people on the inside?"

"The Dysons have people inside the Jackson clan's organization?" Erin demanded, shocked. She had seen what the enmity between the two families was like. She couldn't believe that anyone would cross that line from one to the other. She looked at Vic, but Vic didn't seem surprised by this. If the Dysons had people inside the Jackson organization, Erin supposed that the reverse was true. The Jacksons had people inside the Dyson clan, spying and reporting back on internal operations. Vic had never been a formal member of the crime syndicate. Still, she would have some familiarity with this because of her father's participation.

"Of course," Charley said. "There are people who are related to both, or who have friends, or just want the money. There are moles in every organization."

"Wow. Okay. But I still don't see what that has to do with you drinking."

"Don't you?" Charley raised an eyebrow. "If I'm not part of the Dyson clan, then who is going to talk to me about what's going on?"

"Well, no one, I would guess."

"Yeah. Unless maybe I could do something to loosen their lips."

"Oh."

Charley nodded. She rubbed her temples. "If I can't get a drink, do you think I could at least get an aspirin?"

"I'll ask Terry," Erin agreed. But she didn't move to go get him. She waited for Charley to spill the beans. "So...? Did you find anything out?"

Charley looked at Vic again. "You know you can't take anything that happens inside the clan at face value."

"Not even my pa coming down with a stomach bug or having a heart attack?"

Charley nodded. She looked toward the little window in the door to make sure Terry wasn't standing there. Erin assumed that there was a mic in the air vent shaft overhead, if not a camera providing a live video feed as well. They would need a way to monitor and record interviews. But Terry wouldn't be listening in on a private conversation between two sisters. This was just supposed to be Erin's lecture on straightening up and flying straight. Nothing that he needed to hear.

"What would you say if I told you he was poisoned?" Charley whispered.

Erin and Vic both leaned toward her.

"We already figured he might have been," Vic told Charley. "I got a call... from someone else last night. Something that made us think maybe he had a little help getting sick."

Charley nodded.

"But how would the clan know that?" Erin asked. "If it was Vic's mom...?"

Charley blinked and frowned. "Who said it was her mom?"

Vic looked at Erin. Erin shrugged. Vic had thought that the only one who would have had access to Pa's food and a reason to kill him or at least to make him sick, was Ma. Who else could it have been?

"Who do you think did it?"

"Word is that it was ordered."

"Ordered? By who? The Dysons?"

Charley shook her head. "Would I be telling you if it was the Dysons? That would just be asking to get offed myself."

"Then who?" Vic stared at Charley and Charley didn't answer. "Do you mean by the Jackson clan?" Vic demanded. "That doesn't make any sense!"

"Why not?"

"Why would they put a hit out on one of their own?"

"There are all kinds of reasons. It happens all the time."

Vic shook her head vigorously. "My Pa has been a loyal Jackson for decades. He's a revered member of the community."

"And...?"

"There's no way they would put a hit out on him. He's never done anything against them."

"But he's done things *for* them."

"Yes. Of course. He's been part of the clan forever."

"Near the top. He takes orders from the bosses."

"Yes," Vic agreed. Her tone still indicated that she knew they wouldn't kill him because of this.

Charley massaged the back of her neck. "Vic... I guess you've never actually been a part of the organization, so there is a lot of stuff you don't know. The way that things work."

"I know how things work."

"Some things. But the real inner workings of an organization like that... you don't. Those things are only shared between those who are on the inside."

"You think that my Pa did something wrong. And that's why they would put a hit out on him. That's why someone poisoned him."

"No." Charley shook her head. "I'm not saying that he did something wrong. He did everything right. He did everything he was told to. But *that* is a problem."

"Why? How could that be a problem?"

"Because he knows too much."

"About his own clan?"

"Yes." Charley let Vic think about that for a few moments. "He knows too many things that could get people into trouble. Those guys at the top, they're very sensitive to how much people know about them. How easy it would be for them to end up in prison because someone talked. Someone like your Pa who knows where all of the bodies are buried… so to speak."

CHAPTER 28

"*P*a has never said anything to anyone," Vic said, frowning. "They know he would never say anything. No one could turn him. He would never say anything to the cops or anyone he didn't know was loyal to the clan."

"That doesn't matter. He could still make a mistake. He could still be used. He knows all of the dirt and could use it for his own advancement, or set up a retirement plan with the feds, anything. He knows too much, so…"

Vic shook her head. She was obviously having a hard time wrapping her mind around this. Erin understood what Charley was saying, and it made sense to her. But Vic knew her father, knew his history with the clan, and had notions about how the clan would behave or not behave toward him. She had been raised with the idea that the clan was the highest authority, the one organization that she had to respect and obey. And now, she was being told that the clan had betrayed her. Betrayed her father, one of its most loyal followers.

"I think… she needs some time," Erin told Charley.

Charley looked sympathetic. "Yeah. I guess something like this could throw you for a loop."

"Are you *sure* about this or just guessing?" Vic asked.

"I didn't make it up. It's what I was told. How reliable it is... I don't know. We were both rather intoxicated at the time. And it's only rumor, somebody heard from somebody else... maybe it's not true at all. But your Pa *is* in the hospital."

"And we already had a pretty good idea that he was poisoned," Erin contributed. It wasn't just Charley coming up with a wild tale. It was substantiated by what they already knew.

"But by his own clan? I still can't believe that. And how would they be able to poison his food? He doesn't go out to eat at neighbors' houses. He pretty much only eats at home. Even when Erin brought him cookies that she had baked herself, he wouldn't have any."

Charley looked away. "You'll have to figure out that one by yourself. I don't know who ordered it or who carried it out. Just that there were rumors of an order, and now, he's sick in the hospital. Maybe dying."

"He won't die. They're going to figure out what poison it was, and then they'll be able to give him an antidote. He isn't eating anything else, so he's not getting any more poison."

"And then he'll go home. And then what?"

"Then... he'll be more careful. I'll tell him that he needs to be more careful."

"He's probably already figured that out," Charley offered dryly.

"This is nuts. I appreciate you going to all of this trouble. Sacrificing your body in the name of finding out what happened to my pa," Vic said sardonically. "But I think... you're going a little overboard. There is no way that the clan could have poisoned him."

"Okay." Charley shrugged. "You can think what you like. No skin off my nose."

"We do appreciate it," Erin assured her. She wasn't sure about the part where Charley had gotten drunk with the unknown informant in order to tease out any gossip about what had happened to Pa Jackson. Charley may have learned something while out drinking, but it had probably just been by chance. That made a lot more sense. "Maybe in the future... do your drinking at home."

"But..." Charley's mouth opened and shut. "I was just getting information."

Erin nodded and didn't say anything further.

≈

"Thanks for talking to her," Terry said as he escorted Erin and Vic back out to the front reception area. "I don't know what's been up with her. She's been pretty good lately, and then all of a sudden, she's getting smashed and making a big spectacle of herself. Not someone you want to be associated with your business."

Erin nodded. "I know. I told her that. I think... she'll be better now."

"Good. we'd rather not have to staff the office overnight because someone can't moderate their drinking."

"Yeah. I don't think you'll have any more problems with her."

He kissed her cheek. "Are you going to be home tonight?"

"Yeah. I think we're going to relax here, spend the night, and figure out what to do next."

"What to do next?"

"Uh..." Erin caught Vic's warning gaze. "What we can do to help Vic's family. Her dad is still hanging in there, but her mom is spending all of her time at the hospital. We want to do what we can to make things easier for her. But sooner or later, she's got to go home, too. And we'll have to come back here to take care of Auntie Clem's."

"Ah," Terry nodded his understanding. He put a hand on Vic's arm briefly. "Sorry about all of this, Vic. It must be very stressful."

"Thanks."

"When are you off?" Erin asked.

"Not until eight. You ladies should go have dinner. I'll scrape something up at home after work. You don't want to be cooking."

Erin had to agree. The last thing on her mind was cooking.

≈

Vic nominated the family restaurant. "I need my southern comfort food," she declared. "I need my meat plus three."

Erin laughed. "Family restaurant it is."

"You don't want something different?"

"No, it feels like it's been ages since we were there last. That works for me."

CHAPTER 29

*E*rin drove them there. It was still before the dinner rush hour, so the restaurant was not too full and the waitress took their order right away. As they waited for their meal, the tables began to fill.

"Oh!" Erin waved. "It's Mary Lou and Joshua!"

Mary Lou lifted a hand in greeting. After a moment of hesitation, they came over to Erin's and Vic's table to say hello.

"How are you guys doing?" Erin asked, trying to include Joshua in the conversation as he looked off in the other direction. "How are things?"

"Well, we're managing pretty well," Mary Lou said, smoothing her pantsuit distractedly. "I think... Joshua's feeling a little better, aren't you, Josh?"

Joshua turned his head to look at them. Erin could see that he still had dark shadows under his eyes.

"Hey," he greeted as if he hadn't heard anything else they said. "How's it going?"

Mary Lou sighed.

"Do you want to join us?" Erin invited, gesturing to the other seats at their table. "We'd love to have you."

She expected Mary Lou to demur, but she did not. She nodded, looking determined. "Of course, we'd love to join you," she agreed.

Joshua looked as surprised at her response as Erin felt. He looked down at the chairs as if wondering if he'd really heard her right, waiting to see if she were going to sit down. Mary Lou did. She motioned for him to take the other seat.

"Well. It's nice to have the opportunity to eat with friends," Mary Lou said to Josh, sounding forced.

He shifted his position a couple of times, looking uncomfortable. He shrugged his shoulders. "Sure. Yeah."

"We've been stuck at home so much lately," Mary Lou said. "I told Joshua that we needed to get out and do something. We can't just stay at home all day, not talking to anyone."

Mary Lou couldn't. She had a job to go to. A family to support. Joshua, however, was not going to school and did not have a job to go to. And apparently, not very many friends to pull him out of himself either.

He nodded but didn't say anything.

"I heard that your father was poorly," Mary Lou said to Vic. "I was sorry to hear that."

Vic nodded. "Yeah. It's been kind of tough. But I didn't expect him to survive the first night, and he did, so maybe things will work out. The doctor is getting closer to what made him sick, so then he'll be able to treat him…"

"Oh? I thought he'd had the flu and a heart attack. The flu can hit us so much harder as we get older."

Erin looked at Vic, waiting to see how she was going to answer before offering anything.

"At first, they thought it was some kind of stomach bug," Vic said slowly. "But now… they think that maybe it was poisoning."

Joshua's eyes went to Vic's face. This had definitely captured his attention.

"Food poisoning?" Mary Lou asked. "That can definitely send you to your bed. I remember once when all four of us came down with—"

"No. Not food poisoning. They think that he ate something poisonous. Not something that… had gone bad."

"What kind of poison would a grown man eat? I can understand a child getting into something, thinking that it was a candy or punch, but why would a grown man eat poison?"

They all just looked at each other for a minute. Joshua leaned closer to Vic, eager for her answer.

"He didn't take it on purpose," Vic responded, fiddling with her glass. "It was an accident. Or else, someone intentionally poisoned him."

Mary Lou made an appropriately shocked face. "Intentionally poisoned him. Surely not."

It hadn't been that long ago that there had been a spate of poisonings in Bald Eagle Falls that had not been accidental, and Mary Lou knew it. Maybe she was hoping to block those memories out by denying the possibility of any new allegations.

Joshua's eyes were wide.

"We're trying to figure it out," Vic said. "I don't know… I find it hard to believe myself. It's still possible that it was just some kind of accident. But… there are some rumors that it might not have been."

"People start silly rumors all the time. I'm sure it doesn't have any basis in fact."

"Why would someone poison him?" Joshua asked. "In theory."

"Joshua," Mary Lou said repressively. "Really. It's not in good taste. I'm sure it must have been accidental."

"But if he was poisoned… do you really think he could have been?" Joshua asked Vic.

She nodded. "It's looking that way. I haven't heard back from the doctor yet, but he thought it might be—" Vic looked at Mary Lou and shifted at the last moment, "he thought he might be able to identify it soon. If we know what it was, then maybe we can figure out where it came from."

"And if it was an accident," Mary Lou said firmly.

They all nodded, but they all knew that Mary Lou was the only one at the table who believed that. Or was determined to believe it no matter what the facts.

The waitress came over to welcome the new guests and to take their drink orders. She handed them menus, though, of course, neither of them needed one. They'd been going to the family restaurant since before Joshua was born.

"If he was poisoned intentionally, then who did it?" Joshua asked Vic, lowering his voice as if his mother might not hear it if he did so.

"I'm not sure," Vic said. "My ma made his meals, so I guess she's a suspect. But I don't know... there's a rumor that it might have been... clan related."

"Is he in one of the clans?"

Mary Lou snorted. Joshua turned his head to look at her, surprised. "Victoria is a *Jackson*," Mary Lou told him.

"Oh. I thought her name was Webster."

"She changed it. When she... you know. She's a Jackson born and bred. Her pa, her grandpappy, everybody in her family has been in the clan for as long as anyone can remember. And longer."

Vic shrugged. "Yeah. That."

"Then *you're* in the clan?"

"No." Vic was firm. "I left home. I was never in the clan. I didn't want any part in it."

"But it's your family. You can't not be part of the family."

"I'm doing my best. There's a difference between being part of an extended family and actually being a member of the clan. They're not synonymous. *Close,* but not quite."

Joshua nodded slowly. He looked at his mother and then back at Vic, wondering how much he would be able to get away with. Mary Lou was bound to shut him down before long. She'd already made objections.

"You think it was the clan, don't you?" he challenged.

"No... I don't know. I don't want it to be them. I don't want anything to do with the clan, and I don't want... to have to stand as some kind of barrier between my pa and whoever has it out for him. I just want things to be peaceful and... I don't want him to get poisoned, but if he is, I hope I won't be anywhere around when it happens."

"You think you would be a suspect?"

"I guess anyone close could be a suspect, but I wasn't this time, so hopefully, everyone would know that it wasn't me. I just meant... I don't know what I would do. I chose not to be a part of that life. So would I just stand by and watch? Or would I try to stop it? And if I tried to stop it, would that make me a target? Or get me all tangled up in clan business? I don't want that."

Joshua nodded his understanding. "No. I get that."

Vic looked at Mary Lou and changed the subject. They received their dinners a short time later. Despite her assertion that she needed comfort food, Vic mostly poked at the food and moved it around her plate, only taking one or two bites.

Erin wanted to know how Joshua's life was going, if he was recovering from the trauma of being kidnapped. But it wasn't an easy question to ask and she didn't want to put him on the spot. But she and Mary Lou had both seen the change that had come over him when he started to talk to them about the poisoning. He went from not caring about anything or wanting to be there, putting out an effort to socialize, to being fascinated and engaged. His investigative instincts immediately kicked in and he wanted all of the details.

Mary Lou had been angry with Erin for letting Joshua get involved in the reporting on the ice cream contest, especially when it had turned into a story about Beryl Batcombe's death. Erin could only imagine how furious Mary Lou would be if they let him get involved in a suspected poisoning case.

CHAPTER 30

They did their best to keep the conversation away from the possible attempted murder of Vic's father. Still, it wasn't easy to avoid the elephant in the room. Pa Jackson was the subject on everybody's mind. Even though they tried to be casual and discuss other things, the conversation kept returning to him briefly.

Vic ordered a hot fudge brownie for dessert and took only one bite of it.

"I want it all," she complained, referring to her dinner and dessert, "but my stomach won't cooperate. Everything I eat just turns into a lump in my stomach. And heartburn. Sheesh." She patted her chest. "You wouldn't think one bite could have such an effect."

Erin nodded.

"I can just imagine how it must be for someone with an allergy or intolerance," Vic continued. "To feel like this whenever you happen to get a bit of the wrong thing..."

"If you're lucky," Erin agreed. "Then you might just have to deal with a bit of a stomach upset. And not have to worry about throwing up for days or having a life-threatening reaction."

"Yeah. That would be pretty scary."

"I was reading in an email newsletter I get on food allergies and intolerances the other day about people having anaphylactic reactions to food in the hospital. After they have done everything they could to inform the dietary staff and nurses about their allergies. One girl was admitted with anaphylaxis from eating something cross-contaminated at a restaurant. She had a really bad time of it and had to stay overnight. Then the hospital triggers another reaction the next day with just one bite of her breakfast. And there was a link to another story about a little boy who died because they gave him something he was allergic to. Right there in the hospital."

"How could they let that happen?" Joshua demanded. "I know that mistakes happen, but if they told them what they were allergic to and then they still gave it to them…!"

"I know. What else are you supposed to do? The girl is suing the hospital. And she says that she'll never eat hospital-provided food again. She'll have a family member bring safe food in."

"You would think that a hospital would be safe."

Erin sighed. "You would be wrong."

Vic pushed her brownie toward Joshua. "You want it? I really can't. I thought I could, but it's just too much for my system right now."

Joshua looked at it, then glanced at his mother. "I don't know. It's yours. You ordered it for yourself."

"And if no one else eats it, it's going to get thrown in the garbage. Is that better?" Vic looked at Erin and Mary Lou. "Why doesn't everyone have a bite? Then we can just say I bought it for the table. If you don't like it, you don't have to have any more."

"I'm not worried about not liking it!" Erin patted her stomach.

Mary Lou nodded. "One bite, but that's it. And just because I don't want to offend a friend."

Vic gave her a mischievous look. "I'll have to remember that one."

Joshua watched as Erin and Mary Lou each helped themselves to a bite of the hot fudge confection. Erin's bite was considerably larger than Mary Lou's dainty one and dripped with thick chocolate syrup. Then Erin pushed it back toward Joshua again. "Now you. Pretend you're a food critic for the newspaper. Tell us how you would describe it."

Joshua smiled. He centered the dish before him and took a delicate bite, even smaller than Mary Lou's. He swirled it around in his mouth and smacked his lips.

"A tasty morsel," he pronounced with an attempt at a posh British accent, "with just enough sweetness to counteract the bitterness of the chocolate." He took a larger bite, being sure to scoop up a good amount of the whipped cream topping as well. "Rich, luxurious. High-quality ingredients." His words were slightly slurred by the food in his mouth. He scooped up another bite and stuffed it in. "A must-try at Bald Eagle Falls's premier five-star family restaurant."

Erin and Vic laughed. Joshua used a napkin to wipe away some of the chocolate syrup that had dribbled down his chin. He scraped the dish to get the rest of the remnants of the dessert.

"It's pretty good!"

Mary Lou was smiling, a genuine smile that Erin hadn't seen for some time. It was rare that Mary Lou let herself relax and be happy in the moment. Erin was glad to see it. It was good that she had called them over to the table and good that Mary Lou had accepted.

Back at home, Erin wasn't sure whether to expect Vic to go back to her loft apartment over the garage for some quiet alone time or to Erin's house to hang out until Terry returned home. She hadn't heard whether Willie would be around or whether he was off working on one of his many ventures. Since Vic hadn't been planning to be home, he might have booked other things.

She pulled the bug back into its appointed place in the garage and turned it off. Vic popped her door handle. "Do you need some time? Or do you mind if we hang out?"

Willie had commented before that he didn't know how Erin and Vic didn't run out of things to talk about or get tired of each other after working together all day. But Erin didn't feel like she had to be "on" for Vic. She could hang out in her pajamas and write in her planner, experiment with a new dish in the kitchen, or read through Clementine's genealogies while Vic was there and not feel like she had to carry the conversation or entertain her. Erin imagined it was like being with a sister that she had grown up with, but she couldn't be sure since she'd never had a close sibling relationship like that. Maybe it was just how it was to be with a good friend.

"No problem. Make a pot of tea and we'll put our feet up."

"You're on. I'm going to change into my jammies first, then I'll be right over."

Vic climbed the stairs outside the garage to her apartment and Erin crossed the yard to the back door.

CHAPTER 31

*O*range Blossom began yowling before Erin was even halfway across the yard. She could hear him outside even though the windows were closed. She hoped he hadn't been howling and disturbing the neighbors while she'd been gone. As a kitten, he had cried when left alone for too long, but he had settled down as he grew up.

"I'm coming, I'm coming," Erin sang out to him, fumbling with the keys in her hurry to get the door open and quiet him. She slowed and steadied her hands and unlocked and opened it slowly. Blossom didn't dash to get out the door, but paced back and forth, meowing at her for being away for so long. Erin disarmed the burglar alarm before carrying on. She turned on a few lights and petted Blossom and scratched his ears, waiting for him to finish his lecture on not going away for so long.

"I know, bud. I know. You were afraid I wasn't going to come back. But you remember when I went on the cruise? I still came back, didn't I? I'll always come back. I'm not going to abandon you."

Marshmallow lolloped around Orange Blossom and Erin's legs, nuzzling her and getting his pets and scratches as well. He never seemed to worry as much as Orange Blossom. They had both been born in the wild, as far as Erin could tell, but their personalities were completely different, Orange Blossom much more anxious and demanding, seeming to Erin to be afraid of being abandoned. Maybe his mother cat had left him too early, or something had happened to her. He had still been very small when he had first appeared at Auntie Clem's Bakery. From what Erin understood, mother rabbits left their kits alone for most of the day, so maybe Erin's absences seemed normal to Marshmallow.

Erin gave them both treats and turned on more lights. She planned out the evening in her head. She hadn't spent much time with her planner in the time she'd been in Moose River, and wanted to think through some short-term goals and some new marketing campaigns for the summer. If she wasn't proactive, focusing on these projects, all of the other work seemed to fill in her time so that there wasn't any left for creativity.

By the time that Erin changed into her pajamas and returned to the living room, Vic had arrived, dressed in her nightie with a ruffly wrap around it, and had put the kettle on in the kitchen.

"Long time, no see," Erin teased.

"I feel so much better after changing. How can a little thing like changing out of the day's clothes make such a difference?"

"I don't know, but it does," Erin agreed. She sat on the couch and patted her lap to invite Orange Blossom to jump up, but he ignored her and went into the kitchen to see whether he could coax Vic into giving him additional treats. Marshmallow hopped over to Erin and lay down on her feet. Erin smiled and wiggled her toes. He didn't move.

She opened her planner and glanced over the schedule and tasks she had written in for the next few days. Most of them had now been delegated to Charley or to other employees at Auntie Clem's Bakery. However, she still needed to get on top of the accounting and some other big-picture tasks to keep the business moving forward. She knew if she got behind on her accounting, she would regret it.

"Erin?"

Erin startled and looked up. Vic handed her a cup of tea. "Oh, sorry. I was lost in my planner."

"I can see that." Vic sat down and sipped her tea. Erin brought hers up to her nose. Orange and ginger. One of her favorites. Vic had probably asked her what she wanted and, getting no reply, had just picked one of Erin's standbys.

"Thank you. This is great."

Vic nodded and had another sip of hers. Erin could smell licorice and valerian. Something to help Vic to relax. Usually, she popped an Ambien if she was having problems sleeping or was up late. The tea suggested that she needed more than just sleep, but something to calm her anxious thoughts. It was no wonder she was feeling anxious after the day that she'd had.

"Big plans?" Vic asked with a nod at the planner.

"Well… just holding steady right now. But I want to think of a couple of promotions to do over the summer. Something to keep the kids coming back when they are out of school. People tend to get out of their usual routines and healthy eating falls by the wayside. Families rely more on fast food and heating prepared foods at home."

Vic nodded. "And less on fresh-baked bread and muffins."

"Right. I was thinking maybe a weekly promo… kids have to get their passports stamped each week to get a prize at the end of the summer, and then do some little grab bags for them. Or maybe a fun school supply like a pencil case or notebook cover…"

"That would be fun. What about when kids go on a vacation with their family for a week or two? Then they can't get their passport stamped."

"Yeah. We'll have to work around that. You only need to get eight out of ten weeks, or bring proof of your vacation to get a stamp for the week that you missed."

"That sounds good."

"If we've got the kids coming in each week, then Mom is coming in every week and may as well pick up the usual shopping items. Maybe we can focus on hoagie rolls, because they travel and picnic better than just sandwiches."

"I love hoagies," Vic declared. "We should definitely do more hoagies."

"We can do a variety. Some fancy seed or cheese hoagies as well as the white and brown."

"Awesome," Vic pronounced, and had another sip of her tea.

Erin heard footsteps on the sidewalk outside the house and turned her head to see two figures coming up the sidewalk.

"Company."

She pulled her feet out from under the toasty Marshmallow and got up to answer the door. Jeremy and Beaver smiled and greeted her at the door.

"My sister here?" Jeremy asked. "I saw the lights on."

"Yeah, you bet. Come on in."

The couple entered. Vic didn't get up, staying where she was already nice and cozy. She checked the front of her nightgown and wrap to make sure she was decent. "When did you get back? I didn't know if you were still in Moose River or back here."

Everyone sat down.

"Wasn't a lot of reason to be in Moose River. Once I checked in... well, you were there, and the guys were at the farm, and I didn't figure anyone needed me any too badly. Pa was still hanging on. Figured I might as well get back to work, and if something happened... someone would give me a call."

"Yeah." Vic nodded. "We just came back for the afternoon, but I don't know how much longer I'm going to stay around. If he gets better and they let him go... Ma will be back home and they can take care of themselves."

Erin thought about the possibility that Ma or someone else had poisoned Pa. Could they really take care of themselves? Wouldn't he just be in danger again as soon as he was out? And this time, he would know it. He'd realize that someone had poisoned him. Would that help him to avoid being poisoned a second time, or would it mean that whoever had done it would step up their game? Give him a heavier dose the next time in order to kill him. Or maybe a switch from poison to a more lethal option. A knife or a gun.

"I'm glad it wasn't as bad as we initially thought," Beaver said. "The fact that he's survived this long... that's a good sign. I wasn't sure whether he would live through the first night."

Vic looked at Beaver over her cup. "How did you know about it so fast, anyway? Nobody called me or Jeremy."

"I have channels," Beaver said with a shrug. She chewed on her wad of gum. "I know that the two of you are kind of estranged from the family, but I thought you would still want to know. Then at least you get to decide whether to see him or not."

"Yeah. I appreciate it. I'm not sure I made the right choice in deciding to go see him… but at least I don't have to feel guilty about not going. Better to go and think it wasn't worth it than to not go and think that I should have made up before he died."

"You find out anything interesting?" Beaver asked, looking sideways at Erin to let her know that she was included in the query.

"What do you mean?" Vic asked, as if she really had no idea.

Beaver chewed vigorously, her wide mouth spread in a grin.

"I think that if you found anything interesting, you would know what I mean."

Vic considered, not giving anything away. Erin waited to see what she wanted to reveal.

"I got a call from Theresa."

Beaver's gum cracked like a gunshot. Jeremy leaned forward, gaping at Vic. "You got a call from Theresa?"

Vic nodded. "Yeah. It was a little freaky," she admitted. Her eyes went to Beaver. "I don't know where she is, and we did tell the appropriate law enforcement officer. In case you're wondering."

"Interesting that they didn't think that was important to share with us."

"You're not thinking Jack Ward did anything wrong, are you?" Erin demanded. "He's not mixed up with the clans or Theresa."

"I didn't say he was. I said that it was interesting he didn't share that."

"He probably will at some point. Maybe he just wanted to look around first, before calling people who might tip her off. If we suddenly had a bunch of feds in town, that might have looked suspicious. Better to keep it hush-hush."

"The department specializes in hush-hush."

"Well…" Erin squirmed. "I'm sure Jack Ward isn't involved in anything with Theresa or the clans. The last time Theresa was in town, she stabbed him."

"No," Beaver agreed. She was chewing slowly and thoughtfully.

Erin didn't think for a minute that Jack Ward would take things into his own hands to get his private revenge on Theresa Franklin.

Well, maybe for one minute. He would be tempted, of course. But he was a law enforcement officer and he was good at what he did. He didn't make mistakes like going after Theresa Franklin without sufficient backup.

Not a second time.

CHAPTER 32

"*D*o you think that Theresa could have had something to do with Mr. Jackson getting poisoned?" Erin asked Beaver. "Or do you think that it was just an excuse to call Vic?"

Beaver chewed slowly, considering the question.

"Poisoned?" Jeremy repeated, his eyes getting big. "What are you talking about, poisoned?"

"Oh." Erin looked at Beaver and Vic for help. "I mean... if he was poisoned."

"He was *poisoned*?" Jeremy demanded, his voice getting louder. "Who said he was poisoned? And why didn't anybody say anything before now?" He looked accusingly at Vic and then Beaver.

Vic put her hands up defensively. "We don't know for sure. The doctor hasn't said anything definitive yet."

"Erin sounded pretty sure."

"Well... that's the theory that we're operating under right now. It could still just be the flu."

Erin shook her head. The doctor had said it wasn't the flu.

"But you don't think so." Jeremy turned his eyes to Beaver. "And you don't think so. You knew about this?"

Beaver shook her head. "No. But I can't say I'm surprised."

"Well, I sure as heck am!" Jeremy glowered at his sister again. "How exactly did you come up with this theory? And why didn't you tell me? And Beaver?"

"I haven't exactly been keeping it a secret. Like I said, we called Jack Ward right away. I guess I should have called you, but to say what? We don't know anything. And I didn't know whether you were staying around and wanted to know or whether you were back here and would want to be kept out of it. You didn't exactly tell me your plans."

"You told Jack Ward. You said you told him about Theresa. So is that where this is coming from? This is a Crazy Theresa theory?"

"Umm… yes. That's who suggested it, in a roundabout way. But I think Pa already knew it might have been poison. And I think the doctor would have been looking at that even if one of us hadn't said something. He doesn't think it's just a virus. The police talked to him, and he was talking to Ma and Pa and was going to run some tests, see if he could figure out what it is. If it's a poison."

"What do you mean you think Pa knew?"

"When Erin tried to give him cookies, he refused. He didn't say that he was too sick, just flat out wouldn't eat them and told her not to bring him anything. It isn't like Pa to turn down baking." Vic shrugged.

"He's been trying to eat healthier. That's probably all it is. Or he was feeling sick but didn't want to say so in front of someone he didn't know."

"He made it sound like this health kick is Ma's idea."

Jeremy opened his mouth, then closed it again. He glanced over at Beaver, who was chewing her gum slowly, watching him and Vic closely. At his look, Beaver simply smiled and leaned back in her chair, looking casual and relaxed. Jeremy looked at her, then back at Vic.

"You're not putting this on Ma? That is a Crazy Theresa kind of idea. Ma never poisoned Pa. Why would she?" His tone was incredulous.

"Think about it, Jer," Vic said flatly.

Erin saw the mask he put over his expression. His usual anima-
tion disappeared, and Erin thought he had suddenly become aware of
every eye upon him and every movement or expression he made. She
had seen that kind of studied expression before.

Family secrets.

Abuse.

The need to keep family business within the family.

"Things weren't that bad between them," Jeremy said, his voice
similarly flat. "If they were, she could have left any time she wanted.
There wouldn't be any reason to poison him. That's Hollywood stuff,
not real life."

"Leave him and go where? Leave behind her family, her home,
everything she worked for thirty years to achieve? Live in a shelter
with nothing? Soup kitchen meals? They don't even *have* any of that
in Moose River. She'd have to go into the city. Can you really see her
leaving the farm and trying to make it on her own?"

"They've stuck things out until now. What has changed?"

"I'm not saying that anything has. I'm just saying that it's a possibility. If the cops look at her, they're going to realize she had a
motive."

"No, they won't." Jeremy shook his head. "Who is going to tell
them that? Her? Him? Neither one of them is going to say anything
that would put Ma in the center of a police investigation. He wouldn't
care if she did it or not; he would never rat to the police about it."

"Anyway, no one is saying it *is* Ma. She is just the first one they
would look at. She's the one with access to his food. The one who
started him on a different diet recently. One that would make it a lot
easier to hide a leaf or two of some plant that would make him sick.
But I never said that she did it. Not to you, not to anyone."

She didn't look in Erin's direction. It was still true. She hadn't told
Erin that Ma had done it. Just that she was the most likely suspect.

"But you think it was."

"I never said that."

"You're not answering my question."

"You didn't ask a question," Vic pointed out.

They both glared at each other, but neither one posed the question or Vic's thoughts on it.

"There is a rumor that it was the clan," Erin said, hoping to derail the argument between Vic and Jeremy by focusing them on the alternative theories. They didn't have to argue about whether or not Ma had anything to do with the poisoning if they could show that it was someone else. Most likely.

Jeremy scowled. "The clan? Why would they poison Pa?"

"You probably understand it a lot better than me," Vic said. "You were still with them for a few years after you left school. Me, I just took off. I was never involved."

"It doesn't matter. I still don't know what you're talking about. That doesn't make any sense."

"Char—the person who told us about the rumor said that it was because he knew too much," Erin related. "He's been working with the clan for a long time and, if he decided to talk to the police about any of it, he could inform on a lot of people."

Beaver gave a nod at this. She knew all about informants. From what Erin could tell, she used them quite a bit.

"Pa would never inform on the clan."

"Of course not," Vic agreed. "He's always been loyal. But that doesn't mean that they would trust him one hundred percent. Because they wouldn't. They don't trust anyone that much, no matter how high they are in the organization." Vic stopped and considered her own words. "Right?"

She was telling him how things worked when she had never been in the organization. Basically just regurgitating what Charley had told her. But Jeremy had his own experience to rely on. He would know the truth of the matter better than she.

"Well..." Jeremy shrugged. "I don't know. I don't think they would ever put a hit out on someone in the organization without pretty good reason. And I don't think that just knowing a lot would be a good enough reason. I just don't see it."

"Maybe you could talk to Daniel and Joe. Find out what they think. If they've heard anything."

"They're not going to tell me. Not with me out of the clan. I'd be the last person they would talk to."

"Maybe if you went back, hung out with them a little, got to talking about old times… maybe something would slip."

"You want me to get our dear brothers drunk?"

Vic tried to keep a straight face, staring at her cup and raising it to her mouth for another sip. "I don't think I said that. Did I say anything to anyone about drinking?" Vic looked at Erin. "Did I?"

"No," Erin obliged. "You didn't say anything about drinking."

"I don't know. I still don't think they'd tell me anything. But if the clan had a contract out on Pa, you can bet Daniel and Joe wouldn't be sitting around doing nothing about it. They wouldn't let anyone get away with it. They'd protect him."

He hoped. Erin hoped that was true too. She hadn't seen much of the young men, just a few brief meetings, during which they had not been particularly friendly toward Erin or nice to their youngest sibling. But that didn't mean that they didn't care about their father or the family. If they reflected Pa's attitudes toward Vic, then that just went to show that they honored and respected his opinions.

They would protect him.

Jeremy looked back at Beaver. "So I guess… maybe I should go back to Moose River."

"Not alone."

"You mean with Vic? We'll both be there."

"I mean me," Beaver said and popped her gum. "I think you should have someone to back you up. Keep an eye on things." Her gaze swept over Vic and Erin. "It isn't that I don't trust your Jack Ward to keep the peace down thataway. I'm sure he's a very competent law enforcement officer. But I don't trust him. I don't trust anyone else in a case like this."

"Okay… if you want to come and you can get the time off. I don't know how long it will be. Just a day or two, probably. If he hasn't died yet, then he's not likely to, is he? The doc will find out what it was, and then we'll figure out who it was if it was really poison. And…" He shrugged.

Erin pondered over the unsaid words. They would deal with it?

They would let Jack Ward know and let him make the appropriate arrests? They would warn Pa, and he would know to be more careful of what he ate? It was impossible to tell how Jeremy might have finished the sentence. But he obviously didn't want to do it aloud, so she had to assume that he didn't want his words quoted back to him at any point.

CHAPTER 33

*E*rin heard a car door slam and turned her head to look out the living room window. Terry's truck was at the curb.

"Officer Piper is home," Jeremy observed. "I think that's our cue to head home ourselves."

"You don't need to run," Erin said. "I'm sure Terry would like to have a visit too."

"He'll want some time alone with you. Especially if you guys are going to turn around and go back to Moose River tomorrow." Jeremy looked at Erin, raising an eyebrow.

Erin nodded. "Yes."

"Yeah. So we'd best give him all the time he can get."

Terry opened the front door and was met by Jeremy and Beaver heading out. He made a token protest, inviting them to stay and visit a little longer, but they made their excuses and left. Terry nodded at Vic, still sitting in her chair, teacup drained.

"Vic. How are you doing?"

She yawned. "Had my sleepy tea and a visit and I'm about ready for my bed. You two have a good night."

"You too."

"See you in the morning," Erin told her. "Whenever you're ready."

Vic nodded, yawned again, and left her cup in the sink on her way through the kitchen to the back door. Terry watched until she was up the stairs and inside her loft, then locked the back door and set the alarm.

"You guys have made your decision? It's back to Moose River first thing in the morning?"

Erin nodded. "Sometime in the morning. I don't know if it will be first thing."

"With the two of you, late morning is when the rest of the world is waking up. You'll probably be out of here before six."

"Maybe."

Terry loosened his heavy belt. K9 went over to Erin for pets and ear scratches, knowing that he was now off duty.

"You look tired," Erin told Terry. "Long day?"

"I'm sure it wasn't as long as yours. But I am plumb tired."

"Why don't you have a shower and I'll make you a sandwich?"

He stood there for a moment, deciding whether to argue about it and say that he could make his own dinner, then shrugged and smiled. "Sounds wonderful. Thanks."

Erin thought about Ma and Pa Jackson as she prepared Terry's sandwich and got a cold beer out of the fridge for him. How many times had this domestic scene been repeated in their house, day after day over thirty years? And then one day, Ma just decided to poison him? Decided that she could no longer deal with his abuse or what he was doing in the clan and decided it was time to end it? Had she meant to kill him? Just to make him sick? Or had it not been her at all?

"Those look like some serious ruminations," Terry observed.

Erin forced a smile and placed his plate on the table. She sat down across from him to visit while he ate. K9, who had followed Terry into the kitchen, lay down beside him with a sigh.

"I hear you, buddy," Terry told him. He used the toes of one bare foot to massage K9's neck.

"Would you like me to give *you* a neck massage?" Erin offered.

He looked at her, the dimple appearing in his cheek. "Preferably not with your toes."

Erin laughed. "We'll have to see."

Terry stretched his neck back and forth. "It is a bit stiff. Maybe before bed."

He took a couple of bites of the sandwich. "This is really good. Hits the spot. So… what's up? You were looking very thoughtful."

"You remember when we were talking before? About the possibility that Pa Jackson might have been poisoned?"

"Sure. Did you end up talking to Jack Ward about it?"

"Yes. But not because of our conversation."

"What, then?" Terry took a large bite from his sandwich.

"After that, we got a call from Theresa."

He blinked at her in surprise. "*The* Theresa? Crazy Theresa Franklin?"

Erin nodded. "Yeah. Maybe I should have called you to let you know last night, but there was nothing you could do about it. We were already talking to Jack about it. That's what you would have said to do."

"I might have told you to come back here too, where I could keep an eye on you." Terry reached for Erin's hand across the table and gave it a squeeze. "You know what that woman is capable of."

"Yeah. We talked about it, but we decided to stay in Moose River a bit longer. And I'm home tonight."

"Well…" Terry blew his breath out hard, as if trying to push away all of the emotions that the mention of Theresa's name had brought up and to refocus on the conversation. "What did lovely Theresa have to say?"

"She called about Vic's Pa. Heard that he was in the hospital."

Terry's eyes narrowed. "So, she's local? You know for sure that she's in Moose River?"

"We don't know for sure. Jack was going to check into it, see if they could spot her at her parents' place or anywhere else in town that she might be hanging around. Just because she heard about Vic's pa, that doesn't mean for sure that she's in town. Just that she heard something from the clan or someone else in Moose River. Anyone might have talked to her on the phone. She could be in Canada or halfway around the world."

"I doubt it, though. If she's that wired into the gossip, she's probably close. I don't like this development."

"Me neither."

Terry took a few chugs of his beer. Then he set it down carefully, rotating the can to study the logo. As if that was what he was thinking of, rather than Theresa Franklin and how she had nearly killed him. And came even closer to killing Jack Ward.

"She called Vic to console her about her father's illness?"

"Sort of. And she said that Pa's illness was similar to her parents' illnesses. Their very brief illnesses."

"You said that Jack Ward believed Theresa had killed her parents."

"Yeah. He still thinks so."

"And now… you're worried that maybe she had something to do with Jeremiah Jackson's illness."

"Of course."

"Didn't the doctor say it was the flu?"

"No. He has been looking in other directions. This morning, he said he thought it might be digitalis."

"Digitalis. An organic poison."

"Is that significant?"

"I don't know. I think that organic poisons are more likely to be used by women. But that's only my own personal opinion. And we know that was not the case when Joelle was poisoned."

"Yeah." Erin sighed and traced a circle on the table with her fingertip. "So you think it was Ma?"

Terry's brows lifted high on his forehead. "Ma? No, I was thinking of Theresa."

"Oh. Right. I was just wondering about Ma because she's the closest one to Pa. Handling his food and everything."

"Sure, but after thirty years with him, you think she's suddenly going to flip? I would think she would be resigned to his shortcomings at this point."

Erin considered telling him the story of Mrs. Goodale and the baseball bat. She refrained. "Right. Yeah. So she probably isn't a viable suspect. But she's the one who is there all day. She's the one who makes his meals. I tried to give him a cookie and he wouldn't even touch something that had come from someone else."

"I'm sure there were other opportunities for people to poison him."

"I'm not sure how. It sounds like he's at the farm all day and that Ma is the only one who prepares all of his food."

"I imagine he eats other places too. A restaurant in town. If he's out doing other jobs, then he eats with the clan or on the road. Picks something up at a gas station or diner."

Erin nodded. But that didn't make her feel any better. "How is anyone going to poison any of those other sources? No one can poison a candy bar he picks up at the gas station and eats on the run. If you were going to poison someone, wouldn't you need access to his house? To poison something in his fridge or to sit and break bread with him and add something to his drink at the table?"

"Yes. And they probably have guests for dinner often enough. With all of the clan work that he is said to be involved with, they probably have visitors pretty regularly." Terry's eyes flicked over Erin's features. "You think that his own clan wouldn't have any reason to hurt him?"

"I've already heard the theory that he knows too much and they want him out of the picture," Erin said with a shrug. "I guess I have to accept that it could be true. But if they want to hit him and he's been pretty careful about what he eats, then how does anyone—Theresa or someone else—poison him?"

"I've heard of cases where someone was poked with an umbrella or a needle to inject a small amount of poison that they never even noticed. That would have to be a pretty potent poison, though, and I don't think digitalis would do the trick unless it was really concentrated."

"Which might explain why he survived."

"Maybe. But I doubt if it was any of these super spy methods. Probably someone who walked into the farmhouse and poisoned something without getting caught."

Erin thought about the farm. "There are dogs."

"Dogs are a good deterrent. But they don't prevent people from getting into the house. Especially not if it is someone you trust and invite in."

"Like someone else from the clan."

"Yes. Like someone from the clan. All of the security measures in the world aren't going to help if you invite someone in." Terry's eyes went to the burglar alarm to confirm that the green light was glowing.

"But if he invited someone in, he would be watching them. Making sure that they didn't do anything."

"Maybe. Or maybe he excuses himself to go deal with a pressing issue. Or to the bathroom to wash up before the meal. A little distraction, sleight of hand, and the deed is done."

Erin couldn't imagine her nerves being strong enough to do something like that without getting caught. She would be sending off signals of her intention long before she got the nerve to do the deed.

"They're not like you," Terry reminded her. "Think of Theresa. You don't think she could do it?"

Of course she could. Without a split second of doubt or remorse. She'd been well-trained by the clan to do just that.

"She would have to poison Pa's meal when it was already dished up," Erin pointed out. "Otherwise, she might poison Ma too."

"Would the clan care about that?" Terry stared off into space, considering it. "From what I know of them… they probably would want to avoid any collateral deaths. So, yes, she would want to add it to something already served to Mr. Jackson or something they knew only he would be eating. Maybe he liked Nashville hot sauce and she didn't. Something like that."

"Theresa wouldn't know something like that."

"Whoever gave her orders would."

Erin was skeptical. How would some boss in the clan know what Pa Jackson's personal tastes were?

"They would make it their business to know," Terry said. "And probably he has eaten with members of the clan plenty of times in the last thirty years. You know Vic's tastes, don't you? And all of your customers' tastes?"

"Well… yes. But that's my business. And my best friend."

"And the clan is Jeremiah Jackson's business and his best friend."

Erin nodded. She got up and went to the freezer, where she surveyed the various baked goods on hand and picked out a couple of Terry's favorites—white and milk chocolate chunk cookies—for his dessert. She warmed them briefly in the microwave and put them in front of him. Neither commented on the obvious. That she knew his tastes and he knew hers.

But not because they were work colleagues. Because of their living arrangements. Like Ma and Pa.

"I assume this isn't poisoned," Terry teased, trying to lighten the mood. "As a test run to prove your theory of the crime?"

"No. It's too soon after Pa Jackson being poisoned. It would look suspicious."

Terry chuckled and picked up one of the cookies, taking a big bite.

"Or is that the one I put strychnine in?" Erin pondered. "Oh well, I guess we'll find out. How does it taste?"

"Like one of Auntie Clem's finest."

"Oh. Must be one of the other ones. That's the problem with so many poisons. They're so bitter."

"The amount of sugar in the cookie wouldn't counteract it?"

"I guess we'll find out."

Terry laughed and ate it anyway.

CHAPTER 34

*E*rin had left her phone on silent and, when she picked it up, she realized that she had missed a call. It wasn't Vic or the bakery so, hopefully, it wasn't anything important. But it was a number Erin didn't recognize. She tapped the unfamiliar number. If it was a business, they would be closed and she would get their after-hours greeting and find out. If it was a personal contact, they would probably still be up. Nearly everyone went to bed later than Erin did. One of the challenges of running a bakery.

"Cousins."

"Oh, sorry, it's Erin Price. You had called my phone?"

"You gave me your number in case we had any developments on Mr. Jackson. This is Dr. Cousins, from the hospital."

"Oh, right. Sorry, I forgot your name."

They had given him Erin's number rather than Vic's, as Vic was worried about how she might react if she were alone when she got news of her father. If Erin broke the news to her, then she was guaranteed to have a shoulder for support.

"Thank you for calling back. We don't like to leave messages like this on voicemail."

Erin's heart sank. "Oh, dear. That doesn't sound good."

"He is responding to treatment," Cousins said quickly, realizing that he had said the wrong thing and Erin had assumed the worst. "We are hopeful of a full recovery, as long as his organs have not been too badly damaged."

"Does that mean that you've found… what made him sick?"

"Yes. Can I talk to you, or should I wait until you and Miss Jackson are together?"

"Uh—Webster."

"Sorry?"

"Miss Webster, not Jackson."

"Oh, my mistake. I didn't realize they had different last names." He paused for a moment as if considering this. "Shall I wait, then, or…"

"No, you can tell me. I'll pass it on, and then if she has more questions, she can call you."

"Fine. We were able to identify the toxin as oleander."

"A flower," Erin said, trying to think about what she knew of it. A bushy plant with bright pink or yellow blossoms, if she remembered right.

"Yes. Of course, we don't know what part of the plant might have been ingested. But his blood work did show the presence of dangerous compounds found in oleander."

"You can't tell… what it was in, though, can you?"

"No. By the time he made it to the hospital, he had been vomiting for an extended time. There was nothing left in his digestive system."

"And he hadn't eaten anything while he's been at the hospital—so why did he keep getting sick? Why didn't he recover?"

"These compounds are quite toxic. They continue to cause havoc for some days after ingestion. I read about a little girl who ingested foxglove, which contains similar compounds. Her heart issues continued for a couple of weeks, even with treatment. It was some time before she was out of danger."

"Oh, the poor thing. So now that you know it was oleander, is there anything that you can do?"

"We have a treatment used in digoxin overdose that has also worked quite well in cases of oleander poisoning. We have started treatment already and are seeing an improvement in his heart rhythm. That's a big relief for us. It also gives us options for treating his wonky electrolyte levels."

"And he'll completely recover."

"I can't promise anything. It looks good. But only time will tell whether his liver, kidneys, and heart will recover or whether there has been permanent damage. He is out of danger, and—fingers crossed—he will be out of the hospital and feeling his old self very soon."

"That's excellent news. I'll pass it on to Victoria right away. Thanks for letting us know."

"You're welcome. Always happy to have good news to relate."

Erin hung up the phone. Terry was watching her, obviously having heard at least her side of the conversation.

"They've confirmed poisoning."

"Yes." Erin's voice immediately fell to a more subdued tone, realizing the implications. Pa Jackson would recover, but there was still a poisoner somewhere. In his own home or clan. "Oleander. A flowering shrub. They had a treatment for it and he's already responding. He'll be back home in no time."

"That will be a big relief to Vic."

Erin nodded. "I'm not sure I understand why, though. She didn't want to see him at first and hasn't ever said that she hopes he survives. And the way that he treats her..." Erin shook her head angrily. "It's awful. She'll be relieved, I guess, to know what's going to happen. But I don't know if she'll be glad that he'll survive."

"Well," Terry shrugged. "She feels how she feels. It might be a relief just to know what's going to happen instead of being up in the air about it. It isn't your responsibility to make her happy. Just pass the information along."

Erin nodded. "Yeah. I guess. I'll go see if she's still up."

Terry glanced at the clock on the wall. "She's usually up later than you are."

"Yeah. But she was having sleepy tea before you came. Wants to settle in and get a nice long sleep tonight."

He gave a nod. Erin slipped on a pair of sandals at the back door and gave the quick exit code for the burglar alarm before opening the door. She could see that there was still a light on in the loft and crossed the yard to go give Vic the happy news.

~

"We may as well get an early start," Vic offered, letting herself into the kitchen while Erin made tea. "We're both up."

Erin turned to look at Vic as she put her hair up into a ponytail. She looked tired. Bags below her eyes, a stretched-looking quality to her skin, and hair that showed a few snarls, when it was usually perfectly smooth and sleek.

"You are up early. Are you sure you got enough sleep?"

"No. Not even close. First time that Ambien has failed me. My brain was just so frantic after we talked last night. It wouldn't stop spinning like a hamster on a wheel. Man, if that is what it feels like for you when you are having trouble getting to sleep, I feel for you! I've been spoiled, being able to just pop a pill and get to sleep whenever I wanted to."

"Hopefully, it will just be one night, and you'll be back to normal again tomorrow night. You'll have had a chance to see and talk to him, and maybe he'll even be back home. And maybe you'll sleep in the car."

"I may just never sleep again. If I didn't know better, I'd think I took speed last night instead of valerian. I'm not even talking about a caffeine high. This is way worse than that."

Erin nodded. She knew how tightly anxiety could wind her up. Until she felt like if she had to deal with one more thing, she would snap, and everything she'd managed to accomplish would fall to pieces.

"It will be okay," she assured Vic. "It won't last forever. It can't."

"Yeah." Vic sighed. "So you say. I'm not sure."

Erin put a few slices of toast into the toaster. "Get out whatever you want for tea this morning. I'd recommend something… calming. Maybe chamomile?"

Vic agreed and rifled through the containers of tea to find the one that she wanted. Terry drifted into the kitchen, barefoot and wearing sweatpants. Vic grinned at him. "Lazy day today?"

"I'll probably sleep for a couple more hours. My circadian rhythm isn't exactly matched to a baker's schedule."

"Sloth," Vic proclaimed. "That's one of the seven deadly sins, isn't it?"

"Probably," Terry agreed. "Why don't you look it up? You seem awfully chipper this morning."

"Hyper, yes. Chipper, no. I'm not quite sure how I'm going to be able to sit still long enough for the drive to Moose River." Vic looked at Erin. "You might need to make a pit stop halfway to let me and Nilla out for a walk."

"If you need it," Erin agreed. She looked out the back window to see Nilla in the backyard. "How's he been? He didn't tear everything up as soon as you got home, did he?"

"Nah. Acted like we'd never been away. He slept better than I did."

"Good." They had both been unsure how Nilla would do with the location changes. He was unpredictable, and Vic had been working hard to train him and didn't know how his training would hold up as they took him from the place that had become familiar to him and took him to Moose River. It could precipitate all kinds of behavioral issues. "I'm glad he's been okay. He was very well-behaved while we were gone."

"Good as gold."

Terry looked out the window at the little white dog snuffling around the grass in the dim light of dawn. "He's come a long way since you got him; I'll be the first to admit that. He already gets along with K9. Maybe one of these days, we can introduce him to the other animals. Orange Blossom and Marshmallow are both bigger than him, so they should be able to hold their own."

"Maybe," Erin agreed doubtfully. When Vic had first taken Nilla in, he'd been a terror, like the Tasmanian Devil in the cartoons. If he went nuts around the other animals, thinking that they were prey...

"When you're ready," Vic assured her. "And not a minute sooner."

Erin smiled, grateful for that. "Okay. Good. We just want to be sure… I don't want Marshmallow or Nilla getting hurt."

Terry snuck a cookie from the freezer and didn't even warm it in the microwave before nibbling on it.

"I notice you didn't say you were worried about Orange Blossom getting hurt."

Erin gave him a look. "No."

Orange Blossom had, after all, once protected Erin from a burglar intent on killing her. Erin knew how loud and terrifying he could be. Nilla wouldn't stand a chance.

Vic giggled. The kettle whistled and Vic filled mugs as Erin took the toast out of the toaster.

CHAPTER 35

*A*s Erin had predicted, Vic did fall asleep on the way to Moose River. The problem was, she didn't fall asleep until about ten minutes outside the town limits. And ten minutes wasn't nearly enough sleep. She would be bound to be groggy and feel worse off than she had before falling asleep.

She decided to drive around Moose River for a while. Probably, Vic would wake up the first time she stopped the car for a stop sign but, if she kept sleeping, Erin would keep driving. They didn't have anywhere they had to be at a particular time.

Erin had learned a little of the layout of the town in her previous visits. It was small enough that she didn't have to worry about getting lost. So she was free to explore the more remote corners and crescents that she hadn't been in before. She looked for small businesses that might be fun to visit when they were looking for something to do. Vic wouldn't want to be with her father the whole day. Especially if he continued to behave the way that he had demonstrated so far. If they had a few places to explore, Vic could get her mind off of her family problems for a few minutes.

Erin had been exploring Moose River for almost an hour when Vic woke up abruptly. Long enough that she had been over the same ground twice already, even though she was looking for a street she might have missed the first time around. Long enough to remember the names of most of the businesses and cement them in her mind.

"What?" Vic snorted and sat up abruptly. "Where are we?" She peered out the window, then looked around, her brow furrowed. "Erin?"

"Just driving around a bit. Thought I'd let you sleep."

Vic rubbed her eyes, yawned, and made mutterings under her breath that it was probably better if Erin couldn't hear. Nilla was in her lap, not curled up in a ball as usual, but sprawled on his back, pink belly showing.

"What a silly dog," Erin laughed.

Vic scratched Nilla's ears and kissed the top of his head, flipping him around the other direction.

"Ugh." She let out a long breath. "How long have I been asleep?"

"About an hour."

Vic blinked, looking out the window. "We were almost to Moose River last I recall."

Erin nodded.

"And you've just been driving around town since then?"

"Yeah. How are you feeling? Any better?"

"I am, actually. I think. Got a splitting headache, but that weird hyperactive feeling is gone."

"Eventually, your body can't keep up with your brain and says it's had enough."

"Is that it? Maybe. Whatever it is, I don't like that feeling. Felt wound as tight as a two-dollar watch." Vic slapped her own cheeks lightly. "You should have just woken me up. We could have visited Pa and then gone back to the hotel to sleep."

"I wasn't taking the chance that you might not be able to get back to sleep again. You needed it."

"I know. You're right."

"Do you want to go back to the hotel to freshen up first, or to the hospital, or to the house?"

"He won't be out yet, will he? I think the hospital. Then we can crash at the hotel for a bit before we make any other decisions."

"Sounds good."

Vic yawned again. "I think I need caffeine. Think we could stop at a coffee shop?"

"Sure. I know just where there is one."

She'd driven by it at least two times already, and a couple of times on previous occasions. *Coffee and Key Chains* was clearly a hybrid business. One of those funny little rural businesses that ended up serving two disparate purposes, even though a business major would have had kittens over their business plan. Vic and Erin walked in and looked around.

"You know, I've never even been in here," Vic said with a laugh. "You would think that with how small this town is, I'd know every business intimately. But I always went to the coffee shop close to the school. That's where everyone I knew went. I almost forgot about this place."

Rows and rows of glittering key chains covered the walls of the coffee shop, providing an interesting backdrop to talk about. Erin wasn't sure whether they sold key chains or just collected them. When she got closer, she could see that some of the key chains had price tags on them. There was a key cutting machine in the corner with a spinning display of blanks to choose from. The list of prices handwritten on a sign near the register looked like it had been there for twenty years.

"What an interesting place."

Vic nodded. "Can't beat it for ambience. Let me get a couple of cups to go."

Vic went to the coffee counter and placed her order, zoning out staring at the key chains while she waited for their order to be filled. There were a few customers there ahead of them, older people mostly, and no one seemed to be in a particular hurry. A nice change of pace from Starbucks and other modern shops. Nilla's tags jingled softly as he scratched his ear, sitting beside Vic.

Erin looked down a display of name key chains, scanning for her own. Sometimes she could find it in similar displays, sometimes not. It was hit and miss.

Another patron entered as she figured out that the names ran alphabetically down one column and then up the next, snaking around instead of breaking and starting at the top of each new column. A unique method.

The young man who had entered bumped her as he walked by her toward Vic, then muttered, "Hey, watch where you're going," as if Erin had been the one to run into him rather than just standing there looking at key chains.

She looked at him in irritation as he strolled across the shop to the coffee counter where Vic was waiting. It looked like he struck up a conversation with her. Hitting on the pretty blond, probably. And Vic would be too polite to say that she didn't want to talk to a stranger and that she already had a boyfriend, thank you very much.

Erin drifted closer to them to make sure that everything was okay. If Vic needed a wingman to help to extricate herself from the situation, Erin didn't want to miss any signals.

Vic appeared to be upset, her brows drawing down. She glanced over in Erin's direction, and her expression was pale and pinched. Paler than she had been from the lack of sleep. Erin stepped forward to give her a little extra support and help send the young man on his way.

"Back off," the young man hissed at Erin as she got closer. "I'm talking to Victoria alone."

Erin was surprised. He was probably a friend of Vic's from her school days. Someone who felt possessive toward her or maybe who didn't want his friends to know that he'd been talking to her because of Vic's presentation. Erin looked at Vic to see if she wanted Erin to back off and was met again with the pale, pinched, wide-eyed expression.

Then it all fell into place, everything shifting at once as Erin realized that it was not a young man in the hoodie with the gray hood pulled down low as she had initially thought, but a young woman. A girl of about Vic's age, with mouse-brown hair and a generous mouth. Crazy Theresa Franklin.

CHAPTER 36

"*W*hat are you doing here?" Erin grabbed Vic by the arm and pulled her backward, away from Theresa. "You want to get arrested?" she demanded of Theresa.

"No, so why don't you just shut up, Erin? You're not wanted here. If you make a move toward your phone to call the cops, I'll kill you where you stand."

Erin had no doubt that Theresa would follow through on the threat. Or at least try to. She had failed to kill Erin the last time because the police had arrived too quickly. The same thing could happen again. But she could also use a different method this time. A knife to the heart or a bullet to the head. Those methods were much faster and more certain.

"Leave Vic alone. She doesn't want to talk to you. Are you the one who poisoned her father?"

"Me? Why would I poison the old man? If I took out someone that much higher up in the organization, I'd get my throat slit."

"Unless you were under orders."

Theresa nodded. "Yeah. If I had orders, I could do it." She smiled. "Do you think I had orders?"

"Rumor is that someone did," Erin agreed.

"Well, someone has been doing detective work again. How did

that work out for you last time? Don't you ever learn not to stick your nose where it isn't wanted?"

"I'm just helping out a friend. The police are the ones looking into Mr. Jackson's poisoning. They're the ones you need to be worried about. They can arrest you on sight since you already have outstanding warrants issued for your arrest."

"Warrants for what? You can't prove that I did anything."

"You attacked me and tried to choke me out," Erin said incredulously. "You stabbed Jack Ward and choked Terry Piper and hit him over the head. And you killed Bo Biggles. Who knows what else you've done, but we know that much."

Theresa rolled her eyes. "You have to prove it before a jury."

"Not for you to be arrested. There are already warrants out. Everyone knows what you did."

She shrugged. "I'm pretty good at keeping a low profile." Theresa turned to Vic. "Thought I'd take a page from your book. You like my outfit?"

Vic looked her over. "What do you mean, taking a page from my book?" she asked in a flat voice.

"You know, dressing like the opposite sex. People are looking for a woman? Fine, dress as a boy instead. Everyone is used to seeing teenage boys hunched over in hoodies everywhere they go. No one looks twice."

"I don't 'dress like the opposite sex,'" Vic corrected. "I am transfemale."

"Whatever you want to call it." Theresa gave an uncaring shrug. "We all know what equipment you were born with."

Red blotches appeared over Vic's cheeks in the middle of her pale, white skin. Her lips thinned as she pressed them together. "That equipment has nothing to do with who I am."

"If you can make up whatever reality you want, why can't I?" Theresa laughed. "You like boys now, so I'll be a boy." She leaned closer to Vic, clearly getting into her personal space, looking like she would attempt a kiss.

Erin shoved Theresa away. It was more sideways than backward, which maybe would have been easier for Theresa to recover from. As it was, Theresa's feet got tangled as she was forced to step to the side, and she hopped and flailed around, almost falling.

She clutched at her pocket, face furious. "You don't touch me, Erin Price! Who do you think you are? Just because you're Victoria's employer, that doesn't give you any right over who she is friends with and what she does."

Nilla barked and growled, baring his teeth at Theresa, straining on the leash. Vic kept the leash short, holding him right by her side.

"She isn't interested in you. She has a boyfriend. Just leave her alone. *I will call the police.*" She raised her voice for the last words so that everyone in the store could hear her.

Nilla let loose a volley of barks.

Theresa glanced around. She had said that she was invisible and no one would see her, but if Erin drew attention to her, that was different, and she didn't like it. "Shut up!"

Her hand went still in her pocket, and Erin knew that whatever she had been trying to get a hold of was now firmly in her grip. A knife or a gun? Either way, Erin wouldn't have much of a chance if she pressed things. She might be able to give Vic a little time to draw her weapon and decide whether she was willing to shoot Theresa or not, but Erin was afraid that she had too many doubts. She'd had feelings for Theresa at one time, even if she had been young and inexperienced at the time. She felt sorry for Theresa for what she had been through at the hands of Bo Biggles, an older cousin who had bullied and molested her. Vic might be too nervous to use her gun when Erin and other customers were in close quarters and a stray bullet could hurt someone.

Erin wasn't really ready to chance it. She didn't want Theresa to pull her weapon to use it. She wanted her to calm down. To retreat instead of doing something stupid. She had run before. If she thought that the police were only moments away, Erin was sure she would run again rather than let them catch up to her.

"I know you and Vic are friends," Erin said, her voice low to try to calm Theresa down. Feed her what she wanted to hear. Soothe her. De-escalate. "And you think that I'm standing in your way, but I'm not. But you're moving too fast. You need to give her a chance to think. To come to you. If you keep pushing so hard..." Erin trailed off, shaking her head. "You need to give her time. Remember that she's trying to deal with almost losing her father. There's a lot of family stuff going on right now. *You* know how that is."

Theresa was nodding slowly. She rolled her eyes when Erin said, "family stuff."

"Families are nothing but trouble. I honestly don't know why I put up with mine for as long as I did. What was the point? They were never there for me. Always trying to force me to see and do things their way. They were *weak*." Theresa looked at Vic, looking for some sign that she understood and agreed. "You can't let family drag you down and make you vulnerable and weak. Maybe yours aren't as bad as mine were, but you can't let them control your life. If you care what they think, then you've lost."

And that was Theresa Franklin in a nutshell. Get rid of any close relationships. Don't worry about what other people think. Act for herself and her own selfish desires.

"It's just a really bad time," Vic said to Theresa, finding her voice. "You must understand what it's like. I thought that my pa was going to die. Seeing how my mom is and how the farm is falling to rack and ruin, everything is all mixed up. I can't think about anything outside of that right now."

"You don't need to worry about any of that. The clan holds a mortgage on the farm. Let them take care of it. Why don't you just go away with me? Then you wouldn't have to think of any of it ever again."

"Tempting," Vic gave a wan smile. "But no. I have responsibilities. I'm sorry."

Theresa took a half-step closer to Vic. More careful not to get into Vic's personal space this time, but clearly inviting physical contact, if Vic would respond. "Come on, baby."

Nilla growled again. Vic shushed him. "I have to see to my dad. We were on our way to the hospital. Just thought I needed to top up the engine." Vic motioned to the coffee cups on the counter, ready for her to pick them up. "I really do have to get over there. Find out what is happening."

"Nothing is happening. I guess he'll get better now, and then he'll go home. And you'll have to figure out what you're doing with your life. It's not like you're going to stay here to nurse him."

"No, I won't. But I do want to make sure that they're back on their feet before I leave again."

"Do you know how he got poisoned?" Erin asked, trying to keep her voice casual. "Did you hear the details?"

Theresa turned her head slightly to look at Erin, her expression masked. "I know more about it than you ever will."

"Because you were involved?"

Theresa snorted. "If I was, do you think I would tell you? Ask anyone if they saw me around." A slow smile spread across her face. "No one ever saw me."

Erin tried to suppress a shudder, but goosebumps popped up all over her arms. Theresa relaxed her grip on whatever was in her hoodie pocket.

"I'll see you around. But you'll never see me unless I want you to."

With that, she seemed to slide across the room silently, and then she was gone.

Vic let out a long breath, her hand over her heart. "Is she gone? Oh my. Oh, my, my." She fluttered her hand to fan her face. "I can't believe she found us here. I can't believe that she just walked in here and started up a conversation, like half the police in the county weren't looking for her."

Erin pulled out her phone to call Jack Ward or the police dispatcher. Vic waved her hand, motioning for her to put it away.

"No. Just let her go. Let her run as far as she can so I don't have to worry about her anymore."

"We need to get her put in jail. She can't do anything to you if she's in prison."

"I don't want to have to testify against her. I don't want to have to stand up anywhere in any court in the world and say what I know about her. I never want to face her again."

"But if you don't…"

"No. Just let it go, Erin. I need her out of my life."

Erin slid her phone back into her pocket, feeling helpless. She should be able to do something. She knew she should call the police. They would find Theresa, arrest her, and put her away. Then Vic would be safe from her. They would all be safe from her.

Vic picked up the two cups of coffee, her hands shaking. "Okay. We're all set here."

CHAPTER 37

*E*rin found a parking space at the hospital and pulled the yellow bug in and turned it off. She sat there for a minute, muscles shaking and heart still racing. Vic was doing a pretty good job of looking casual and unaffected by the encounter with Theresa. Still, Erin knew that she must feel at least as shaky as Erin did. Not a great time to visit her father.

Vic put her coffee cup up to her lips and took a long sip, watching Erin. "That's good stuff. Have some. You'll feel better."

Erin wasn't sure that caffeine was the antidote to the combination of fear, relief, and bewilderment she was feeling. But it was all she had. She picked up her cup—unsure why Vic had gotten her a large when she never had anything that big—and had a sip.

It was unusually good coffee. She had made a good choice. It was probably better than the mainstream coffee place, and certainly better than whatever swill they were trying to sell at the hospital.

"It's good," she told Vic, who was watching her with concern.

"It is," she agreed. "Thanks."

"For what?"

"For standing up for me. I was... I don't know why it's so hard for me to just tell her to back off. I feel so... inadequate about the whole thing. I don't owe her anything. There's no reason I wouldn't be able to tell her to just leave me alone. Maybe if I wasn't giving such mixed signals..."

"You are not giving mixed signals," she told Vic firmly. "You have told her and signaled to her that you are not interested in a relationship. She is the one who won't listen. And just now... that was just so that we could get out of there in one piece. She knows that you're not interested in her. The two of you are not going to run off together somewhere."

"I just think... she doesn't understand that we're over. That relationship was finished a long time ago, and really it never even got off the ground then. She's had such dysfunctional relationships with her family, and Bo, and who knows what else she had to put up with. It's understandable."

"That doesn't mean she has any right to threaten you. Or to keep calling or showing up to talk to you when you've made it clear that you don't want to be with her."

"No, I know." Vic looked out the window and gave a shake of her head. "And I know what you're thinking. I talk so tough, and then when it gets down to it..." She touched in the neighborhood of her bra holster under her shirt. "When it gets right down to it, I didn't do anything. So much for shooting her without a second thought if I ever saw her."

"You couldn't have. Not in there. Someone else might have gotten hurt. And you'd be in jail instead of going to see your pa."

"I might prefer sitting in jail to this."

"If you want, we can go back to the hotel. Just hang out there until we hear something. If they release him, we can just pack up and go home."

Vic didn't even take the time to think it over. She just shook her head. "No. I gotta do this."

"If you're sure." Erin popped her door handle, not giving Vic any more time to think it over. "Let's go in."

Vic followed quickly, letting Nilla out first and keeping him on a short leash to ensure he couldn't get in any trouble.

"Let's do this," she agreed.

Pa was sitting up in his bed when they got there. His face was ruddier than it had been the last couple of times they had been there. He was definitely looking stronger and more like himself. Ma was sitting up in her chair, not hunched or relaxed like she had been before, but straight-backed and rigid, holding her purse in her lap, looking ready to dash out at any time. Erin wondered whether she'd had any sleep in the time that Pa had been in the hospital, other than the few times she had dozed off in her chair. She would undoubtedly be glad to get back to the farm.

"What are you doing here?" Pa growled.

"The doctor said that you were doing better." Vic stood casually, her body language relaxed, looking him over. "The treatment must be working; you're looking a lot better than you did."

"There's nothin' wrong with me. A bit of the flu. Sometimes it hits you harder."

Vic didn't argue that it had been poisoning rather than the flu. "You should be careful. The flu can kill people. Especially older folks. Retired, like you."

"I'm not retired."

"Oh? I thought you were. Not too much going on at the farm anymore. I thought that maybe you and Ma were relaxing and enjoying your golden years now."

"We're not that old. There's still plenty going on at the farm that you don't see."

Erin wondered if that meant that it was being used for clan purposes. Theresa had said that the clan had a mortgage on it. They might be using the property as a way station for the drug business, some kind of warehousing operation, almost anything. There could be outbuildings full of munitions. Or an underground bunker. Erin had learned that things weren't always what they seemed. Sometimes, there was a whole separate business going on that no one knew about. Or only the few people who were in on it. She flashed a look at Vic. Maybe they should go back to the farm and have another look around before Pa was released. They wouldn't get the opportunity again.

Ma sighed. Erin and Vic looked at her.

"Tell him that if he wants to have a retirement together, now that all of you boys are grown, then he needs to eat better. Take care of himself."

Obviously, she wasn't referring to his getting sick from being poisoned, but to the new diet she had been putting him through before he got sick. Vic looked at her father to see what he had to say about this.

"Ask her why I would want to spend my retirement chewing on leaves and getting no enjoyment in my life?" he growled in return.

Again, the old married couple who seemed to only be able to communicate by sniping at each other. This time not even speaking directly to each other, but passing messages through an intermediary, like children.

"How much longer are they planning to keep you here?" Erin asked Pa.

He glared at her. "I don't see why you're here. Don't you have a bakery to take care of?"

"I have employees. It's being looked after."

"You ought not to be here."

Vic ignored this exchange and looked at her mother. "I was going to see if you needed me to bring you anything. But I guess if Pa is being released today?"

"I think he will be. They could still keep him another day, but…" Ma looked at Pa with watery eyes.

"It's probably best to get him out of here," Erin agreed. "He'll be more comfortable at home."

"It's none of your business where I feel more comfortable," Pa snapped. "It won't be up to you."

"Of course not," Erin agreed.

He appeared a little taken aback by her agreement.

"We'll see you later then," Vic offered. "Back at the house."

She paused for a moment, as if unsure what to do next. Erin thought that in the normal course, she might have given her mother a kiss on the cheek. And might have also given her father a handshake or some other farewell. But she didn't approach either of them, letting the moment wash over all of them awkwardly.

CHAPTER 38

$\mathcal{E}$rin and Vic strolled back out to the car. There was no need to be in a hurry. Vic sipped her coffee, lost in thought. Nilla pattered at her side, looking around with interest, his little nose wiggling as he sniffed the air, drinking in the smells of the place.

Erin wished that her own nose wasn't quite so sensitive. It must be that much worse for a dog, but dogs seemed to enjoy disgusting smells rather than being sickened by them. As soon as Erin had entered the hospital, she had been able to smell the cleaning solutions, stale smells of dinner, and the heavy odor of bedpans and diapers over everything else. The hospital was clean, no worse than any other she had been in. She knew from experience that the smells from a hospital could be overwhelming.

She was glad to take a deep breath of fresh air when she left the hospital, even if it was tinged with exhaust from the traffic and cigarette smoke from the people standing outside the exits. Not as bad as in the city. That was one thing that was definitely better about living in a small town like Bald Eagle Falls or Moose River. The air was so much cleaner.

If you didn't mind the smell of manure when the wind shifted.

"Let's go back to the hotel before the farm," Erin suggested. "We can get everything packed up and check out and not be charged for another day. And then when you're ready to go home, everything is in the car and we can just head straight for the highway."

"Sounds like heaven," Vic offered. "Good idea."

She obviously didn't have any plans to stay in town once Pa was home and he and Ma had everything they needed. Once Pa was released, Vic could check that box on her mental "good daughter" checklist and could go on with her life once more.

"Wait a minute," Vic said, putting her hand on Erin's arm as she reached for the gear shift.

Erin turned to her to see what she had forgotten. They both had their purses. They hadn't forgotten Nilla, who was settled in Vic's lap. Anything Vic wanted to say to her parents could be said later, when they were all back at the farm.

Vic nodded toward the hospital. Erin looked, but didn't see anything remarkable.

"What"

"That boy. There." Vic nodded again toward a figure in a hoodie. Erin's heart sank as she looked closer, thinking it was Theresa. But it wasn't. The clothing was slightly different from what Theresa had been wearing a few minutes earlier. The figure was taller, though slim, like Theresa. An actual teen boy, Erin thought, rather than a woman pretending.

He turned his head slightly. It was Joshua Cox.

Erin swore under her breath. "What is he doing here? Mary Lou is going to kill me."

"He must have driven himself." Vic looked around for his car. "Mary Lou probably doesn't have any idea that he's gone."

But Erin had seen Mary Lou's face when they had discussed Pa's poisoning over dinner. She had seen Mary Lou's worry that Joshua was again going to investigate something dangerous. Get more cred as an investigative reporter by publishing an exciting story in the Bald Eagle Falls weekly. Attempted murder. Poisoning. Organized crime. He couldn't really write anything dangerous to the Jackson clan, since he didn't actually have any inside information. But he could make a nuisance of himself, and Erin happened to know that the clan did not like people poking around in its business.

"Should we talk to him?" Erin asked, putting her hand on the door.

Vic shook her head. "No, don't. He's not going to listen to anything that we say, and then we'd have to admit to Mary Lou that we had seen him and knew what he was up to. If we don't talk to him, nobody has to know that we ever knew he was here."

Erin wasn't sure how that was any better. If Mary Lou asked, Vic would have to either admit that they knew he was there or lie about it. Lying would be a breach of her moral compass.

But Vic was right that Joshua wouldn't end his investigation just because they told him to or told him how upset his mother would be if she found out or if he got hurt. Teenagers thought they were invulnerable. Nothing would happen to him if he were careful.

She hoped that he was right.

~

It didn't take long to pack up their room at the hotel and check out.

"What if he doesn't get out today?" Vic asked, looking around.

"Then we can check back in. Or go home. Or stay at the farm. Whatever you want. But I bet that he'll check himself out today even if the doctor doesn't think it's a good idea. He had that look in his eye."

Vic looked amused by this. "And how do you know what look my pa has in his eye?"

"I've seen enough sick people decide they don't want to be in the hospital anymore. They all get that look."

And usually, it turned out to be okay. People fared better at home in their own surroundings than they did in the hospital, where sleep was disrupted, there were dangerous infections, and they were uncomfortable. Home soothed the soul.

"Back to the farm, then?" Erin asked. "Or did you want to pick something up for lunch first?"

"I'm not ready for lunch. Are you?"

Erin shook her head. "No. I'm good."

She drove the now-familiar route to the Jackson family farm and looked around. She had only been to the house so far. She hadn't seen anything out of place or that hinted at anything criminal taking place on or around the property. But she had been confined to the house.

"Why don't you show me around?" she asked. "It's probably the only chance I'll get to see the rest."

Vic raised her brows. "I thought you were a city girl."

"I am. So, wow me with your rural roots."

Vic smiled. "Okay. But you're not really dressed for farm work."

"I'm not actually going to do any work. Just have a look around while you do the work."

She wasn't dressed up, but she supposed that her shoes were not exactly the best for walking through fresh manure and whatever else she might find out there. Vic shrugged and motioned to her.

"Let's go, then."

Nilla was already pulling excitedly on the leash toward the barn. Apparently, he had enjoyed visiting the cows or other animals the day before when Vic had not confined him to the house.

"Nilla. No. Heel," Vic ordered.

The dog pulled on the leash for an instant longer, then he stopped and waited for Vic to catch up. He fell in at her side as she stepped by him.

"Good boy, Nilla! Good job."

They walked down to the barn. Erin could hear the mooing of the cows, loud and insistent.

"They haven't been milked," Vic observed, irritated. "You'd think Joe and Daniel could do *something* around here."

Erin watched as Vic went about the farm chores, explaining a little about what she was doing. And she looked around the barn for any locked doors or stores of goods with a tarp pulled over them. There wasn't anything suspicious. After the cows were taken care of, she and Vic continued on to the chicken coop and Vic checked their feed and gathered eggs. Nilla barked once as they approached, but when Vic told him "no," he stopped and just stayed at her side, watching the birds intently. Erin knew he was just spoiling to run after them and chase them all over creation, but he remained firmly glued to Vic's side.

"He's being really good."

Vic nodded. "Last time, he went after one of them and got pecked. He's not going to do that again any time soon."

"The chicken went after him?"

Vic nodded, laughing. "They might not go after one of the big farm dogs, but Nilla's so small, I think they know they can gang up on him."

Nilla made a quiet woof, as if he couldn't quite contain himself, and then just stayed there, staring at them.

Erin looked around. "So are there sheds or storage units anywhere? Or is this it? Just the barn and the chickens."

"There are a couple of other buildings. A garage for the tractor and stuff. An old grain silo." She gave Erin a sideways look. "Why?"

"Have you been there this week? Looked to make sure that everything is in order?"

"No. I didn't check them out. What are you thinking?"

"I was just wondering… Theresa said that the clan held a mortgage on the farm. I wondered if they were using it to… store anything."

"Nah, I can't see Pa allowing that."

"If he's that far in debt with them… they could threaten him. 'Let us use your barn or we take the whole farm.'"

"I don't know, Erin. We can look. But don't expect to find anything."

"I didn't expect to find tunnels under the bakery, either."

"Well… no," Vic admitted. "That was kind of a surprise. Okay, come on, Nilla. We'll go explore the other buildings. Just to be sure."

She led Erin around the barn where the cows were now quiet and contentedly chewing, through a stand of trees, to another barn or large garage. Vic reached for the handle of the small entrance door and twisted the handle. Erin had been fully expecting Vic to find it locked. Vic opened the door and reached around the wall to turn on the inside light switch. Erin craned her neck to see over Vic's shoulder. But there was nothing to see. No bales of heroin. No hot merchandise. Nothing incongruous. Just farm equipment and machinery. Erin walked around, looked under a couple of tarps and into a couple of side rooms. But everything was on the up-and-up. Perfectly normal. She sighed.

"You don't need to look so disappointed," Vic laughed. "And we've still got the silo!"

"Yeah." Erin didn't dare hope to find anything there. It was just going to be sitting there empty, maybe just a rat's nest and a few cobwebs present to lend it some ambience.

"Come on," Vic invited with a laugh. "Let's go look."

They turned off the light and closed the door. Vic led Erin through another stand of trees to the grain silo. The trees must have been the ones Vic had mentioned before that Pa had planted since she had left home. Nilla chased a squirrel and tried a couple of times to dig holes at the bottoms of trees, but he attended when Vic corrected him and followed again at her heel.

Erin was holding her breath as Vic led the way into the silo, even though she had already decided that they were not going to find anything. Vic turned on her phone's flashlight app to shine it around the cavernous darkness of the silo and shook her head. "I don't see anything."

Erin examined the ground for any sign that something other than grain had been stored there recently, but there was nothing to indicate that it had been used at all. It seemed to have been sitting there empty for several years.

She looked at the interior walls of the silo with her own phone light and found all of the children's names written at various levels. Vic's "dead name," James, was the lowest. She turned to look at Vic, smiling.

"Yeah, those were our heights," Vic said. She walked over and looked down at her name. "Can you ever believe I was so small? I was cute, too."

"I'm sure you were!"

Vic touched her name, then shook her head. "Well, if you're done exploring…"

"I guess I am. If there's nowhere else you can think of to hide a drug-running operation or a trailer full of hot merchandise."

"If I was doing that, I'd take them out in the hills somewhere."

Vic waved her hand toward distant trees. "A property no one is using. Just back a trailer into the dense trees. No one will see it."

"I just thought they might be using this land for something. But… I don't know what else it could be. Why would they want to advance a mortgage on it?"

"Just to help Pa out, I assume. If he didn't have the stability, he couldn't do anything for them. He'd have to move somewhere else or find another job, and there isn't much in the county. If they wanted to keep him working for the clan…"

"Is it that important for him to work for them?"

Vic contemplated this as they walked back toward the farmhouse. "I think… it is. More for looks than because Pa has any special talents. He's a Jackson. Part of the patriarchal line. So he should be high up in the organization. If they don't have Jacksons in the top positions, it's hard to convince people that it's still the clan. With Pa Jackson there, everyone knows, this is still the same clan."

Erin considered this, nodding slowly. "And what if he died? Then they wouldn't have him anymore."

"Then they'd go to the next in line, I guess. Luckily, I'm not a Jackson anymore."

"So, Daniel or Joseph?"

A nod from Vic.

"I don't even know which is older. Which of them would it be?"

"Daniel is older. But the two of them are always a unit, so I guess they'd both advance. Be hailed as the leading lights of the Jeremiah Jackson family." Vic wrinkled her nose. "I just can't see those two actually being in charge of anything. I guess they would just be soldiers until they've actually earned any responsibility. But in name… they would be representing the family."

CHAPTER 39

As they got closer to the house, the dogs started barking and Vic yelled at them. Erin saw a truck parked behind the yellow bug on the gravel pad. It did not look like one of the beaten-up farm vehicles that Daniel and Joseph drove. It was big and black and in better condition than the farm trucks. Erin's stomach tightened. A visit from the clan? Ma and Pa back from the hospital already? She didn't feel ready to deal with any of them yet.

But as they grew closer, Vic suddenly picked up her pace, striding quickly toward it. A man opened the truck door and stepped out. It was a split-second before Erin recognized the figure. A man with his skin stained dark from his mining and mineral refining processes.

"Willie!"

Vic hurried up to him and threw her arms around him in a tight embrace. Willie grasped her body and swung her in a circle, lifting her from the ground. Nilla started to bark and growl excitedly, not sure what to think of this behavior.

"Shaddup, Nilla," Willie told him sharply.

Nilla backed away, his barks quieting, but still growling a little to tell the man that he didn't like it.

"Nilla, it's okay. You know Willie," Vic told him. "Though…" she put her hand alongside Willie's face. "It has been an awfully long time."

"A couple of days," Willie admitted. "How are you doing?"

Erin knew that they had spoken on the phone, but that wasn't quite the same as a face-to-face visit or sleeping under the same roof. She missed Terry too, even though she had slept with him the night before. There was so much going on, so much emotional stuff, that she wanted him there, looking after things.

"I'm fine," Vic said. "Pa should be getting out today. Then... everything will be back to normal. We've checked out of the hotel, so we're ready to go home once I'm sure that everything is settled."

"And they're sure that it was poisoning?"

Vic looked at Erin. She stepped closer.

"The doctor said that they detected substances in the blood that come from oleander. It's a flowering bush. And I guess it acts like digitalis on the heart, and they use the same treatment as for foxglove poisoning."

"So this wasn't something that he just got accidentally." Willie looked at Vic, assessing what she thought of this.

Willie had been the one to recognize when Erin had been poisoned and rushed her to the hospital. She owed him her life. If he hadn't been so quick to react, she would not have made it in time.

"Mom has been feeding him more salads, but oleander isn't something that you pick thinking that it is lettuce or spinach," Vic said, giving a grimace. "If it was in his food... I don't see how it could have gotten there accidentally."

"If it had been mixed in with a salad, do you think he would have eaten it? Wouldn't he have recognized it as something foreign?"

"I don't know. Maybe? I probably would, but if he's just forcing down this salad because that's what Ma gave him to eat, and he's not really tasting it, just trying to get it down... He wouldn't necessarily notice that a couple of leaves looked and tasted different. He'd just think it was supposed to be that way."

Willie nodded.

Vic sighed. "Theresa said that it was a hit. That there was a Jackson clan contract out on him."

"I've heard similar."

"When we saw her today—" Erin started.

Vic lifted a hand to stop her but, of course, it was too late. She'd already said it. Erin's face burned. Vic rolled her eyes and shook her head, knowing that now she was going to have to explain. She probably hadn't even been planning to tell Willie after everything was over.

Willie's eyes went to Vic. "When you saw her today?" he repeated.

"We... ran into her at the coffee shop. That is... Erin and I were at the coffee shop and she came in. I don't think she was actually there to get coffee."

He looked from one of them to the other, eyes quick to catch any facial expressions or indications of injuries. Crazy Theresa Franklin, soldier for the Jackson clan. Vic's former girlfriend, with warrants out for her arrest for assaults, confessed murderer of Bo Biggles.

"How did that go?" he asked in a flat, neutral tone.

"Well... there was no bloodshed," Vic said lightly. "You'll be happy to know that no weapons were discharged or even drawn. Just a civilized conversation."

Erin rolled her eyes. Willie probably understood that it had definitely not been a civilized conversation.

"Why is she here? Is she back at her family's place?"

"I don't know." Vic looked at Erin.

"Jack Ward was going to look around for her," Erin contributed. "He said he would check her place. Put surveillance on it for a while and see if she showed up. But Theresa said... that we would never see her unless she wanted us to."

"The two of you aren't exactly trained in counter-surveillance," Willie said with the hint of a smile. "She's probably right about that. But that doesn't mean that no one will see her. The police are better trained. Others in the clan might know where she is."

Erin was expecting Willie to reach for his phone to call the police or to ask whether they had made the call or not. But Willie didn't. Maybe he just assumed that they had. Erin had just said that Jack Ward would be looking for her. Willie didn't need to know that it was her first contact that they had reported, not the second.

Willie's eyes were on the road, checking for any approaching vehicles.

"You should probably go," Vic said. "They wouldn't like it if anyone saw you here."

He kissed her. "I'd stay here with you if I could. Try to make things easier."

"But you being here would not be easier," Vic admitted. "It would just cause trouble. I'm sorry you can't stay, but…"

"I know."

He kissed her again, longer this time. Erin watched Nilla, investigating every rock and blade of grass, while she waited for them to finish their goodbye. Nilla looked up suddenly, and Erin saw a puff of dust at the farthest part of the road she could see before it curved around and disappeared in the trees, where it later met the highway.

"Someone is coming."

Vic and Willie separated, and Vic looked down the road, eyes sharp. They all stood watching for a minute. Erin's stomach was tight and she felt a little sick. All of the anxiety was doing a number on her digestive system.

A beaten-up station wagon resolved out of the cloud of dust, and Erin let out her breath in a puff. She knew that vehicle.

"Beaver?" Vic asked, her brows coming down and pinching together.

"That's her car," Erin agreed.

"It must be Jeremy. Maybe his car is in the shop."

Jeremy's clunker was even more beaten-up than Beaver's. Erin had a strong suspicion that he'd paid a hundred or two for it at the auto wrecker's yard. But it ran. Usually. Erin was glad she now had a more reliable vehicle and didn't need to worry about breaking down on the highway.

The farm dogs started up again. Vic waved her arm at them. "Shaddup!"

When the station wagon pulled onto the gravel pad behind Willie's truck, they could see that both Beaver and Jeremy were in the car, with Beaver in the driver's seat. She rolled down the window as the dust settled, her well-muscled, tanned arm resting casually on the windowsill.

"The gang's all here," she commented, chewing her gum.

"Well, not everyone," Vic said. "Ma and Pa and the boys aren't here yet, but I expect to see them before too long. I'm surprised to see you here."

Beaver shrugged. "Thought I'd tag along with Jeremy."

"It might not be the best time to introduce a new girlfriend," Vic cautioned. She got a little pink and turned to look at Willie self-consciously. "Willie just stopped in to say hi. He's leaving again before the others get here."

Willie smiled. "Well, if Beaver is staying, maybe I will too."

"Please *don't*," Vic requested, putting her hand to her head, rubbing the space between her eyebrows. "It's just going to cause more trouble. They're already riled up enough by me staying and poking my nose into things. You being here just emphasizes my gender and they're going to start in about how you're corrupting me. You know how they were last time. And being a former member of the Dyson clan... that's all I need right now. Please go before anyone else gets here."

Willie gave her one final peck on the lips and climbed up into the cab of his truck. "Unless you want to play 'monster truck rally,' you might want to back up and give me some space to get out," he called to Beaver.

She cracked her gum, grinning. She looked at Jeremy. "You want to play?"

"I'd like to get back to Bald Eagle Falls in one piece!"

Beaver chuckled. "Spoilsport." She shifted the car into reverse and pulled out from behind Willie and to the side of the gravel road. Willie's engine roared into life. He backed past Beaver's car, made a quick and efficient three-point turn and headed back toward the highway.

Vic shook her head, watching him go. "There goes the sweetest and most aggravating man I've ever dated."

Beaver left the car pulled to the side so that others could get in and out and stepped out. Jeremy got out and walked around the car to her.

"Mind if I take a look around?" Beaver asked.

Jeremy looked uncomfortable. "Uh… I'm pretty sure Pa wouldn't want me letting a federal agent wander around the property. And I don't own the property or live here, so I probably can't give you permission anyway."

Beaver shrugged. "A technicality. I could work with it."

Jeremy shook his head, his blond wavy locks dancing, looking much more serious than usual. "No. Let's just stick around here. Together."

Beaver studied Jeremy, but didn't argue. So that was why she had come with Jeremy? To use her connection with the family to investigate when she didn't have enough evidence of something suspicious to get a warrant? And it was probably nothing to do with her current cases or mandate.

Though maybe it was. Beaver had been the first to hear about Pa's illness and hospitalization. So perhaps she was already involved with an investigation into the clan on some level.

They all stood looking at each other for a minute, then Vic motioned to the house. "Let's go in. May as well get comfortable."

CHAPTER 40

*N*ot that it was really possible for them to all get comfortable. Beaver was the only one who looked even remotely comfortable waiting for the rest of the Jacksons to show up. Even though he was usually very laid back and must have approved Beaver's idea to come along with him, Jeremy was possibly regretting that he had. He kept looking at her and then looking around the room as if to check that there was nothing illicit that she might fasten onto and request a warrant for.

Vic and Erin both knew that there would be fireworks when Ma and Pa got home and found Vic there. And Beaver. They might not guess that she was a federal agent, but having a stranger in their house would probably be an issue. Erin didn't know if they already knew about the woman their son was dating or not. He had never talked about Ma and Pa in front of Erin.

There were some half-hearted attempts at conversation, observations about the weather or rehashing what they already knew about Pa being poisoned, and people playing on their phones or checking to see if they could get enough of a signal to check their email.

Eventually, they all heard the dogs outside start barking. Vic got up to look out the window. "It's them."

Erin tried to calm the pounding of her heart and sloshing of her stomach. They weren't, after all, going to do anything to hurt Erin. Pa might insult her, but he wouldn't hurt her physically like he might Vic. If Vic wanted to be there, she was the one who needed to think about those consequences and how to best protect herself. At most, Erin was going to have to listen to arguing and yelling. She'd dealt with that plenty of times before in plenty of different families. Families were dysfunctional. In her experience, more of them were dysfunctional than not. Maybe poor relationships were actually the norm, and looking for anything else was just chasing rainbows.

There were a few bellows of "Shaddup!" from outside, and the dogs quieted. From where Erin was seated, she could look into a small mirror on the wall and see the image of the window reflected. Ma was driving the old pickup. Pa was in the passenger seat. The two oldest boys were in the bed of the truck and jumped out nimbly as the truck rolled to a stop. There were booted footsteps and loud laughter from the kitchen. Daniel and Joseph strode into the living room first and looked around.

"The whole family together," Joseph observed, giving a low whistle. "Well, it's been a couple of years now, ain't it?"

Daniel's eyes skipped from one person to another, spending more time on Erin and Beaver than his siblings. He stopped with his eyes on Beaver, examining her. He turned to Joseph and raised an eyebrow.

"And who are you?" Joseph demanded of Beaver.

Pa Jackson moved slowly into the room, with Ma bringing up the rear, looking around at everyone worriedly.

"Uh, everyone," Jeremy said, his grin tighter and more strained than usual, his natural playfulness gone, "This is Rohilda Beaven. She and I are… seeing each other."

Beaver stood up and reached her hand out to Daniel, the closest one to her. "Beaver. People call me Beaver."

"Beaver?" Daniel repeated. He took her hand and gave it an uncertain shake. "What kind of name is that for a lady?"

Erin saw Beaver's fingers tighten over Daniel's, and he winced.

"No one said I was a lady," Beaver told him, smiling and chewing her gum.

Daniel's eyes went over her clothing. Olive green tank top. Cargo pants with lots of pockets. A bulky coat that Erin knew contained several different weapons carefully tucked out of sight.

"What are you, army?"

Beaver shrugged. "Just a bum. Pick up jobs here and there when I need them. Part-time treasure hunter."

Erin nodded. That part, she knew, was true. Beaver actually did go hunting lost treasures. Sunken ships, lost gold, caves in remote areas. She'd never filled Erin in on her exploits in any great detail but, every now and then, she would mention a treasure she had hunted for, or even one she had found. Mostly, she did not succeed, but that was the nature of finding hidden treasures. No one expected to succeed every time, or even half the time. She did her research, gave it her best shot, and returned home from another trip to a faraway country, happy with her adventure.

At least, to hear her tell it. Who knew how much of what she said was true and how much of it was fiction, like what she had just told them about not having a steady job?

"Treasures," Joseph repeated. "Ever find one?"

"A couple. Every now and then." Beaver flashed a look in Erin's direction, remembering the treasure that Erin had found. Erin could understand how treasure hunting could become addictive. One big find every now and then just whetted the appetite for more, even if she didn't need it.

"No such thing as treasure," Pa snapped, walking slowly with the assistance of his cane, aiming for his chair, the one that Beaver had been occupying. "A man gets ahead with hard work. Not trying to find the easy way out. You get out of life what you put into it."

It was sad to think that he believed this to be true. If the farm was so deeply mortgaged that he was in danger of losing it, then what did that say for all of the hard work that he'd done in his life? That he hadn't tried hard enough? That he was a failure? Hard work was no guarantee of success; Erin knew that. She'd learned that lesson many times.

No one else offered to shake Beaver's hand. She sat on the arm of the chair that Jeremy was in.

"Is everyone staying for dinner, then?" Ma questioned, clasping her hands together in front of her and looking around at all of them.

Vic looked around at the family. "I can help you out, Ma. I just want to make sure you guys are settled and have everything you need." She glanced at Daniel and Joseph and didn't say that she didn't trust them to take care of themselves, let alone anyone else.

"I've been making dinner all of these years by myself. I don't need any extra bodies in the kitchen."

"Let me do something. I'm not going to sit around while you work. You've been taking care of Pa at the hospital this whole time."

Ma suddenly seemed to become aware of her dress, worn and slept in for several days at the hospital at Pa's bedside.

"I need to change into something fresh. And freshen up."

"I'll get started in the kitchen," Vic told her firmly. "Take some time to clean up and you can take over."

"I'll help," Erin offered quickly. She wanted to be out of the way of any crossfire and in the kitchen, where she was most comfortable.

Ma stopped and looked at her sternly, shaking her head. Vic held up a hand to stop Erin. "You're a guest. You stay and visit."

"You're a guest too," Erin pointed out.

"I'm not a guest. I'm family. You just visit. You know Jeremy and Beaver."

She didn't say that they would protect Erin, but Vic's meaning was clear. Erin hesitated. She really preferred to be in the kitchen. She hadn't planned on being left in the lion's den while Vic took off and did something else.

"Here." Vic reached out to hand Erin Nilla's leash. "Keep an eye on this little terror for me. He can't be in the kitchen."

Erin was grateful for something to do, even if it was just symbolic. Nilla was behaving himself perfectly well at the moment and would have been fine in the kitchen.

Ma and Vic went in different directions.

"What's that beast doing in the house?" Pa demanded, really noticing Nilla for the first time. He was out of the way, tucked under the chair that Vic had been sitting in. Being quiet and watching everything going on around him. "There are no animals allowed in the house. We don't believe in pets. Animals belong outside or in the outbuildings. Not inside the house."

"Nilla's fine," Vic sang out as she walked into the kitchen. "He's only here for a little bit, and then I'll take him home. He's not staying."

Which meant that Vic wasn't staying either, but no one seemed surprised by that.

"We don't have animals in the house," Pa repeated sulkily.

No one paid him any attention.

The two older boys turned their attention to Beaver and Jeremy.

"How old is she?" Daniel demanded as if Beaver weren't sitting right there listening. "She's gotta have ten years on you."

"What difference does that make?" Jeremy countered. "Who cares how old anyone is, as long as we get along?"

"Maybe I don't like some *cougar* attaching herself to my little brother," Daniel sneered. He looked at Joseph, giving him the eye.

"She can't even support herself?" Joseph contributed. "Living the life, being supported by Jeremy's hard work? I thought women were so big on equality these days. Making their own living and not relying on someone else to bring in the bacon?"

Erin happened to know that it had been Beaver who had put down the initial deposit for Jeremy's apartment and who contributed the lion's share to their shared expenses. But Beaver gave no sign that she intended to fight the allegations. She'd said she was a bum and would stick to that story.

"We happen to like our arrangement," she told them, and popped her gum. "And I like a younger man. You boys..." Beaver looked them over and shrugged. "You're a bit too old. You've settled. Someone Jeremy's age, he has more..." She looked Daniel up and down. "More *energy*."

Jeremy was flushing, but he didn't protest. He just laughed, tossing his long blond hair. "And I like a more experienced woman," he contributed. He tried for a salacious look at Beaver, but laughed too much to pull it off. She patted his cheek.

"She might be a little *too* experienced," Joseph warned.

"Trust me, you can't be too experienced," Beaver returned.

Erin admired her for being able to hold her own. She'd always hated being teased and mocked, and had never been able to come up with good responses in the face of it.

Pa grunted. "You know who's too old?" he demanded, not bothering to join in on the innuendo-laced observations of Beaver and Jeremy. All eyes turned toward him, and Erin had a sinking feeling she knew where he was going to go. "That William Andrews." He looked toward the kitchen where Vic was working. "Seduced James. Led him away down sinful paths. He's nearly as old as I am! Twice James's age. It's people like that who corrupt our children, leading them down to the devil's own ground."

"Victoria," Erin corrected, trying to keep her voice steady. "Not James. And he didn't lead her into anything. She has the right to choose who she is interested in. Who she has a relationship with. It's none of your business."

She was glad that Willie had heeded Vic's plea and had left before the Jacksons returned home.

"And you," Pa turned his anger on her now. "An atheist. Leading him away from God. Telling him that it doesn't matter what he does. You're just as bad, if not worse, with your godless ways."

"I've never discouraged Vic from believing in her god. It's got nothing to do with me. We don't discuss religion at all."

"If you were a decent, God-fearing person, you would set her back on the right path. Tell her how to make things right between her and God. And her family."

"If you were a decent, God-fearing person," Erin snapped back, "you wouldn't be involving yourself with organized crime and encouraging your children to follow in your footsteps."

Pa's face flushed a deep red, and Erin thought that was it. She'd killed him. She'd caused another heart attack, and this was the one that would kill him. Daniel's and Joseph's mouths were hanging open.

"You know nothing of our lives or our family," Pa spat out. "How can you sit there in judgment on us when you know nothing about us?"

"How is that different from what you're doing to me? If you really believe in your Christian god, then why don't you do the things he taught?"

"Let's just cool down," Jeremy suggested, raising his hands to stop them and playing the peacemaker. "I don't want this to turn into a free-for-all. Erin would win for sure," he joked.

"I didn't invite you into my home," Pa told Erin. "And you are not welcome here. Ever."

"Great. I'll be out of here as soon as Vic is ready to go."

"Pa," Jeremy protested. "Whatever happened to hospitality? You think Ma would want you treating company like this?"

"I didn't invite her here—"

"You didn't invite any of us here. We're here because we were concerned about you. And Erin is here because she wants to make sure that Vic is okay. That you don't treat her like you did last time they came here for help."

"I'll do whatever I decide is necessary to keep James in line. He's my child. I don't stop being his parent because he turns eighteen. I'm still responsible for telling him when he screws up and doing whatever I can to get him back on the path of righteousness."

"You never did figure out there's more to raising kids than beating them."

There was only silence in response to Jeremy's comment, as everyone gaped at him.

CHAPTER 41

*E*rin heard Ma Jackson walking from the bathroom to the kitchen, where Vic was working. She didn't think that either of them had any idea of the conversation that was going on in the living room.

Or maybe they did. Maybe they both knew exactly what would happen after they left the room.

"Spare the rod and you spoil the child," Pa Jackson told Jeremy and the room in general. "It takes more than talking to raise children up to the Lord."

"Well, you never spared the rod," Jeremy acknowledged. "No worries there."

Eventually, the tense little group was told that dinner was ready. They all moved into the kitchen, where leaves had been added to the little kitchen table and chairs scavenged from every room to seat them all.

The last thing that Erin felt like doing was sitting down to eat. But she couldn't think of a polite way to tell Vic that and get her to separate from her family and go back home to Bald Eagle Falls, where she was loved and respected.

There were still plenty of people in Bald Eagle Falls who disapproved of Vic's gender identity and made no bones about the fact. But there were also people who loved her and would never do anything to hurt her, and that was who Erin wanted to surround Vic. Not the people gathered around the table who thought that she was some kind of abomination.

Ma sat down with a sigh, eager to take the load off of her feet. "Thank you for your help," she told Vic, looking at her but not addressing her by name. "And for everything that you gir—that the two of you did while Pa was in the hospital. I can tell that someone was here looking after things. It's nice to come home to a clean house and kitchen and not to have to worry about everything that has been neglected."

"Of course, Mom," Vic acknowledged. "That's why we came."

Pa grunted and maneuvered himself into his chair at the head of the table. "Still dunno why you would come when you weren't invited. When you were told to stay away."

But he didn't make any move to get his shotgun, which he had threatened on the previous visit. And he didn't tell them that he wouldn't sit and break bread with them.

Erin sat down beside Vic, as far away from the others at the table as possible, and directed Nilla under her chair. Nilla whined at not being given any of the delicious foods he could smell, but was eventually induced to do what he was told and lie down quietly.

There was a big green salad, as well as meat and potatoes and various other Southern staples. Erin took a small bit of salad and potatoes and tried to spread them on her plate to look like more than it was.

Joseph, sitting across the table from her, examined her plate. "Don't tell me you're one of those vegan freaks," he demanded. "We eat *meat* here."

Erin shook her head. "Just not very hungry. I had a big breakfast."

A lie, of course, but a polite one. Meant to keep the peace. She watched the dishes go around the table. Pa passed most of them on. He took some of the salad, but not a large amount, and examined the dressings that Ma had put on the table. So maybe the dietary changes were his idea, or he at least agreed with them.

But after a lengthy blessing of the food, during which Erin was afraid everything would go cold, she noted that Pa wasn't actually eating. Like Erin, he pushed the food around his plate and watched to see what everyone else was eating. His eyes were sharp and calculating. Not exhausted after his hospital stay. Not dulled by whatever medications they had given him. Carefully considering all of the bits of data that he gathered.

Was he waiting to see which of them might get sick? Who might try to add something to the food while no one was looking? Or was he just "off his feed" due to his illness or his meds?

Toward the end of the meal, Pa got up from the table without comment and moved slowly across the kitchen with the help of his cane. He put a few cubes of ice from the fridge ice maker into a tumbler, then pulled down a bottle of whiskey from the cupboard.

He didn't offer it to anyone else.

Erin's stomach clenched as he poured himself a drink and put the bottle back away. He picked up the glass.

"Wait!" Erin warned, jumping to her feet and making everyone else startle.

Pa looked at her, his eyes wide, surprised by her behavior. "What?"

"Don't drink that!"

Around the table, everyone exchanged looks.

"Has anybody else had a drink from that bottle?"

Pa shook his head. "Of course not. That is my anniversary bottle. Jack Daniels Bicentennial. It's eight hundred bucks a bottle. No one else touches it."

Erin looked around the table at everyone else. Had Daniel or Joseph snuck a swig while he'd been in the hospital? If anyone else had sampled it that he wasn't aware of, then she might be wrong.

But no one looked guilty or amused by his assertions. They had all been raised to fear him physically and, perhaps even on his supposed deathbed, they had been unwilling to take the chance of a beating.

"If you're the only one who has drunk from it, then that could be what was poisoned."

Pa considered this, looking down at his glass. "You think so?"

"She's right, Pa," Vic chimed in. "If there's anything that you have eaten or drunk that no one else has... that could be what the oleander was in."

The family was awkwardly silent, not sure how to discuss the fact that Pa had been poisoned.

"Haven't the police tested everything for poison?" Beaver asked, frowning.

Ma shook her head. "They wanted to come and test everything, but I told them that we had already thrown out everything that we had eaten that night. That there wasn't anything left for them to test."

Why had she done that? There had been plenty of leftovers in the fridge when Erin had cleaned it out. Surely some of it had been from the meal at which Pa had been poisoned.

But Pa had made it clear before that even talking to the police was prohibited. Jeremy hadn't allowed Beaver to look around, even given how close they were. Pa still maintained a great deal of control over his family.

"It's an eight-hundred-dollar bottle," Pa protested, looking at it. From what Erin could tell, it was nearly full.

"You could have a sample tested," Vic suggested. "If there's no oleander in it, then you're okay. But if it does..." She shrugged.

If it contained oleander, then Pa would have to dump it out.

"Where did you get it?" Jeremy asked. Something that Erin had been wondering but, as an outsider, had not been comfortable asking.

"An anniversary present from the clan."

"Anniversary?" Jeremy repeated. "Your anniversary is in July."

"Not my wedding anniversary," Pa snapped, as if Jeremy were stupid. "A *clan* anniversary."

A *clanniversary*. Erin tried to suppress an inappropriate smile when the portmanteau came into her head.

Who knew that the clan would be so sentimental? She wondered how long Pa had been involved with them and exactly what anniversary the bottle was in celebration of. But then, she probably didn't actually want to know.

"So the clan might have poisoned you," Vic said, sounding relieved. She was probably still worried about the possibility that the poisoner could be her mother.

"The bottle was sealed. No one in the clan could have poisoned it."

"There might be a way to tamper with it and re-seal it."

Pa shook his head at Vic. "It wasn't tampered with," he told her flatly.

If it hadn't been tampered with before he had received it and it had oleander in it, then someone had come into his home and done it. An outsider? His wife? A guest he'd welcomed into his home?

Pa's eyes went around the table, dark and suspicious. Eventually, he fished the ice cubes out of his glass with his fingers and tossed them into the sink. For an instant, he was going to lick off his fingers, then realized what he was doing and rinsed them under the tap. He banged around the cupboards to find an empty jar, which he poured his drink into. He screwed the lid on tight. He looked around at them again.

"Nobody here poisoned you," Daniel said finally. "Why would any of us do that?"

Pa's expression didn't soften. If anything, it became more frozen and mask-like. He returned to the table and sat down. He poured a glass of water from the jug that everyone else had been drinking from, but didn't eat anything.

CHAPTER 42

hey retired to the living room again after the meal, everyone feeling full and satisfied after the hearty meal. Except, of course, Erin who hadn't been able to eat anything, and Pa, who was too careful to allow anyone to poison him again. If he didn't start eating again at some point in the near future, no one would need to poison him, because he would waste away to nothing. Erin had seen starvation and malnutrition before. It was not an easy way to go. They needed to find out who had tried to kill Pa so that he could start eating again.

Nilla was whining and nosing at Vic.

"He needs a walk," Vic announced. "I'll be back in a bit."

"I'll come along," Erin offered, not about to be left alone with the family again. Beaver murmured something to Jeremy, and they got up as well.

"You leaving?" Pa demanded.

"No. Not yet. Just getting some fresh air." Jeremy patted his stomach. "Work some of this meal off. Ma, you're as good a cook as ever."

Ma smiled wanly. "It's too bad none of you ever took to cooking, other than…" Ma looked at Vic and shrugged. "I hope that *she* can cook." Ma nodded at Beaver, too awkward to call her by her nickname, but unsure what else to call her.

Beaver smiled and chewed her gum. Erin had seen her pop several sticks into her mouth after dinner was finished. That woman had a real addiction. "Cook? Not a lick," Beaver told Ma frankly.

Jeremy laughed.

Vic let Nilla lead them out of the house. Erin breathed a sigh of relief to finally be out of the stifling atmosphere.

"Whew. I think I needed a walk worse than Nilla does."

Vic grinned at her. She was still tense. Doing her best to act as if everything were normal and she was on good terms with her family but, of course, they all knew that wasn't true. It was just a facade.

"Good call on the whiskey," Beaver told Erin. "I think you're probably right on the money."

Which made Erin wonder why Beaver herself hadn't suggested it. Because she didn't want to give away that she had any law enforcement training? Because she would rather that Pa took poison and was out of the way? Sometimes the best thing for law enforcement was to let the bad guys kill each other off. Less time and money than going through investigations and trials that took years and might not lead to incarceration or only to a light sentence.

"But who do you think put it there? Do you think he's right that it wasn't tampered with and that it was someone in the home who poisoned him? Or do you think they dosed it before they gave it to him? That sounds a lot more efficient."

"It is possible to recap and seal a bottle if you have the right equipment. But that is very rare. It's much easier to put something into a bottle after it has been opened. You don't need any special training or equipment for that."

"No. But then it would mean that it is someone who was in the house."

Beaver nodded. They continued to walk, Nilla leading the way. He was heading directly for the trees. The new ones that had been planted. The grass around the bases of the trees was dying, black as if it had been burned.

Vic kicked at the grass, frowning.

"Did someone try to poison the trees?" Erin asked. "You couldn't poison a tree with oleander. You'd have to use some chemical." She sniffed, bending a little lower to the ground. "I don't smell gasoline or anything like that."

"And we all know how sensitive your smeller is," Vic acknowledged. "It's weird. Why would someone want to poison Pa's trees?"

"It might be natural. Some kind of… infestation."

"It doesn't look like bugs," Vic disagreed. "There are no marks on the grass. Or on the leaves of the trees. What are these?" She fingered the buds on the branches. "Are they nut trees?"

Jeremy nodded. "Hazelnuts."

"So Pa thinks he's going to save the farm by selling hazelnuts? And what, the clan doesn't want him to make money, so they tried to kill the trees and then kill him? None of this makes any sense."

Nilla was sniffing eagerly around the trees, his nose pressed into the dying grass.

"Nilla," Vic protested, trying to pull him back. "What if there are chemicals in the grass? Something that could hurt him?"

"I don't think there are," Jeremy contributed.

"What? How would you know? It looks like something must have been sprayed on them."

"Not sprayed on the trees," Erin pointed out. "Just on the grass. The trees still look healthy."

"Maybe they used the wrong chemical."

"I don't think it's a chemical," Jeremy repeated.

Vic again gave him a sideways look. He sounded fairly sure of himself, but the evidence seemed to be against him. They could all see how the grass around the trees was dying out.

Nilla scratched at the dirt, trying to dig a hole. They watched him, shaking their heads at how intent he seemed.

"Maybe there are mice," Erin suggested. "Or worms. Something that he can smell."

"Get away from there!"

They looked up to see Pa making his way painstakingly across the ground, leaning heavily on his cane.

"Get that darn dog away from there! You want him killing my trees? Don't let him dig there!"

"He's not hurting anything," Vic protested.

"If they were your trees, you could let him dig them up, but they're not. Get him away from my orchard!"

Pa's face was suffused with blood, whether because of the difficulty getting across the field with his cane or from anger, Erin wasn't sure. And she didn't want to wait to find out. And she sure wasn't going to be anywhere in range of his cane.

Vic tried to pull Nilla back and, when that was a problem, she bent down and picked him up. He kicked and squirmed, yipping and whining in protest.

"Sorry, baby," Vic told him. "You can't dig over here. We'll take you somewhere else where you can dig when we get home."

"I don't need you kids messing around out here. In fact, you don't need to be here at all. Why don't you go back to Bald Eagle Falls?"

"Ma's going to need some help with the clearing up," Vic said firmly, and they all started to make their way back toward the house. Maybe once the dishes were clean, Vic would be ready to go home. There wasn't much more she could do. She'd have to admit that she was done and leave her mother to deal with Pa again. Erin could understand her reluctance to leave her mother with the man. But she also really wanted to go home and just leave the ungrateful Jacksons to themselves.

As they headed back to the farmhouse, Erin could see that Pa Jackson was having trouble walking that distance. She had worked in a number of personal care positions, and she could see that he had overexerted himself. He probably thought that he had a lot more energy than he did. A heart attack could be a difficult obstacle to get past. And he already had whatever was wrong with his leg as well. It seemed stiff and painful, and he was not managing well with the cane.

"Do you need a hand?" she asked tentatively. "Or to take a break for a minute? You're still not fully recovered."

"I'm just fine," Pa snapped. "The day I can't get around my own farm…"

"I don't think your doctor would want you overexerting yourself. I know you're a strong man, but you've been sick and not able to eat for days."

Pa paused. He looked at her, standing a few feet away from him, and at Vic and Jeremy hurrying on ahead without realizing that they were leaving Erin and Pa behind.

"You need to mind your own business," Pa told her. "You were not asked to come here or to interfere with my business."

"I'm not trying to interfere. I just don't want you having another heart attack because you're too bullheaded to listen to your doctor."

"Who's bullheaded?"

"You are," Erin told him firmly. And stayed well back from the cane.

"You are somethin' else," Pa said, shaking his head. "I ain't the only one around here that's bullheaded."

"No, I don't think so," Erin agreed. "It definitely runs in the family."

He chuckled. "Give me your arm, then."

Erin didn't get closer or offer it. She had offered to help him, she realized, but she wasn't going to get that close to him. He could get one of his sons to help him if he really needed it.

"You're not touching me. I've seen what you can do with a cane."

Pa looked taken aback by this, looking as if he didn't have the slightest idea what she was talking about.

"Do you want me to get one of the boys, or do you just want to take a break?"

He put both hands on his cane, using it to balance himself and rest. "I'm fine. Just a break."

Erin nodded, waiting with him. Vic looked back when she reached the house and realized that Erin wasn't right with her.

"Pa? Everything okay? Erin?"

"Just be a minute," Erin told her. "Just having a talk."

She couldn't tell if Pa appreciated her saying that they were talking rather than resting. His breathing started to slow and he wasn't quite so red.

"I'm not a feeble old man," he told her.

"No. I don't think you are. The doctors didn't even think you would survive the first night. You've been able to fight this and get better against all kinds of odds. That's not feeble."

"Can't walk all the way across the field and back," he grumbled, looking the short distance that he had covered,

"You had, what, three heart attacks? And you haven't been eating. Once you start eating, you'll start to get some energy back. Open a can of beans and eat straight from the can. Then you know nobody has tampered with it."

He looked at her sideways. "Yeah, suppose that's right."

"Have a nap when you get in. Everyone is all visited out. Your wife needs a rest too and she's not going to get one until you do. She's just going to keep pushing herself. You don't want her to have a heart attack too. Women do, you know, and they're a lot more likely to die from the first one."

Pa started walking again. Erin walked with him, still keeping far enough away from him to make sure that he couldn't grab her or reach her with his cane. Just because he'd stopped growling and barking at her, that didn't mean she was going to forget what kind of a person he was.

She knew that his behavior could turn on a dime.

CHAPTER 43

o Erin's surprise, Pa did retire to his room to sleep, which reduced everyone's tension level significantly. Vic was helping Ma in the kitchen, but shooed Erin out and told her that since she was a guest, she wasn't allowed to help. She also told Daniel and Joseph to go take care of the animals. With Ma there to glower at them with her hands on her hips, they obeyed with only minor grumbling, quiet enough that Erin couldn't make out their words.

So, Erin retired to the living room with just Jeremy and Beaver, which was a much more comfortable situation. They had both been in her living room many times while they visited and she worked on her planner or genealogy or browsed through the Bald Eagle Falls weekly.

She sat down and sighed, squirming around to find a comfortable position. Nilla settled on the floor beside her quickly. Despite Erin's restlessness, the dog was snoring lightly in just a few minutes.

"You have something on your mind," Beaver said to Jeremy.

"Me? No, just relaxing. That dinner was enough to put anyone into a food coma."

But Beaver was right. Jeremy didn't look sleepy; he looked worried. Erin supposed that going home to a dying father and the rest of the Jackson family was enough to upset anyone. Though with Pa on the mend, she thought that he would be more relaxed now.

Jeremy caught Erin's look and laughed. "No need to look so serious, Erin."

"No? You were looking pretty serious yourself. And that's not like you. At least anxiety is my natural state."

He chuckled at that. "Just my digestion," he claimed, patting his stomach. "I never know when to stop."

"You must be worrying about who poisoned your pa."

Jeremy looked at her, then up at the ceiling. "That's for someone else to worry about. Pa and the police. And if he won't help the police with their investigation, then he's on his own. There's not much I can do. I'm not staying here to protect him. If he's bothered someone enough that they want to kill him, then he'd better figure out who that is and why and put a stop to it. Me? I have no idea. And I don't think I want to know. It's clan stuff, and I'm out of the clan."

Or so he had claimed a number of times, but Erin wasn't sure whether it was the truth. She suspected he still had a few ties, even if he wasn't actively working for them anymore. It would be hard to make a completely clean break from an organization like that. Particularly when they were literally his extended family.

"Looking forward to getting back to Auntie Clem's?" Beaver asked Erin. "And, of course, the illustrious and devastatingly handsome Officer Piper?"

Erin shook her head. "That might be a little melodramatic. But yes, I am looking forward to getting back into the swing of things, and my own bed and surroundings. And Terry."

"But everything has been running smoothly?"

"Yes. We've got some good employees who are more than capable of running things, as long as there are no major disasters."

"And Charley?"

"And Charley. I haven't heard any more about her from Bella or Charley herself, so I assume everything is okay."

"What happened?" Jeremy asked, raising an eyebrow at Erin.

Erin looked at Beaver, wondering if she knew any details or if she had just been making an idle inquiry as to how Auntie Clem's and Charley were doing.

"She had some…" Erin tried to figure out how to say what she wanted to tactfully. "She'd heard some things from the Dyson clan. Just… rumors. She decided that alcohol would be a good way to loosen people's tongues and, apparently, she went a little overboard."

Jeremy laughed. "Only Charley. How overboard? Was there any dancing involved? Wardrobe malfunctions?"

"I have no idea, and I don't want to know. I know she was picked up for public intoxication, but I don't know what she was doing at the time. Probably best that I don't."

Jeremy continued to snicker. Erin shook her head and dug her planner out of her purse. She could plan her next week, since she would be back in Bald Eagles Falls and everything would be back to normal again.

Ma and Vic finished cleaning up after the meal, and Vic insisted that Ma go lie down and start catching up on the sleep she'd been deprived of while at the hospital. Ma made a couple of protests, but only a couple, on the way to her room. She never even paused in the living room. Erin smiled and looked up from her planner as Vic sat down with a sigh.

"That's the same noise as I made when I sat down."

"I guess there's a lot of it going around," Vic acknowledged. "How are you? Are you too tired to drive tonight?"

"No, not at all. I'm fine."

Vic nodded.

"Does that mean you want to go back tonight?" Erin asked.

"Yeah, we may as well. Pa's home. If we stay here, it's just more work for Ma instead of less. Go home and they can go back to normal. Whatever that might mean. I'm worried about the whole poisoning thing… I mean… if they don't find out who did it—and Pa doesn't seem too inclined to let anyone look into it—then it's probably just going to happen again. I don't think I'll come back again next time."

Jeremy nodded his agreement to this. "It might sound mean, but… we've got our own lives, and he's got his… and that's always included working with the clan, doing things that put him at risk for being killed or arrested. If he's not going to get out, tell them he wants to retire, then you and me can't change that. Nothing we can do."

The sound of the kitchen door slamming open made Erin jump. She turned to look at the doorway from the kitchen as Daniel and Joseph hurried in, their work boots clomping loudly on the kitchen floor.

"What is it?" Vic demanded, jumping to her feet. "What's wrong?"

"It's that dang dog!" Daniel growled.

Vic's eyes jumped to Nilla, lying on the floor curled up in a ball, perfectly peaceful.

"There's been a mangy dog around here for a few weeks," Joseph clarified. "Gone wild. Causing all kinds of trouble with the critters. Well, he's dug his way into the chicken pen."

"Oh, no!"

"We could use some extra hands," Daniel said. "Me and Joe can catch the chickens that have escaped and get them back into the pen. They know our voices; they don't know yours. If you two can go after the dog and take care of it…" Daniel's gaze indicated Jeremy and Vic.

Jeremy got up immediately. "Yeah, of course," he agreed. He disappeared down the hall and came back with a shotgun. "Point us in the right direction."

"You can't shoot it!" Erin protested.

Daniel rolled his eyes. "City girl. Things aren't the same here as in the town. Here, if you got a critter breaking in and mauling your animals, you kill it. There's no dog catcher. No rehabilitation programs for dogs gone rogue. You track it and you kill it."

"We haven't been able to run it down yet," Joseph said. "But Jeremy and Ja—they have always been the better trackers."

The four siblings headed for the door. Beaver got to her feet in a movement that looked lazy, but was fluid and graceful, a sign of what great shape her body was actually in. "You don't mind if I tag along?"

Everyone looked at Erin, who would be left alone while they took care of rounding up the chickens and hunting the dog.

"Go," Erin made a shooing motion toward them. "I'm not going to be any good to you out there."

"You're okay on your own for a bit?" Vic asked worriedly, glancing toward her parents' bedroom, even though it was out of sight.

"I'm on my own plenty, in case any of you have forgotten," Erin said, laughing. "I've got my planner. I won't even notice you're gone."

CHAPTER 44

*E*verything was quiet as Erin sat in the living room by herself with her planner with Nilla snoozing quietly by her feet. Ma and Pa didn't make a sound in the bedroom. Considering all that they had both been through, Erin would be surprised if they didn't sleep for several hours straight, maybe even on through the night. A nice long sleep to make up for the deficit they were running.

Nilla raised his head, ears pricked forward, looking toward the door. Erin heard the soft click of the kitchen door latch. Nilla growled low in his throat.

"It's okay, boy," Erin soothed.

Nilla's gaze was fixed on the doorway between the kitchen and the living room. Straining her ears, Erin could hear footsteps on the tile. Her stomach muscles clenched.

"Hello?" She called in a welcoming voice. It was probably just neighbors or ladies from the Jacksons' church checking in on them. Small communities were like that. People made an effort to check up on those who were sick or injured, made casseroles, tried to help ease the burden of a family in difficulty. "Who's there?"

The two figures who appeared in the doorway were not church ladies.

Daniel and Joseph.

Both of them stood there looking at her. Serious and forbidding. Erin cleared her throat nervously. "Did you... get all of the chickens rounded up already?"

"Yeah," Joseph agreed. "It was pretty easy."

Erin was getting bad vibes from them. They entered the room, closing in on her.

"Don't know why you had to come here in the first place," Daniel said. "If you and Jamesy aren't an item, then why are you always joined at the hip? He could have come here on his own. He didn't need you along."

"I wanted to support Vic," Erin said firmly. She shrugged. "I don't know why that should bother you. What's wrong with me supporting a friend?"

"Because you're too nosy." Daniel stepped forward. "You don't back off when you're told. You call the cops. You... change things."

Erin took a deep breath in and let it out slowly, counting like it was one of her tai chi exercises. "I'm just being a friend. Trying to help y'all out. I know what it can be like when someone is sick. Especially a provider, someone you rely on."

"Provider," Joseph snorted. "He's no provider. Not anymore. He gives up on the farm and starts planting trees. He's off his nut."

"His hazelnut," Daniel offered, snickering. This earned him a glare from Joseph. He fell silent.

"He's running the farm into the ground," Joseph continued. "The only provider this family has right now is the clan. The old man has no idea what he's doing. Things have been going downhill for a long time, but the last few years..." Joseph shook his head. "Jeremy and James are too young to understand. They don't see it. By the time they're old enough to care about this old place, it will be too late."

"So you—" Erin choked on the words. "You decided to take matters into your own hands? To get rid of your own father because you didn't like the way he was operating the family farm?"

"You're stupid," Daniel snarled at her so harshly it made Erin jump.

She blinked at them, trying to figure it all out. What had they done? And what were they planning to do with her? They wouldn't be confessing to her and then driving her home, that was for certain.

"What do you mean?"

"The clan knows all about it. They have the big picture. They can see what's going on here. Pa's been getting more erratic at work. They said maybe he's getting Alzheimer's or some kind of dementia, you know? Going nuts. What if he talks to the wrong person? Says something because he forgets who he is and isn't supposed to talk to. All while running our inheritance into the ground."

"Always planting and pruning those stupid trees." Joseph contributed. "Do you know how many bushels of hazelnuts it takes to support a farm like this? There's no way. He could spend the rest of his life planting hazelnut trees and it wouldn't save the farm."

"Especially since he's not going to have a 'rest of his life,'" Daniel agreed. "It stops here and now. We protect the clan and we protect what's ours."

"By poisoning your father?"

"It's not like that," Joseph assured her. "You city folk put dogs down with a needle. Or murderers. They even got 'end of life choice' or 'death with dignity' laws in other states now. Tennessee is behind the times. In a few years, it will have one too. But that will be too late for Pa."

"So, what, this is just euthanasia?"

"End of life choice," Joseph repeated.

"Whose choice? Not his! He didn't decide that he wants to die."

"That's because he's losing his mind. If he understood what was happening to him, that would be his choice. His and Ma's."

"Is your mother in on this too? I don't believe you."

"No, I'm just saying that if she had a choice, that's what it would be. So we have to help out. We can give him peace."

They both stood there, looking at her. Erin shook her head. She didn't know whether to get up and try to escape the house to go find Vic. She had no idea what direction they had gone in.

But she knew there was no point. They weren't there just to complain. She was a liability. They had diverted Jeremy and Vic so that they could take care of the liability. Maybe they had intended for

Beaver to stay behind too. Then they could take care of both interfering women at the same time.

"How exactly do you plan to explain this to Vic?" Erin
demanded. "I just keeled over? Or am I going to disappear?"

"Disappear," they said together, and snickered.

"Exactly how are you going to explain that? I decided I couldn't
wait for her to get back and... what?"

"Decided to run an errand?" Daniel said with a shrug. "But...
something happened to you. One of those 'into thin air' things that
everyone talks about it. You were there," he motioned to the chair
Erin sat in, "and then... gone."

"No one will ever know," Joseph agreed. He tilted his head
slightly. "It's too bad you and James are so close. It was good for him
to have a friend. But... you should have just kept yourself to
yourself."

"I didn't do anything," Erin said in frustration. If she were going
to be harmed for interfering in something, then it could at least be
something she had been actively pursuing. She hadn't been investigating Pa's poisoning. Not really. She'd just been hanging around,
supporting Vic, asking the questions that came up naturally. The only
thing they had called the police about had been Crazy Theresa's
phone call. The actual information about Pa's illness being caused by
poison had come from the doctor, not Erin.

It would be one thing if she had been interrogating people about
who had a reason to kill Pa or who had had access to the food and
drink in his home.

She hadn't done that. Not exactly.

"Was it in the whiskey?" Not that it mattered now. Pa would have
the whiskey tested, and then he would know. And he would know
who'd had access to it. It was true that anyone could have walked into
the unlocked farmhouse while he was not there. But one of them was
usually there. And there were the dogs. Though they were sometimes
penned and could probably be managed with an offering of food and
a stern "shaddup!"

If it had been Daniel and Joseph, they would know whether it
was in the whiskey or something else. Erin assumed that it would be

in something that only Pa would eat or drink. They hadn't wanted to poison their mother as well.

"Yeah," Daniel agreed. "In the whiskey. Thought he'd drink more of it. But with this new diet stuff, I guess Ma told him to lay off the sauce."

"I think the Bicentennial was a mistake," Joseph disagreed. "At eight hundred dollars a bottle, he ain't gonna drink the whole thing in one night. You saw how much he poured. Barely covered the ice cubes."

"Should have put more juice in it. Then it wouldn't matter."

"He would have tasted it. Te—the boss said it's bitter."

"He'd just think it was the drink. How does he know how expensive whiskey tastes? I've had some of those expensive wines, and they taste awful." Daniel made a face.

"I dunno." Joseph swept the topic to the side with a sweep of his hand. "Get up. Let's go."

"Please..." Erin looked around, trying to come up with an argument, to find a weapon, something. There were vases and lamps, heavy books on a bookshelf that looked like they hadn't been touched in decades. Nothing that would help her fend off the two men. They were armed. Two men who had grown up with violence and had seen it in the clan. As far as she knew, they were only low-level gang members, but even low-level soldiers were trained to kill. "You don't need to do this. We're going back to Bald Eagle Falls right after this. We're on our way home."

"Maybe you were, maybe you weren't. But either way, you know too much. You should have stayed in your bakery."

It wasn't the first time Erin had been told that. Hopefully, it wouldn't be her last. But things were not looking too good.

As Joseph stepped forward and reached out to grab Erin by the arm, Nilla came to life, jumping forward and growling. He snapped at Joseph, trying to bite him through his pant leg, growling and holding on. Erin looked for an escape. Nilla had provided the distraction she had needed once before, and maybe if she could make it to the car...

But Nilla was no pit bull. Joseph yelped when the dog bit him, but then shook his leg, dislodging him, and tried to kick him to get him out of the way permanently. He grabbed Erin by the arm and hauled her to her feet.

"Stupid dog. Why would James get such a stupid, girly mutt? He's grown up with dogs. He knows that little fluff ball isn't going to be any use for anything."

"Nilla's owner was killed," Erin protested. "Vic rescued him. And she's been training him really well…"

She was on her feet and turned around, looking for some way out of the situation. If she had been in a movie, she would be able to instinctively turn her tai chi practice into martial arts fighting moves. Or she would be carrying a gun in an ankle holster. Or a bra holster like Vic's. Nilla would dart in and distract them, and Erin would… do something heroic.

But she didn't. She just stood there, looking at Joseph and Daniel. Their eyes were dead, their expressions flat. Doing what they had been told to do, without allowing themselves any humanity.

"What does Theresa have to do with it?" Erin asked, stalling, hoping that something would occur to her, or Ma would wake up and emerge from her room to get them all a cup of tea. Anything that would slow or stop what was going to happen.

"Theresa?" Joseph shrugged. "Nothing, really. She wasn't the one who…" he trailed off, looking at Daniel.

"It wasn't her deal," Daniel agreed. "Why would she be involved in that? But she knows things. She's… helpful to have around."

She knew things? Like how to poison her own parents? Yes, Theresa had helpful experience in that kind of thing.

"Helpful," Joseph agreed. "And…" he darted a sideways look at his brother, "entertaining."

Daniel's brow furrowed. "Entertaining?"

Joseph snickered.

Daniel looked at his brother, leering. Gloating.

Joseph's mouth dropped open. "Not you too!"

"Me too?"

"Yeah." Joseph blew out his breath in a whistle and rolled his eyes. "You gotta be kidding me. You never told me that the two of you…"

"She said not to. Just… keep it between her and me." Daniel shook his head and called Theresa a nasty name. But maybe an appropriate one if she'd been playing both brothers simultaneously.

For a moment, Erin thought that maybe this was just the distraction she needed. She could slip away while they fought about Theresa, just the way they did in the movies. But in all of the fights and other situations she had tried to slip out of in the past, it had never worked. Real life was much messier than thriller movies.

And, as it turned out, the boys weren't going to have a jealous fight over which of them Theresa liked better or who had seen her first. They shrugged it off as unimportant and turned back to the job at hand, getting Erin to wherever they were planning to take her.

Where would they take her to make her disappear, as they had suggested? There were thick woods, caves, wells, abandoned properties, all sorts of places where they might plan to dispose of her. They would have to get rid of the car too, or they wouldn't be able to sell the story that she had just gone off to do some errands while she waited for the others to get back. A bright yellow beetle was harder to hide than one small woman. But that didn't mean it couldn't be done. A nice deep lake somewhere. Clementine's bug would never be seen again.

Joseph dragged Erin through the doorway into the kitchen, making another comment to Daniel about Theresa as they walked through it.

"Y'all can let her go and put up yer hands."

CHAPTER 45

The three of them turned as one toward the source of the voice.

Beaver stood leaning against the wall, where she couldn't be seen from the living room and was behind them as they walked into the kitchen. She was chewing a big wad of gum, as usual, and, in her right hand, she held a gun trained on them.

Daniel and Joseph did not immediately raise their hands. Daniel barked out a laugh and reached for his own weapon in a concealed belt holster. Beaver pointed her gun directly at his head.

"I wouldn't do that if I was you. A shot in the head at this range will drop you on the spot. And make a big mess of your ma's kitchen. I don't imagine it will be the first time blood has been spilled in this room, though. It should wipe up pretty easily."

Daniel stopped, his hand on his weapon, eyes calculating as he tried to figure out just how much time he had before Beaver would be able to shoot him. Considering all she had to do was squeeze the trigger, he apparently decided not to chance it. He might not know that she was a federal agent, but he could probably tell she was familiar with a weapon. Beaver's clothing suggested military, which, from what Erin understood, was accurate; she had been in the Airborne forces for some unspecified length of time.

"What's going on?" Joseph demanded. "I thought you were out with the others, going after that dog." Despite the danger that they were in, Joseph's lips pulled into a grin at that suggestion.

Clearly, there had been no dog.

Beaver chewed on her gum. "Tracks looked like human, not dog. No blood in the pen that showed the chickens had been attacked. I figured I'd let the others look and make sure Miss Erin was okay."

"Then I guess I'll have to take care of both of you," Joseph blustered.

Unlike his brother, he had a split-second to try to get the drop on Beaver before her gun would be on him. Daniel might die in the process but, with Beaver's attention focused on him, Joseph might just have a chance.

And maybe he didn't care what happened to his brother. He would get a larger portion of his father's estate, if he had left anything to his children. He wouldn't have a rival for Theresa's attention, if he was really interested in her. He would be the sole heir to his father's position in the clan, rather than having to compete with Daniel for it.

"How about you put up your hands."

Erin's eyes jumped to the kitchen door. She hadn't heard anyone else drive or walk up, but Terry stood on the other side of the screen door, in full uniform, his gun out, pointed directly through the screen at Joseph. Erin didn't suppose the screen would do much to alter the path of the bullet or slow it down. Not like going through the door's metal panel.

"You'll have to help with the clean-up," Beaver warned in a casual, friendly tone. "I wasn't necessarily going to shoot both of them. I figured this one," she nodded to Joseph, "would surrender once I popped his brother."

"I'll deal with the inconvenience," Terry told her.

Erin waited. She could feel Joseph softening his hold on her arm. She wanted to warn Beaver or Terry, tell them that he was getting ready to move and they'd better be ready to follow through on their threats. But her voice was paralyzed. She could barely breathe and couldn't move her feet or her body to get her farther from the boys or drop to the floor so that Beaver and Terry both had clear shots without worrying about her getting caught in the middle.

Joseph slowly started to raise his hands in the air. Daniel made a sort of a *huh* sound, eyeing his brother and the two opponents, trying to work out a way that he could get himself out of the situation. Eventually, he copied his brother and lifted his hands in surrender.

"All the way up," Terry told them.

The two young men reluctantly raised their hands as far as possible, arms against their ears.

"Either of you twitches and you're dead," Terry warned. "And there's no one here who's going to say that you didn't ask for it."

Neither of the brothers moved.

Terry reached down and opened the screen door with a flick of his wrist. "Go in," he told K9.

K9 obeyed, snaking in through the narrow opening and heading straight for the subjects, ears pricked forward, eyes intent. He didn't even appear to glance at Erin, and his tail didn't wave like it usually did when he greeted her. This was K9 at work, focused on the dangerous job at hand. Erin watched K9 as Terry opened the screen door the rest of the way and entered, as did Daniel and Joseph. They might laugh over Nilla's attempts to attack, but it would be a different story if a trained police dog took one of them on.

Terry approached Joseph and gave him a quick pat-down, removing his gun from its holster and also turning up a utilitarian jackknife in his pocket and a second gun in an ankle holster. Terry took Joseph's hands one at a time, pressed them together behind Joseph's back, and then applied the handcuffs. He patted Joseph down more thoroughly and turned out his pockets, looking for anything else that might be dangerous or suggestive of a crime.

After Joseph was secured, Terry looked at Beaver, waiting for her to do the same with Daniel. "If you want to take care of this one too...?" Beaver suggested.

Terry frowned, but went through the same procedure with Daniel. Erin guessed that Beaver didn't want to give herself away as a law enforcement officer. The fewer people who knew that, especially people connected with Jeremy and the Jackson clan, the better. Once they were cuffed, Terry pushed both men into kitchen chairs and turned to Erin.

She could finally move and melted into his arms. "I'm sorry," she apologized. "I didn't know what to do. I wanted to help, but I couldn't move."

"You did just fine, Erin. Staying still when there are weapons drawn is just the right thing to do. No heroics. Freeze and wait. That's all I want you to do." He kissed her hair, then turned her face up toward his and kissed her lips, warm and reassuring. Erin held on to him tightly, her body starting to shake like she had hypothermia. He rubbed her back and squeezed her and murmured reassuring things.

After a few minutes of this, he clicked his shoulder mike. "All clear."

Erin didn't have any time to wonder what that was about. It took about three seconds for Vic to get in the door, traverse the kitchen and grab Erin away from Terry.

"What happened? Are you okay?" Vic looked her over, as if expecting to see stab wounds or bullet holes. "You're okay? What happened?"

But it would seem that she already knew or guessed what had happened because she went for the nearest brother, Daniel, and slapped him across the head. Not just his cheek, like in the movies, but his ear and half the side of his head. Daniel's head snapped to the side, and he let out a bellow of pain and protest. Vic moved to Joseph. Terry and Beaver were both too slow to stop her. Joseph reared back to avoid a slap, and Vic came back with a left cross to his chin that nearly made the chair tip over backward. The thud of the contact made Erin wince.

"Now, Miss Victoria," Terry intervened, "I can't have you assaulting my detainees." He stepped forward and nudged her gently back so that she was no longer within reach of either of them. Both boys were whining and protesting their injuries.

"You can't tell me he's a girl with a punch like that," Joseph insisted, working his jaw slowly to make sure it wasn't broken. "*Miss* nothing!"

"Mind your manners, or I'll let her have another go."

Joseph decided not to push his luck.

There were other people pouring into the kitchen through the screen door, and Erin, overwhelmed by everything that had happened, was having trouble making sense of who was there and why. She knew that she shouldn't distract Terry while he was on duty, but she reached for his hand, and he took hers and stepped closer to her.

"Okay, Erin?"

"I'm just…a little dizzy," Erin explained, although that wasn't the right word for her confusion and disorientation.

"Let's get you a place to sit down for a minute." Terry guided Erin over to an empty chair at the table. Daniel and Joseph were no longer sitting there where they had been. Erin saw Willie standing at the fridge, putting ice cubes into a zip-top bag while talking to someone else beside him. Jack Ward was there, giving instructions to a few of his police officers. Erin frowned at Terry.

"Could you arrest them? Are you allowed?"

"Because I'm not in Bald Eagle Falls? Yes, it's allowed. I heard what they said and saw them holding you against your will. I don't actually have to be in my own jurisdiction for that. Besides which, I was under the direction of Jack Ward, and he does have jurisdiction."

Erin nodded, only vaguely understanding his answer with the way her brain was whirling. Willie handed the bag of ice not to Joseph for his jaw, but to Vic, who put it over her knuckles, wincing and talking to Willie animatedly. Willie saw Erin watching them and nudged Vic in that direction. They both approached, and Vic sat down in one of the other chairs, looking at Erin critically.

"A bit crazy here, huh?"

"Yeah." Erin breathed in slowly, held her breath, then released it, counting the seconds. She did it again, trying to relax her muscles as she breathed. "Are you okay? Is everybody okay?"

"We're fine," Vic assured her. "We all figured out pretty quickly that there was no wild dog and came back, but Beaver was the only one Jack would allow back into the house. Jeremy and I had to stay outside."

"Where's Jeremy?" Erin looked around for him.

Vic glanced around and shook her head. "I guess he decided he didn't want to be part of this circus. Or the cops wouldn't let him in. I told Jack there was no way he was going to be able to keep me out and he'd better not even try once everything was secure."

"And…" Erin looked at Terry. "How did you get here? How did you know what was going on? I don't know how you got here when you did."

"Willie texted me."

Erin blinked at this. "Willie?" She looked in his direction. "How did he know? And how could you get here so fast?"

"I told him as soon as I knew that you two had run into Theresa Franklin face-to-face," Willie explained.

"Something you should have done," Terry pointed out.

Erin's face warmed. It seemed like so long ago, but it had only been a few hours. It seemed like another life altogether. "Sorry."

"That was my fault," Vic confessed. "I wouldn't let her call anyone. I didn't want… I just wanted Theresa to disappear, and not to have to deal with her. But I guess… that's just wishful thinking. Not reporting her to the cops isn't going to keep her away from me."

"No, it's not. But if warrants for her arrest on felony assaults and murder don't keep her away, then adding a BOLO isn't going to help much either. Jack was already looking for her. There wasn't much more he could do. But I wasn't going to stay away. I could stay with you and make sure you were safe, something that he couldn't do."

Erin rubbed her temples, nodding.

CHAPTER 46

"What is going on here?" Pa's angry voice cut across all of the conversation and activity in the kitchen. Everyone stopped talking and looked at him.

Everyone in the room either knew Pa or knew who he was. And that meant no one wanted to talk to him. They all looked at Jack Ward. He sighed and shook his head, then approached Pa.

"Mr. Jackson. I apologize for all of this. As it happened, we were able to make two arrests in regard to your poisoning and attempted murder."

Pa's eyes swept the room. Joseph and Daniel were no longer there, but he probably had a pretty good idea who it was that had spiked his whiskey. His mouth turned downward in a pronounced frown.

"You had no right to be on my property. You can't come in here without a warrant!"

"I assure you, no laws were broken in coming here and making this arrest. When someone is in imminent danger, there are laws that allow us to enter a property."

"Imminent harm. I was back from the hospital. I'm just fine; nothing was going to happen."

"Well, your safety was certainly a consideration. But so was that of Erin Price. She was being held against her will and had been threatened with violence. The two young men freely admitted that they planned to kill her and you."

"Bragging about something and doing it are two separate things," Pa said sternly. "They didn't do her any harm."

"We have enough to hold them and to try them for both their actions against you and against Miss Price. They're going to go away for a long time, Jeremiah. You may as well figure that out now."

Pa stopped arguing, scowling blackly. "I want all of you out of here. This is my private property."

"Can we get everyone out of the kitchen?" Jack raised his voice above the hum of chatter that had started up again. "Out of the house, please, unless there is a specific reason for you to be here."

They all started for the door.

"Off of my property," Pa insisted. "I don't need cops all over the place. You got no reason to be here now."

"We are investigating an attempted murder and a kidnapping with intent to murder."

"You've got everything you need here. You got no need to search anywhere else on the property. None of it has anything to do with that."

Erin thought about the empty silo and the barns. What was it Pa didn't want anyone to see? Was it just a matter of principles, or did he have something to hide?

There was probably evidence of his work with the Jackson clan in the house somewhere. Written instructions, computer files, maybe illegal weapons, drugs, or some other kind of contraband. Just because Erin hadn't found it, that didn't mean it wasn't there. Vic might have intentionally kept her away from anywhere that Pa was likely to be hiding anything illegal. She could appear to be showing Erin all of the likely places while knowing that Pa had another secret hiding place that she didn't show Erin for her own safety.

Though as it had turned out, Erin's ignorance of what was actually going on was no protection. The brothers or the clan had still decided that she was being too nosy and needed to be taken out of the picture.

"I want everyone out of here and off the property," Pa repeated, leveling a look at Erin and Vic. "Everyone."

"Let's get on our way," Terry suggested. "Are you okay? Can you walk?"

"I'm fine." Erin brushed away his attempts to help. "Really. I'm okay now."

Vic took Nilla's leash from Erin's hand, and Terry walked her outside, hovering in case she was unsteady on her feet, but Erin made it under her own power.

Once outside, she saw Jeremy and Beaver talking. Jeremy made a motion for her to come closer, though the gesture might have been aimed at Vic behind her rather than Erin herself. But he didn't wave Erin off and, when Vic joined them, he started walking across the field toward the hazelnut trees, jerking his head for them to follow him.

Erin breathed a sigh of relief as they got farther away from the hustle and bustle of the police. Their vehicles were all parked behind Erin's, so she wasn't going to be able to get out of there until the majority of them were moved.

"Pa told me a few years ago that the value of the farm is in the land," Jeremy commented as they approached the trees.

Erin and the others just nodded. Of course it was. It wasn't the buildings that made the farm property valuable. It was its potential for growing crops. As Moose River grew, the property might gain value because of its potential for building new communities, but they were too far away from town for anyone to be considering development yet.

Some properties also had oil or minerals, but Erin hadn't seen any caves or any sign of wells or excavations where they might have been mining for something near the surface.

They reached the trees. Nilla started snuffling around again, very interested in the trees and the dying grass. What did he smell that was so captivating?

"They use dogs to find them," Jeremy commented.

Erin looked down at the earth, not understanding. "To find what?" She suddenly thought of cadaver dogs and Theresa's missing parents. Or others that the clan might have disposed of if any of the stuff about organized crime portrayed on TV was correct. Her stomach muscles clenched and she shook her head, not wanting to know. "No... never mind. Forget I asked."

Jeremy raised his brows, looking puzzled. "What?"

"What do they use dogs for?" Vic asked, pressing the question.

"Truffles."

"What?" Erin asked blankly. "What did he say?"

"The mushroomy ones, right?" Beaver asked, chomping on her gum. "Not the chocolate ones."

Jeremy gave her a disbelieving look. Beaver flashed him a grin, letting him know that her ignorance was pretended. "Yes," Jeremy shook his head at her comment. "The mushroomy ones."

"You think there are truffles here?" Erin asked, looking down at Nilla, who was scratching at the ground. Vic pulled him back and Nilla protested. He *really* wanted whatever smelled so good under the ground.

Jeremy nodded. "They have a few patches of them at Crosswood Farm." Crosswood was where he acted as a guard protecting valuable crops. Up until then, Erin had only thought of that being ginseng. However, she remembered Jeremy saying that they had other crops as well.

"They have truffles?"

"Some." Jeremy looked at the row of trees. "Not this many."

"Well... what are truffles worth?" They were expensive, she knew. But how much?

"About nine hundred dollars a pound."

Erin looked down at the blackened grass. "But how do you know how much is here? How do you know there's any, if Nilla isn't a trained dog?"

"Truffles are a fungus that grows in the roots of certain kinds of trees," Jeremy explained. "One of them... hazelnuts. They don't harm the trees; they are symbiotic, not parasitic."

Erin nodded, fascinated. He'd obviously picked a lot up at Crosswood Farm, even if his job was just to guard against intruders.

"The grass around the trees is dying because the truffles leach nutrients out of the soil." Jeremy scuffed at the grass with the toe of his shoe, but didn't dig down into it to find the truffles.

"So…" Erin looked at the long line of trees with rings of dying grass beneath them. "Your dad isn't just growing hazelnuts. It looks like that's what he's doing, but he actually has another crop under the ground."

Jeremy agreed, putting his arm around Beaver's waist to pull her close. "I think someone figured it out, though."

"Daniel and Joseph thought he was going senile, planting hazelnut trees that weren't worth enough to sustain the farm."

"But someone knew."

"Whoever told them to poison him."

Beaver chewed her gum, thinking on this. "If Jeremiah was gone, then the clan could enforce their mortgage to take over the farm, and no one would be any wiser about how much it was actually worth. They buy it for pennies when it's producing a hundred thousand dollars a year."

"The old man is a lot wilier than he looks."

"You think when he told you that the value of the farm was in the land, he was trying to tell you about it?" Vic asked.

"It was around the time that he started planting trees. I never thought anything of it. I wasn't interested in running a farming operation."

"Would you be now?"

"I don't know. Not yet. In a few years… who knows? But not right now."

"If Daniel and Joseph go away for trying to poison Pa… that just leaves you and me."

"Then we'd better hope Pa can avoid getting killed for a few years. I don't know about you, but I'm not ready to settle down to farming yet."

CHAPTER 47

erry dropped Vic and Erin off at the back door of the bakery and watched them go in. His truck remained behind the bakery while Erin and Vic turned on the lights and checked to make sure everything was in order at Auntie Clem's. Erin pulled out her phone and texted Terry to let him know that they were okay. She heard Terry's truck engine rev and then pull out.

"He's pretty paranoid about Theresa showing up here," Vic observed.

Erin nodded. "Yeah. He doesn't want me to go anywhere alone until she's found and taken into custody. But she's vanished into thin air again. It could be months or years before they manage to arrest her." Erin looked around once more, a little nervous because of Terry's repeated need for reassurance. "She's not going to come here. She never has before."

"No. She wouldn't have any reason to," Vic agreed. Neither of them pointed out the fact that Crazy Theresa's behavior was impossible to predict. Chances were, they would never hear from her again.

For a year or two, anyway.

Maybe less if Pa Jackson suddenly got sick again.

They threw themselves into the usual morning routine at Auntie Clem's. There was plenty to be done, though the other employees had been sure to leave the batters that needed to soak overnight all prepped for them, and the kitchen was spick-and-span with everything in its place.

Once they were in the swing of things. Erin found it easier to put Theresa and Pa and everything else that had happened out of her mind. Jack Ward and his police department would take care of it. There was no need for her to worry about anything. He'd assured her he would do everything within his power to track Theresa down and make sure that she was put behind bars. Like Daniel and Joseph.

Bella stopped by on the way to school to ensure that they had found everything in order and didn't need her for anything. Erin asked a couple of questions about inventory supplies to make sure she knew what would need to be ordered. Bella assured her that everything had gone smoothly during their absence, and Erin and Vic could easily take a longer vacation if they needed it.

What Erin needed was not a vacation from work; it was to get back to it. And with Easter just around the corner, they needed hot cross buns and cut-out cookies for the children and maybe some handmade chocolate-dipped marshmallow eggs.

Bella prepared to leave. She paused. "Oh, and your sister called. I forgot to write it down."

"Charley? Did she help at all while I was gone?"

"Charley was fine, other than those couple of days when she was out of touch. And she wasn't scheduled to be in those days, so it was okay. No, I meant the other one… *you know.*"

"Reg?" Erin asked in surprise.

Bella nodded. "Yeah. It was kind of a weird call."

"Well, yes, That's to be expected from Reg. They're all weird calls. If I got a normal call, then that would be weird."

Bella laughed. "Anyway. I don't know if she really wanted anything. She wanted to know how you were doing, if you were okay. I told her everything was fine. She said she needed to hear your voice… actually, I think it was that she could hear your voice. It was all a bit muddled, and I had customers to serve."

"She could hear my voice?"

"Something about hearing her sisters' voices. Does that make any sense?"

"No... not really. But that's Reg for you." Erin hoped that Reg wasn't hearing voices. That was a bad sign and might herald a breakdown. "Well, I'll give her a call tonight and see how she is."

Bella nodded. "Okay! See you later. I'll stop by and help close."

"You've been taking care of everything for the past week. You don't need to do that."

"See you later," Bella said, smiling.

On the way out the door, she nearly bumped into Joshua, coming from the opposite direction.

"Hi, Josh. How are you doing?"

"Good, thanks. How about you?"

"Great," Bella chirped. "Hey, will I see you back at school next semester? I miss having you around."

"Yeah, maybe," Joshua said. He turned his head and watched her walk down the street toward the school before turning back to see Erin and Vic watching him.

He walked into Auntie Clem's, his face turning a little pink. He held up a copy of the Bald Eagle Falls weekly paper. "I didn't know if you saw."

He held it so that they could see the headline: *Investigation into the Poisoning of a High-Ranking Clan Member.* And of course, it had Joshua's headshot and byline beside it.

Erin bit her lip. "Wow. It's great that you got another story into the paper."

He nodded proudly.

"But... do you think it's safe to be reporting on the clan?" Erin asked tentatively. "They don't exactly like to be in the spotlight."

Joshua shrugged. "It's not investigative journalism if you don't make someone uncomfortable." He looked down at the paper. "It's what I want to do. I know Mom won't like it. But... I can't just stay home being scared. I needed to get back out there and face my fear. And I'm okay. I'm still in one piece."

Erin hoped that Mary Lou would still be on speaking terms with her and Vic. They hadn't encouraged him to report on what had happened to Pa Jackson. But she couldn't deny that Joshua would likely never have heard anything about Jeremiah's poisoning if he hadn't been connected through Vic.

"Well... I'm glad that you're feeling better... it's important to face our fears. Just... don't be too reckless."

Joshua smiled reassuringly. "I won't," he agreed. "I'll be just as careful as you."

Craving more gluten-free goodness from Auntie Clem's Bakery?

Get your exclusive copy of

Recipes from Auntie Clem's Bakery

a special collection of my favorite gluten-free treats.

 Gluten-free/grain-free
Vegan
Low allergen

Download your bonus now

Did you enjoy this book? Reviews and recommendations are vital to making a book successful.

Please leave a review at your favorite book store or review site and share it with your friends.

Don't miss the following bonus material:
Sign up for mailing list to get a free ebook
Read a sneak preview chapter
Other books by P.D. Workman
Learn more about the author

DON'T MISS A THING! GET THE LATEST NEWS AND A FREE EBOOK

Your First Taste

PDWORKMAN.COM/SIGNUP

PREVIEW OF CUT OUT
COOKIE

ABOUT CUT OUT COOKIE

Who cut out Crazy Theresa?

Erin once again finds herself sandwiched between a friend and her partner's police investigation when Willie Andrews is accused of killing Crazy Theresa Franklin.

Willie couldn't have done it.

At least, Erin doesn't think so.

He isn't talking to her about it, or to anyone else. There are plenty of other people who might have killed Crazy Theresa. She had enemies. But which one had managed to catch her off guard?

And can Erin ensure that one of her friends does not end up in prison for it?

⭐ ⭐ ⭐ ⭐ ⭐ *The author has the ability to pull you into her story and keep you firmly rooted there until the end. Her characters are interest and have depth. She isn't afraid to explore the areas of our society that many would rather sweep under the rug.*

Like baking mysteries? Cats, dogs, and other pets? Award-winning and USA Today Bestselling Author P.D. Workman brings readers back to small town Bald Eagle Falls for another culinary cozy mystery to be solved by gluten-free baker Erin Price and her friends.

Have your gluten-free cake and eat it too. Sink your teeth into this sweet treat now!

CHAPTER 1

*E*rin heard Terry's truck engine as he pulled in front of the house and parked. She rubbed a hand across her forehead, trying to ease the muscle tension that was giving her a headache. Orange Blossom meowed a protest as she got up out of bed, removing his favorite warm body. She scratched his ears and continued past him to the front door. She reached it at the same time that Terry opened the door and put out his hand to enter the security code into the burglar alarm panel.

Her presence there made him startle, and she saw his hand jump to the holster on his hip before he was able to process who it was and that he was safe. He let out his breath and let K9 in before shutting the door behind him.

"Scared the crap out of me, Erin!" He punched the code into the alarm so that the siren wouldn't start blaring, then took her in his arms and gave her a firm hug and a kiss on the top of her dark hair. "What are you doing up?"

"I haven't been able to sleep. Too restless. I thought I'd get up and have a cup of tea with you and see if that would help me settle in."

Terry nodded and escorted her, one arm around her shoulders, into the kitchen. His brown eyes were smiley and he kissed her on top of the head. "Always happy to have a bit of company. But you need to make sure you get enough sleep."

Erin pushed a dark lock of hair back from her face. "I'm not sleeping right now, whether I'm in bed or out of it, so I might as well do something to help myself relax."

There was the patter of footsteps as Blossom realized they were in the kitchen and galloped in looking for food. He started to yowl noisily for a treat.

"Calm down," Erin told him. "You'd wake the dead."

"Or at least the neighbors," Terry agreed. He shifted his duty belt before sitting down. "We don't need any more nuisance calls because you're making too much noise."

Erin went into the pantry to get a treat for the noisy orange feline and skimmed a few across the floor for him to chase and gobble down. She grabbed one of the gluten-free dog biscuits they offered at Auntie Clem's Bakery and gave it to K9, who was standing patiently waiting for it. He took it politely in his lips, then stretched out on the floor beside Terry's chair to munch on it. Orange Blossom arched his back and hissed at K9, but the dog took no notice.

"How about you, Marshmallow? Do you want a carrot?" Erin called out. There was no movement from the living room, where the bunny was probably snoozing behind the couch. "You see? Marshmallow knows that it's time to sleep, not to eat," she told Blossom, who yowled for another treat. She gave in and got him one more.

After that, she closed the pantry door to signal that there would be no more treats. She washed her hands and put the kettle on, then got out their favorite mugs and put a basket of assorted teabags on the table.

"How was work?"

Terry ran his fingers through his short, dark hair. "Pretty quiet today. A couple of reports of a prowler, but nothing there when we checked it out. Kids, maybe. Or just shadows in the trees."

"Any of those reports from Adele?" Erin asked. Adele lived in the summer cottage in the woods behind Erin's house and acted as a groundskeeper, ensuring there were no trespassers or teens hanging out, causing trouble. It was an arrangement that gave Adele a place to live and the ability to practice her Wiccan observances in private so that she wouldn't be driven out of town by her Bible-thumping neighbors, as she had been from other towns.

"No, nothing from Adele. She can take care of most trespassers on her own."

A shotgun in hand was a remarkably effective deterrent. There were other places to hang out and be rowdy.

As Erin poured the boiling water into their mugs, she saw Terry's eyes jump to the window. Looking out from the brightness of the kitchen into the dark night, they couldn't make out very much, but Erin saw the ghostly glow of a white dress drift across the yard. Blond hair, a slim figure. Victoria Webster, Erin's employee and best friend, in her nightgown, taking Nilla out for a tinkle, she guessed.

"It's just Vic."

Erin put the kettle down on a hot pad and went to the back door. She opened it and turned the back door light on. "Vic?"

"Sheesh, you trying to scare the life out of me?" Vic's voice was sharp, a departure from her usual calm Southern drawl. She swore under her breath.

Erin's stomach tied itself in a knot. Everyone seemed to be jumpy. "I'm sorry, Vicky. I didn't mean to startle you. I was just up with Terry, and…"

"I wouldn't be up if I didn't have to take this critter out for a walk," Vic growled, reaching down to pet the fluffy white dog. "I'd be in bed, where you should be. I know it's not a regular day at Auntie Clem's, just the ladies' tea after church services, but you still need to sleep sometime."

"I couldn't sleep tonight. Figured I'd get up and have some tea with Terry."

"And wake up half the neighborhood with that cat."

Erin shook her head, surprised by Vic's response. She was normally cheerful, even when she was short on sleep. A calm, grounding presence, which was just what Erin needed most of the time. Even though Vic was younger than Erin, she often seemed more mature. Maybe because of the life she had lived with her family, part of the notorious Jackson clan, or as a result of the discrimination and even hate that she'd had to deal with after coming out as transgender.

"Do you want to come in for some tea?" she offered. "Valerian or chamomile?"

"No. I'm going straight back to bed as soon as His Majesty is finished with his business out here."

Erin nodded. "Okay. Sorry about scaring you; I didn't mean to."

"I know. It's okay. You just startled me with the light suddenly going on."

Erin gave Vic a little wave and shut the door. She hesitated whether to turn the light off or leave it on, and decided to leave it on. She would be able to see that Vic was safely back in her loft over the garage before she and Terry went to bed.

Terry raised his brows as Erin returned to the kitchen table and sat down. "She seems a little on edge."

Erin nodded. "Nilla probably woke her up. You know what it's like being awakened from a sound sleep."

"Yes, I suppose. But she's usually more in control than that."

Erin sipped her sleepy tea, hoping that it would calm her overactive thoughts and allow her to get a rest before morning when her body would wake her up, whether it was a baking day or not.

"I've noticed she's been kind of moody since we got back from seeing her parents in Moose River. She's been under a lot of stress."

"Having to deal with the revelation that her brothers were trying to kill her pa for the clan—that kind of stress?" They both sipped their drinks, thinking about it. "Yeah," Terry agreed. "I think we can give her a little bit of latitude for that one."

Erin watched K9 chewing on his biscuit. Orange Blossom was creeping closer, watching for his opportunity to steal what was left of the treat or to lick up the crumbs from the floor and K9's face.

"Do you want something to eat?" she offered Terry. "I can make a sandwich or rewarm some pasta."

"No, I'm fine. I'll eat when we get up in the morning."

"Nothing? A cookie?"

He smiled, the adorable dimple in his cheek making its appearance. "I can't very well say no to a cookie."

Erin got up and went to the fridge to see what was in the freezer. "We've been making a lot of sugar cookies cut out in Easter shapes. Do you want one of those?"

"Sure. Got a bunny?"

"We've got bunnies, eggs, lilies, lambs…"

"You'd better give me an assortment so I can do a quality check," Terry suggested, smiling, the dimple even more prominent. *Officer Handsome* Vic was fond of calling him.

Erin defrosted several Easter cut-out cookies for him. Terry tested them seriously, gazing out the window.

"There must be a security light out. The backyard shouldn't be that dark."

Erin looked, then nodded. "You're right. If someone other than Vic had been out there, I wouldn't have been able to tell who it was. Someone should check into that." She gave him a wry smile. He would, of course, check to see which of the bulbs was out and replace it. He was very determined to see that Erin was as safe as possible, especially when he was on shift and she was home alone.

Things had happened in the past. They didn't want a repeat.

CHAPTER 2

𝓘t was a bright, clear day, already warm when Erin got up in the morning, at a time which she would have considered late any other day of the week. But as Terry had said, all she had to worry about on Sunday was the ladies' tea after the Baptist ladies' church meetings. She didn't bake early Sunday morning; she either made something for the tea on Saturday or pulled something out of the freezer. It wasn't really the baking that the ladies came for, but the gossip session. A little fellowship after their services.

Erin's aunt, Clementine, had held the Sunday tea for many years when the storefront was a tea shop rather than a gluten-free bakery. Eventually, as her health had failed, she had been forced to shut down the business and the weekly get-together. After her death, a private investigator had managed to find Erin and told her that Clementine had left everything to her. They had been estranged for many years, since Erin had been put into foster care after her parents' death and had grown up mostly in Maine and on the eastern seaboard, nowhere near Clementine in Tennessee.

Erin rubbed her forehead and the bridge of her nose. She had been unable to kick the headache and knew that it was most likely tension. She should be relaxed now that she was back in Bald Eagle

Falls, but she'd been struggling with sleepless nights, and the fatigue that was building over the weeks never left her.

She wasn't actually sure how she had ended up moving from Tennessee to Maine as a child, when foster parents were not usually allowed to take children across state borders. But one of the early families that she had been with must have managed to get permission when the father's work transferred him north. Maybe they had been planning to adopt her at the time and some social worker had pulled out all the stops to try to make it work.

But Erin had never been adopted. A forever family had not been in the cards for her.

Erin set out the tray of cookies that she had set aside for the ladies' tea and turned to go back into the kitchen. Vic was coming out at the same time, her eyes down on her phone, and the two of them nearly collided.

"Whoa, I'm sorry," Vic apologized, shoving her phone into an apron pocket. "I wasn't watching where I was going. I thought you were still setting up."

Erin held Vic's arm to steady herself for a moment, then smiled and shrugged. "It's a wonder we don't do that more often."

Vic nodded vaguely. She looked at the small area at the front of the store with a couple of tables surrounded by chairs. "What else do you need? I've got the coffee perking and water heating in the boiler. Cookies. Plates." She laughed. "How about teacups?"

"That might be a good idea," Erin agreed. They were both so scattered it would be a wonder if the tea went off without some kind of snag. She hadn't used the checklist for the ladies' tea in a long time. Still, it was safely stored in a sheet protector in the operations binder, accessible to all employees. Maybe she ought to pull it out to make sure they hadn't forgotten anything. Like the tea.

Erin shook her head as she continued to gather the things they needed together. And she did flip open the binder to make sure they hadn't missed anything obvious. After the number of teas she and Vic had held, everything should be automatic. And usually, it was.

They weren't quite ready when the ladies started to come in the door. Erin focused on not running or appearing hurried as they arranged the final details. The best way to make people think that you were behind or unprofessional was by rushing. Instead, she carefully finished setting everything out, nodding to each of the women and addressing them by name. No one seemed to notice anything awry.

Once everyone had served themselves and was sipping tea and eating cookies—those who allowed themselves such indulgences—Erin took a deep breath and let it out slowly, trying to slow her breathing and heartbeat and to enjoy the moment. She had come to look forward to the ladies' teas, the final cap to her busy week, a time that was slower and allowed her to socialize and relax.

"We were mighty sorry to hear about your family troubles," Melissa told Vic, combing her dark brown curls away from her face with her fingers. Melissa always had the lowdown on the juiciest gossip, drawing from both doing part-time administrative work for the police department and from her relationship with Davis Plaint, in prison for the deaths of his brother and Bertie Braceling. Davis was the one, Erin suspected, who had passed on any word of Vic's "family troubles" to Melissa. Certainly, it hadn't come from Terry, who knew he couldn't rely upon anything he mentioned around Melissa remaining confidential. He wouldn't have passed any of Vic's private information on to her, and it wouldn't have been in the records of the Bald Eagle Falls police department because it had happened in Moose River.

"Well… thank you, I'm sure," Vic said hesitantly. It would be ungracious not to acknowledge and accept Melissa's condolences. Still, she didn't want to discuss any of the sordid details in front of the other ladies. And who knew how much Melissa had already told them? Vic wouldn't know until she started getting condolences from others as well.

"Yes, we were all sorry to hear," Lottie Sturm chimed in.

Her tone clearly indicated that she was holding something back. "But what could be expected from the Jackson clan?" or "We always knew you came from bad stock," or something along those lines. Lottie was one of the women who would never accept Vic for who she was. If she was polite to Vic, it was only because she knew Erin would eject her from the bakery if she weren't.

"How is your poor mother?" Melissa asked, oblivious to Vic's discomfort. "It must have been such a trial for her, your pa being so sick. I heard he was on his death bed."

Vic nodded reluctantly. "I'm sure she's doing better now that everything is back to normal. Pa was lucky to recover. It was pretty perilous for a while there."

Melissa gave a little gasp and covered her mouth in horror. But her eyes were dancing and it was obvious that she was enjoying the drama and having Vic as a captive audience.

"We were all praying for him," Cindy Prost chimed in. She was sitting beside her daughter, Bella, who was one of Erin's best employees. Even though Bella was still in high school, she had a good business mind. She was very responsible and often had ideas for Erin to try out to improve areas of her business. Cindy glanced sideways at Bella to make sure she heard and approved of this comment. Erin had her doubts that Cindy had prayed about anyone in Vic's family. Unless she was a closer relation than Erin thought. Many of the families in the area were related, and the Prosts and Jacksons had been around for long enough that Erin was sure the families' genealogies probably connected at several different points.

"We sure were," Bella agreed, and her words sounded genuine. She'd held down the fort while Vic and Erin had been in Moose River, and she had expressed her good wishes for Vic's father and the family several times. Erin never sensed the same insincerity in Bella as she did in Cindy.

Vic too sensed this and nodded real appreciation to Bella. "Thank you for that. It was miraculous that he survived."

Erin knew that sooner or later, one of the ladies was going to bring up Vic's brothers and their actions. She looked at Vic and cocked her head slightly, as if listening carefully.

"Vicky, would you mind getting the phone in my office? I can hear it ringing."

Vic stared at her for a moment in confusion. There was, after all, no phone in Erin's tiny, closet-sized office in the back. There was a wall phone just inside the kitchen doorway so that if a customer called, they could answer it from either the front or the back, but that was the only hard-wired phone in the bakery. Erin used her cell phone for everything else. Then understanding came into Vic's eyes, and she nodded and hurried into the back, out of the reach of the ladies' pointed questions and comments. If Erin needed a hand with anything in the front, she knew that Bella would jump in to help. Vic could hide out in the back and tidy away anything that had been left out in the kitchen.

The atmosphere in the bakery deflated as everyone watched their prime target retreat and disappear out of reach of their barbs. Lorrie Sturm gave Erin a glare, understanding that Erin had intentionally removed Vic from the line of fire.

"It was so kind of you to go to Moose River with Vic," Mary Lou commented. She took a sip of her tea. She had not taken any of the cookies, always mindful of her figure. "You are always looking for ways to help people."

Erin's face warmed at the compliment. She wasn't quite sure how to respond. It was true; she did the best she could to help those in need. But she was too modest to like having this brought to everyone else's attention. She shrugged and looked away. "Thank you."

Conversations shifted and the focus moved away from Erin and Vic, since they would not indulge the women's interests. After draining a cup or two of tea, the ladies started looking at their watches and excusing themselves. Bella hovered as her mother made movements toward the front door.

"Can I help you clean up, Erin? We can wait for a few minutes."

"No, it's okay," Erin assured her. "There's not much to do. I'll see you next week."

"You sure?"

"I'm sure. Take care. Thanks for coming, Cindy," Erin raised her voice slightly to acknowledge Cindy's departure as well. Not a "see you soon," but more of a "don't let the door hit you on your way out."

Bella gave Erin a grin and scurried after her mother. Mary Lou was the last to leave, though usually she was one of the first, staying for just long enough to satisfy the others that she had made an effort.

"You can tell Vic that it's safe to come out now," Mary Lou said dryly. She patted her iron gray bob, though she didn't have a hair out of place.

Erin acknowledged this with a smile. "Vic! All clear!"

Vic poked her head out the door and looked around. She nodded at Mary Lou. "Sorry about that," she apologized, her cheeks growing pink. "It was a longer call than I expected."

Erin gave an unladylike snort. "Hopefully, by next week, they'll have moved on to other things. Or maybe you should give someone else the shift next week. They're bound to have something else to gossip about in two whole weeks."

"Maybe I will," Vic agreed.

Mary Lou gazed at Vic for a moment in silence. "I do wish you the best with your family," she said eventually. "I hope that... y'all will find some peace."

"Thanks." Vic blinked, her eyes swimming with tears. "I hope that too."

Mary Lou nodded once, smoothed invisible wrinkles on her pants, and left the bakery. Erin flipped the sign to Closed and locked the bolt on the door without a word, and they each moved quietly around each other to gather up the few things that needed to be put away.

"I swear, I thought things would be better this week," Erin sighed. "I thought that giving them a couple of weeks would head off any problems."

"Things must be too quiet in Bald Eagle Falls." Vic swiped at the corners of her eyes when she thought Erin wasn't looking. "We'll have to stir up some trouble!"

❧

Cut Out Cookie, #17 in the *Auntie Clem's Bakery* series by P.D.
Workman can be purchased at pdworkman.com

❧

ABOUT THE AUTHOR

P.D. Workman is a USA Today Bestselling author and multi-award winner, renowned for her prolific output of over 100 published works that span various genres. With a knack for crafting page-turners, Workman captivates readers with everything from cozy mysteries like the Auntie Clem's Bakery series to gripping young adult and suspense novels.

A prolific reader and writer since childhood, P.D. Workman crafts emotionally powerful stories that don't shy away from hard topics. Her books tackle mental illness, addiction, abuse, and trauma with raw honesty and compassion, giving voice to the often unheard. If you crave authentic, character-driven page-turners that hit deep and stay with you long after the final page, you're in the right place.

With each new release, fans eagerly anticipate another thrilling blend of thought-provoking storytelling and relatable characters that define P.D. Workman's brand as an author of unforgettable page-turners—gripping tales that leave a lasting impact long after the last page is turned.

> P. D. Workman, does not shy from probing the deep psychological scars of childhood trauma, mental illness, and addiction. Also characteristic of this author, these extremely sensitive issues are explored with extensive empathy, described with incredible clarity, and portrayed with profound insight.
>
> — —KIM, GOODREADS REVIEWER

Some of Workman's titles have been translated into Spanish, French, Portuguese, German, and Italian.

Workman began writing at an early age and is a prolific reader as well as writer. She is also passionate about teaching and learning, expresses her creativity through art and cooking, and loves exploring the Calgary parks and green spaces where the Parks Pat Mysteries are set. She was a legal assistant for many years and has done extensive charitable work.

Workman was born and raised in Alberta, Canada, and is married with one adult son.

∾

Please visit P.D. Workman at pdworkman.com to see what else she is working on, to join her mailing list, and to link to her social networks.

∾

If you enjoyed this book, please take the time to recommend it to other purchasers with a review or star rating and share it with your friends!

tiktok.com/@pdworkmanauthor

facebook.com/pdworkmanauthor

x.com/pdworkmanauthor

instagram.com/pdworkmanauthor

amazon.com/author/pdworkman

bookbub.com/authors/p-d-workman

goodreads.com/pdworkman

linkedin.com/in/pdworkman

pinterest.com/pdworkmanauthor

youtube.com/pdworkman

Find P.D. Workman's books at

PDWORKMAN.COM

Scan the QR code below